Sarah Armstrong's debut novel, *The Insect Rosary*, was published by Sandstone Press in 2015. Her short stories have been published in Mslexia and Litro, and she teaches undergraduate and post-graduate creative writing for the Open University. Sarah lives in Essex with her husband and four children.

By the same author

The Insect Rosary

THE DEVIL
IN THE
SNOW

SARAH ARMSTRONG

SANDSTONEPRESS
HIGHLAND | SCOTLAND

First published in Great Britain
Sandstone Press Ltd
Dochcarty Road
Dingwall
Ross-shire
IV15 9UG
Scotland

www.sandstonepress.com

The publisher acknowledges subsidy from
Creative Scotland towards publication of this volume.

ISBN: 978-1-910985-54-0
ISBNe: 978-1-910985-55-7

Cover design by Antigone Konstantinidou
Typeset by Iolaire Typesetting, Newtonmore
Printed and bound by Totem, Poland

For Claire Armstrong and Steven Digby

GRETA

The priest told them to run and leave the room full of blood behind them. He said it was to save the rest of the village, that they had brought it on themselves.

The snow clagged around their boots and around the wheels of the cart. My great-grandfather hauled it by hand, piled with a mattress and a chest of drawers still with the clothes in it. Next to this Edith, my grandmother, crouched, just five years old, clutching her two-year-old brother. A fall onto the bitter ground would kill them and do the devil's work for him. And he was the reason they were running, away from his hoof prints and the blood he'd spilled. No-one ever talked about what happened in that room.

My great-grandmother had to walk, forty-seven and pregnant again. A family curse. No woman gave birth before her forties, not her daughter or her granddaughter. We all had one girl and one boy. Her pregnancy only held until Bath, where they were going to settle, but the stories kept coming. The hoof prints which had ended at their door had been seen in Exmouth, Torquay, Weymouth and Lincoln. They hadn't got far enough away. The mark was on them and they had to keep running. They knew that the same snow which held the prints of the devil's hooves also held their own tracks.

Once my great-grandmother could walk, after the loss of the baby, they put everything back in the handcart. What my grandmother most remembered was how the tears froze to her cheeks, the holes in her shawl and the gaps in her boots, which ate the snow when she had to walk. She always made sure she had a good pair of boots and a thick shawl after that, just in case, and she would stand in the snow and wait. I would watch her from the window, staying close to the fire. When it was my mother standing out there in her good winter coat and thick leather boots, I knew it would be my turn one day.

They left Totnes on the 9th of February 1855, fleeing eastwards, and there was still snow on the ground when they arrived in Essex. They were heading to Suffolk, the land of Our Lady, but they stopped short somehow, their tracks leading to Coggeshall. My great-grandmother was thought nearest to death, but in fact my great-grandfather was the one to go. If he hadn't died, maybe my grandmother would have waited until two boys, or three, had asked for a kiss and made a choice between them, the only choice she would ever be given. But she didn't have the luxury of choice, neither did my mother and nor did I.

On my eighth birthday my father was out, as usual. He drank, like my grandfather, and it did for him in the end too. My mother sat me down at the table and frowned, just a little, to show she was being serious.

'Make a fist,' she said, and she made one too. My hand

was smooth like a sea-worn rock. Each of her knuckles looked like a cracked walnut. 'Now, starting with the little finger lift each one to the sky in turn.'

I did it with the first, but the second finger got stuck halfway.

'I can't,' I said.

'Really try,' she said.

'I am trying.' My finger ached but it wouldn't rise above an awkward arch without pulling the other fingers with it.

'Now, this is how things are supposed to be,' she said. 'The middle finger is God and the laws of nature. The little finger is society and the laws of man. The second finger is you. You should never do anything that isn't right in the eyes of God or man, do you understand?'

My finger still hurt but I nodded.

She continued, 'Most importantly, if you ever meet anyone who can move every finger independently I want you to run faster than you ever believed you could. Understand?'

I thought I did. In any case, I nodded.

She stood up and sighed. 'And never marry a man who refuses a drink.'

All the men in my family were born or became alcoholics. This sounded like a terrible rule to follow. I nodded again, and decided to ignore all of her advice.

I've thought about how I should have had the same mother–daughter conversation with Shona, but instead I tried to explain it all. She never needed another reason to laugh at me. And listening didn't do me any good.

My mother loved stories. She went to the pictures at the Regal and Empire in Colchester and sometimes bought magazines with pictures of film stars. She even named me

3

after Greta Garbo. My mother told me fairy tales too, about the green children of Woolpit, strange and small creatures who camouflaged themselves in the trees and grass, the giant of Brockford, the merman of Orford and the dragons of Wormingford.

There was no happy and righteous ending to my mother's fairy tales. No happy ending for me either. My mother knew that. It's why she told me all the stories of the strange children of the woods and men of the sea and black devil dogs, no matter how much I begged for princesses. She was preparing me from my birth to be aware of the monsters and threats that no-one else would believe. These were the forms the devil could take as he moved among us. And I was prepared, but not convinced. I thought, if I needed to, I would be able to recognise a threat when I saw it, like a ten-foot giant or a fish-scaled dragon. I would have run from green-haired women and bull-horned men, from wizened child-like figures in the centres of thorn trees. She should have known that the devil always looks like the thing you think you want.

I didn't think that the threat would come to me while I was listening to The Beatles in a record shop. I didn't think it would be a nineteen-year-old boy crippled by a shy smile and a slight tremor to his hand when he held mine.

Only the craftiest devil would stammer when he asked for a kiss.

1

SEPTEMBER 2011

Shona always felt relieved when she'd left Rob to get back to his life. She could feel herself slipping into the role of wife, rather than lover, if she stayed too long. The state of his room did make her feel better about her own house, untidy as it was. She tried to feel a little guilty for not having picked up shoes or emptied the dishwasher or, as Cerys kept pointing out, having sorted the last three weeks' worth of washing. It would all keep. It would all need doing again tomorrow, whether or not she did it today.

She checked one last time that she had her mobile and keys, threw her leg over the bike and paused to unwind her wool scarf a little. Outside was warmer than inside, although the sky was still brutally clear. She decided to cycle the long way so she could go flat out on the fields by the school. Here, on the roads, she cycled slowly, enjoying the mild chill of the wind. There were leaves gathering in the gutters and a sense of bonfires to come, yet the schools had only just started their year. Only the week before honeysuckle had tingled in the air.

She turned into Victoria Road and stopped pedalling, putting one foot down. That boy was there again, where she'd last seen him a couple of months ago and two or three times before that. Dominic? That sounded right to her. He'd said something about the 1960s which she hadn't quite understood. She had always regretted not telling anyone he was there. Not that she knew who to tell, but he was, maybe, sixteen – or older? It was hard to tell.

The bike wheels clicked around as she slowly coasted towards him. He didn't look up. He was dressed in old clothes again that looked slightly too big for him, jeans and only a T-shirt. His hands were placed, palms upward, by his side, and his knees bent up as he leaned against a tree. As she got closer, she could see goose pimples on his arms and his bare feet buried slightly into the soil.

'Hey,' she said. 'Are you all right?'

He opened his eyes. 'I've been waiting for you.'

'Have you?'

He nodded. 'I've been waiting.' He held his hands close to his face. 'I think I've been here a while.'

'Why are you waiting?' she asked.

He put his hands back by his sides.

'Is there someone I can call for you, let them know where you are? It's Dominic, isn't it?'

'I have been waiting for you. I have to get my instructions.'

Shona waited to hear what they were but he carefully placed his hands on his knees and his head dropped forward. She rested her bike against the tree and crouched down next to him. There were bruises on his cheeks, cuts on the backs of his wrists, his eyelashes surprisingly long and dark.

6

'Do you think that I might be the one to give you instructions?' she asked.

Dominic lifted his face. 'I think I need to stay with you.'

Shona bit down the automatic 'no'. He needed help and she had to help him. It had to be a 'yes'. Just until she found out what kind of help he needed.

She said, 'I think you could come home with me for a little while to warm up. And we can decide what to do.'

'Yes,' he said. 'It is you. Meghan sent me to tell you that there's a message for you, when you're ready.'

Shona swallowed. 'Meghan?'

He nodded and she waited, but he didn't say anything more. Meghan. How would he even know her name?

She stood up and held out her hand to him but he raised himself from the missing paving stone where the tree grew. As he got up he grabbed a handful of soil and put it in his pocket.

He pointed back the way she'd come. 'I suppose you don't want to go the quickest way. Past his house. He might be looking.'

She looked back down the road and back to him. 'Have you been watching me, Dominic?'

'So many people are watching you.'

His hazel eyes blinked once and he smiled. She shuddered. She didn't want to know what he meant by that.

'I'm Shona. I'll get you a cup of tea and then we'll make some calls.'

He nodded. She wheeled her bike onto the pavement and walked home past Rob's house, watching Dominic. He didn't look at her or Rob's house.

Shona walked him down the alley at the side of her house, past the recycling boxes, to the back gate. She leaned the bike against the fence and unlocked the back door.

'Are you hungry?' she asked. He nodded.

He sat down at the kitchen table and looked across and past her, out of the back window. She pulled things from the fridge and wondered why she had agreed to this. Dominic ate everything she put in front of him, cheese and bread and cucumber, not fast but with commitment, and then laid his head down on the table like a toddler having a nap. She remembered napping like that at primary school after drinking the milk through a stripy cardboard straw.

She knew she should call the police or some mental health team, but she didn't. He'd said Meghan. And she knew what the chances were, and how people were tricked into this kind of thing all the time, but she hadn't sought him out. He'd found her. If there was even the slightest chance at all, she couldn't ignore it. The best thing would be if he didn't say it again and she could wave him goodbye.

She waited for a sign that he was pretending so that they could start to talk about where to go next, but he really was asleep. She sat and watched the fluctuations of his breathing, the fluid movement of his eyes beneath the lids. Finally, she forced herself away.

In the back room she turned her phone on and a found a message from her friend Mariana. She always called on Tuesday, but she'd been in Portugal for the last two weeks and Shona found it easy to fall out of a habit. Mariana was the kind of person who would know what to do. Shona phoned her back and immediately decided not to tell her. She'd come round. Any excuse.

Shona could hear Mariana's bracelets rattling as she dramatically, but invisibly, gesticulated. She couldn't concentrate, reciting to herself, don't tell her, don't tell her.

'Are you sure you're OK?' Mariana was saying.

'Yes, I'm sure. I just don't know …'

'I don't know what? Shona?'

'Yes?'

'Have you collected Jude? I can't hear him. I can usually hear him.'

Shona looked at the clock. 'Shit!' She disconnected. The boy was still asleep on the table. She'd have to leave him there.

She collected Jude from the school office, thirty-five minutes late on the second day of his first full week. He looked quite happy, swinging himself around in the head teacher's chair. The head wasn't quite so contented and made it clear that she was only postponing a pep talk about time management or consistency for five-year-olds because she wanted to go home today. Jude was smiling and pleased to see her and Shona was happy to leave.

Shona carried Jude home on her back for a treat to celebrate not getting told off. She clasped her hands under his bum as a seat but he still held on a little too tightly. By the time they got back her windpipe felt bruised.

She opened the back door and remembered. Dominic was still asleep.

Jude sat by him, as Shona had done, watching him.

'Who is he?'

'I'm not sure. He's called Dominic.'

'Are we going to keep him?'

'He's just going to stay for a little while.'

Jude raised his eyebrows. 'In our room?'

'No.'

Jude frowned. 'Cerys' room?'

9

'No, He's just here for a couple of hours. We haven't got any room, have we?'

Cerys had one bedroom while Shona and Jude shared the other and the walk-in office attached to it. The locked, little-used front room downstairs belonged to her husband, Maynard. The attic had a pull down ladder and a lot of dusty rubbish.

'He'll go soon,' she said. She thought again that she should phone someone, but he'd said Meghan. She needed to hear the rest of that and, when he left, that would be her chance lost. She played it back in her mind, trying to convince herself that he had said something else, but it was always Meghan.

She heard the front door close as Cerys let herself in. Dominic stretched and sat up. Shona froze. What convinced Jude wasn't going to work on her.

'Mr Cartwright wants to see you last at Parents' Evening,' she shouted from the hall. 'I wasn't going to bother, but he asked. I wrote it on the sheet.' Shona could hear the school bag drop to the floor. Cerys stopped in the doorway and stared.

She'd taken off her school tie, untucked the blouse and shaken her long brown hair free. Her skirt was rolled up at the waist, revealing thin legs with thick fist-like knees. Her nose, which seemed to have been growing out of sync with the rest of her face, was settling now, straight and pretty. Cerys still hated it.

'Hi,' she said. She wasn't talking to Shona or Jude.

Shona looked at her. She hadn't seen Cerys smile like that for years, open and happy. Dominic smiled back and Shona watched Cerys blush deep on her cheeks.

She hadn't thought this through. She hadn't thought what a boy like this would do to a fourteen-year-old. He was beautiful in a girlish boy band way, with large eyes and longish hair. How had she not noticed?

'Dominic, I think I should call your parents now.'

'There's no need.'

'They'll be wondering where you are.' Shona could sense Cerys fidgeting behind her.

'I'm eighteen. I told them I'd be away for a while.'

'Of course he should stay, Mum,' said Cerys. 'We've got room.'

'Do we?' Any minute now Dominic would start talking about instructions and Meghan, and then Cerys – what would Cerys do? Shona looked at her again. Cerys wouldn't say a word. She was ready to jump whenever he told her.

Dominic stood and stretched again. 'I slept on it. I'm going to stay in the shed.'

Shona thought about it, although it wasn't a question. 'And your parents?'

'I'll let them know.'

Cerys, still blushing, turned and went upstairs. Shona knew she'd be calling her friends, spreading the word. Shona knew this couldn't really happen; she couldn't let this boy sleep in the shed. But, to be honest, she didn't need another fight with Cerys. She would be the one who would cause trouble over it and if it was fine with her ... And Jude?

She didn't think it would be more than a day or two, just long enough for him to tell her about Meghan. And, please God, he'd be gone before Maynard turned up.

She laid out the spare duvet and blankets on the floor of the shed and threw a pillow on top.

'This doesn't seem right, Dominic. Wouldn't you rather sleep on the sofa? It's fine for a night or two.'

'This is where I need to be.'

He looked around the shed. It wasn't a working shed, luckily. Neither she nor Maynard had ever been interested in storing paint pots or bits of wood that might come in handy. All of Jude's outside toys had been given away except for his scooter, and that tended to stay in the hall, his football in his room.

She heard a giggle. Jude was peeping around the door.

'Back inside, Jude.' He walked away slowly and she pulled the door to. 'Dominic, you mentioned someone called Meghan before.'

'Yes.'

'Do you know who that is?'

'Yes.'

'Can you tell me what it is? The message?'

'Soon. Mastery is coming, and then you will know.'

Shona noticed his eyes looked different. They had seemed hazel before, but now they looked blue. He placed one hand on her arm.

'Don't worry. I'm not here for Cerys. I know you're worried about her.'

'OK.' She believed him but had a strange dizzying sensation that, back in her house, it would sound stupid when she thought about it. Why would he say that? She shook it off. 'When you said people were watching me, did someone tell you about Meghan?'

'No.' He yawned and looked young again, not even eighteen. More like twelve, tired and grumpy.

She knew she'd get nothing from him tonight. 'You don't need anything else? A drink, a toothbrush?'

'No.'

Shona walked to the back door and turned around. Jude was hiding by the side of the shed. He groaned and followed her inside.

Shona could hear Cerys' music playing in her room. She settled Jude on the sofa in front of the TV and dithered at the bottom of the stairs. She needed to say something to Cerys, but didn't want it to sound as if she was accusing her of anything, not even a crush. It was so easy to offend Cerys these days and she wanted to do this right.

There was a noise behind her as Maynard turned his key in the lock. He looked surprised that she was standing by the door and they both just stared for a moment.

'Are you waiting for someone?' he asked.

'No.' Shona's heart fluttered. 'Why are you here? Did Cerys call you?'

'No.'

Maynard waited for another moment and then walked past her. He opened the front room door with another key on his weighty key ring and went to close it behind him. He wasn't carrying an overnight bag, but Shona asked anyway. 'Are you staying tonight?'

'Yes. And maybe tomorrow. If Cerys hasn't eaten, she might like to go out for a meal. Has she?'

Shona hated his polite, 'I'm so civilised' voice. As if she wouldn't remember what he had said and what she'd said back. She put on her most prim voice. 'Why don't you go and ask her?'

'I will.'

He closed his door.

If Cerys was going to tell him she would, regardless of whether Shona tried to keep them apart. Shona went into the back room and sat on the sofa next to Jude. She took his fingers out of his mouth, kissed his coarse blond hair and put her arms around him.

She whispered into his ear, 'Maynard's here. Don't be scared of him, he won't come near you. I won't let him.' Jude leaned in towards her and put his arms around her stomach.

'He always shouts at me about my stuff.'

'He's an idiot. I didn't know he was coming, sorry.'

'He makes Cerys cross with me too. When he's here, she doesn't like me. I don't like Maynard.'

'I don't either. One day he'll go and we can take back the front room,' said Shona. 'We'll put your name on the door and fill it with all your stuff.'

They went quiet as they heard the door to the front room open and heavy steps up to Cerys' room. There was a muttering of voices and flutters of steps, Cerys bubbling away and Maynard guiding her out the door. Silence.

'Total shit,' said Shona. She turned to Jude. 'That's a not-for-school word, OK?'

Jude nodded. 'Total shit.'

'I'll make some dinner.'

'Music, music, music.' Jude switched the TV off and checked which CD was in the machine. 'This one?'

'David Bowie. That's perfect, start dancing and I'll catch you up.' Shona went through the fridge and freezer, pulling out all the nicest food so that Maynard couldn't eat it. They would feast on tiger prawns, with rice, maybe, and smoked salmon on toast. And Maynard liked sardines, so sardines on toast too. 'Shall we have everything on toast, or do you want rice too?'

Jude jumped into the doorway, lion-posed. 'I want rice too.' He bounced away. Shona wished she could put a lock on the back room that only kept Maynard out. She hated the way Jude cringed in front of him.

14

Her mind wandered back to the shed but she refused to check it. Check him. It all felt made up now she was inside with Jude, cooking and being normal. She almost asked Jude whether it was real, but he was dancing away school and Maynard, and she didn't want to interrupt. She missed spending time with Cerys like this, silliness and thoughtless love which didn't have to be careful about which words it used. She tried to be normal with Cerys, tried not to buy her affection, but Shona still felt she was always waiting for her to choose which space she wanted to occupy. Hers or his.

It was all about spaces, with both Shona and Maynard. When Maynard stayed, he removed Jude's shoes from the shoe rack and chucked his coat in the bottom of the under stairs cupboard so he didn't have to see it. Maynard spoilt Cerys with clothes and meals and hi-tech knick-knacks. Shona said nothing. It was that silence that kept her with Maynard until Cerys was old enough to choose.

2

Shona finished buttering the toast and stared out of the kitchen window at the one she'd worked out must be Rob's bedroom. She thought it was, anyway, but it was hard to tell which was his house from the back. She thought back to what Dominic had said about people, so many people, watching her. He'd been in the shed for a week now and there'd been nothing else. No message and no oddness. Nothing she could quite put her finger on, and yet he made her nervous. Her skin tingled sometimes and it reminded her of standing in front of her father. It was fear. Had she never been scared since then? She'd been furious, devastated, happy, but not fearful. She was lucky. She had been lucky. The thought of Dominic scared her and she knew she should run from him, but she hadn't. It could never end well when she denied her instincts.

People are watching. Dominic had repeated that last night. After, thinking about it, she felt both scared by it and stupid for believing him. Yet at the time it all seemed to make sense. He made sense. And then there was Meghan.

She believed he knew something about Meghan, even if she didn't know how. Somehow she never seemed to ask the right questions when she was with him. They fluttered into her mind once he was out of sight. It wasn't like her at all. Normally she was so sure of herself she would question anything.

A movement drew her gaze down. Dominic was standing in the doorway of the shed. She thought he was frowning, but his lips smiled. She waved and he let himself into the kitchen. He looked like a piece of summer blown in through the door, sun-bleached ends to his hair which reached down to the neck of his T-shirt, and baggy combat trousers which skirted his bare feet. She'd felt silly shopping for him, or maybe embarrassed like he was a dirty secret. As though if she bought him clothes she was asking him to stay. But he stayed anyway. And sometimes he went to work. Shona had gone to see him there, just to see if he was telling the truth.

Dominic joined her at the window. The slow blue sky stretched over the luminous roofs around them. A steady breeze drove the smell of the sea through the open door.

'It's beautiful, like it's still August,' said Shona. 'I can't believe that Jude has to go to school. What a waste of a day.'

'Don't take him.' Dominic helped himself to a piece of toast. 'Do whatever you need to do.'

'I have to take him,' Shona murmured.

'Then take him.'

Jude scraped his chair back and joined them at the window.

'We could go to the beach,' said Shona.

They stood side by side as Shona made and unmade her decisions.

'Are you busy today, Dominic?'

17

'No.' She could hear his smile.

She turned to look at Jude. She shouldn't ask him, it wasn't his decision or his responsibility.

'I'll phone the school. And I have to confirm the visit with Jimmy. What else was I supposed to do today?' Her mother had left messages, but she was in no rush to see her. She crouched down to talk to Jude. 'It's just this once, OK? School is really important and you have to go, really. Even on birthdays and things.'

Jude nodded. 'What about Cerys?'

'She's gone to meet her friends already.'

Shona knew that Cerys would say no if asked to come with her and Jude, but knowing Dominic was going might be different. She'd caught her hanging around the shed a little too often, just in the hope of Dominic being there. One afternoon there had been five teenage girls sitting on the grass, giggling. It was best if Cerys just went to school.

She whispered to Jude, 'Go and get changed.'

Jude kicked off his school shoes and ran upstairs.

'Why are you whispering?' whispered Dominic, his toast half eaten.

'I'm not sure,' she whispered back. 'I'm just wondering whether I should phone Callum's mum. We've been meeting them on the way. Just bumping into her, but still. Maybe I should.'

'Phone her then.'

'But she might think it's really bad.'

'Don't phone her then.'

Shona looked at him. 'You're no help at all.'

He smiled. 'I know.'

In his slightly too-tight shorts Jude looked like the toddler he suddenly wasn't, according to everyone but Shona. She could still see the baby he was in the way he drank seriously from a juice bottle. She could see the unsteadiness of his progress through the rock pool as well as the way he approached the waves with the confident arrogance of the teenager he would become.

She'd spent all summer worrying about him starting school, that he wasn't ready and would be overwhelmed and diminished by being one of many. It was the last summer that they could see an end to, a definite stop date in September. She'd never worried much about taking him to every session at nursery. There was no obligation to as far as she was concerned, even if the women running it weren't so sure. Ever since they started having Ofsted inspections they'd taken it far too seriously. No-one really cared about their reports apart from them. People just wanted their children to have a couple of hours of fun while they did something else. Or Shona did, anyway. Now, dropping him off and picking him up from school, it was Shona who felt overwhelmed and diminished. When she phoned the school, she had to give Jude's full name, his teacher's name and what year he was in. He was one of many and she was one of many, many mothers.

Jude turned and splashed water towards her. He was fine, seemed fine. Or maybe she'd only been seeing what made her life easier.

She joined him at the line where sandy shells became acres of dark mud.

'Do you like school, Jude?'

'Yep.'

'Do you like lots of children, do you play with everyone?'

'I like Callum. He's naughty. He gets told off.'

Shona decided that if there was a problem, if Jude was unhappy, she'd know. She didn't need to know that he

19

gravitated towards the worst behaved boys in the class. Callum's mum, Thea, seemed nice and sometimes it was best just to leave it at that.

Shona took Jude's hand and walked him along the shoreline. Dominic lay by the crumbling cliffs, his eyes open and his head resting on his crossed arms. Jude stopped at the high tideline of rocks, brittle with barnacles, and screamed every time his stick stirred up a crab from the sand. Shona caught a couple of tiny sand-coloured ones and tried to get him to look at them but he turned away. The second she put the crabs back and they buried under a stone he stirred his stick again.

She sat back from the rocks, trying to arrange her hands so that they didn't get cut by the oyster shells. Her sandals were full of sand, scouring her feet smooth, but there were too many stones to try walking without them. Jude didn't seem to feel them like she did, his gritty socks left next to his shoes. She thought of the things she should have brought from the garden, the spades and bucket with the broken handle. She closed her eyes and listened to Jude splashing.

They'd mostly gone to Clacton over the summer by train. Cerys had been whisked off to Crete by Maynard and returned bronzed and even ruder than before. In past years, Shona would have worried than Maynard wouldn't return with her but their stalemate still held. He wouldn't take her and Shona wouldn't tell.

Clacton had been a bright and busy distraction, not like Mersea. Here the cliff behind didn't shelter them from the wind entirely, but curved it around them with the bitter smell of the sea and salted hair. She heard a splatter. Jude was throwing small stones, trying to hit a larger one he'd jammed upright. His sunhat, a little too large, had finally fallen off and he refused to put it back on again. The sun wasn't strong but he couldn't go back to school with sunburn after being supposedly sick.

Shona led him back to the bags and nudged Dominic's arm.

'We'll have to go and find some shade for a while. Jude needs a nap and probably an ice cream.'

Jude, red-faced, was drinking from his juice bottle but the spout kept falling from his mouth as his head nodded back from sleep. He crawled into her arms and she arranged herself so her shadow protected him from the sun. She looked at Dominic properly. He clearly hadn't been listening. Or hearing. His eyes looked at the sky and she looked up to see what he was watching. Dozens of sand martins darted above them, across the clear sky, in and out of their nests in the cliffs. Unlike the hovering, screaming gulls, their hunt and return was silent, almost mathematical, based on curves and angles of speed. She tried to follow one for a short time but her eyes quickly became tired. She couldn't tell the birds from the black specks floating in her vision, and closed her eyes.

She hadn't been to Mersea for a long time, not since she thought of Colchester as the big city. She thought of how, while she was at the sixth form, she had sat on a rotten pier and eaten kiwis with her friend Steven, who lived in Peldon, reading Eliot and watching the dark skins float off like solidified jellyfish. Then they'd gone back to get drunk with Claire, and waited for the ghost to play the piano.

She jerked awake. It was only early, about half past eleven, but both boys had been lying for hours in the sun. She hadn't been organised, brought sunshades or anything

21

sensible, just an old bottle of sunscreen and two towels. They had come on the bus, to an unmarked bus stop she had to somehow memorise to get back again. It was an impromptu visit, she had plenty of excuses for why she wasn't prepared, but she still felt negligent. She felt that she looked negligent, although only two other people had passed them since they arrived, as far as she knew.

She saw the sweat build up on Jude's forehead and upper lip. He was always a hot sleeper, his dreams steam driven.

'Dominic, I need to cool Jude down. Can you come back up with me for a bit?'

He didn't move.

'Dominic.' She touched his arm. 'Can you hear me?'

He looked awake and there, but he was somewhere else entirely. She felt that tingling sensation in her stomach as she examined his fierce expression and moved away. Jude flung one arm out and shifted uneasily. Shona decided to risk it, to take him to the café and come back for Dominic. She tried to justify it to herself as she carried Jude along the path that took her to the top of the cliff. Dominic wasn't her child or her responsibility. He chose to live with her and had no claim on her as she had no claim on him.

There was a long grass field, with trimmed and longer sections, and finally the car park and the café. He would be there, and if he was gone he was gone. He was eighteen, after all. She paused in the café doorway. He was only eighteen, still a teenager. She forced herself through the door.

Loaded with drinks, three sandwiches and packets of crisps and no bag, she had to wait until Jude woke up so she didn't have to carry him too. Thea texted a couple of times, wishing Jude a speedy recovery from his fictional stomach ache. She should have invited her and Callum along. She wouldn't have been judgemental about it, maybe. Then again, when Cerys was first at school Shona had tried as hard as possible to play everything right, to take her to the right groups and prompt a temporary interest in a range of activities. She would never have allowed her to skip school, not for a birthday, not for a dentist appointment. Everything was beyond reproach as far as Cerys went, apart from the deeply unhealthy hatred between her loving parents. She texted Cerys a couple of times, but she wasn't replying. Cerys would have replied to Dominic in a second though. Shona had seen how she waited in doorways for him to notice her.

Shona tried not to imagine what Dominic was doing alone on the beach. She'd been thinking of what could have brought him to her, and had fixed on the idea of the summer riots. All those children who had been caught up in the excitement of chaos and had their lives restricted by convictions, their futures crossed out. He didn't seem the type in some ways but, from what she'd read, there hadn't really been one. They didn't see themselves as political or dissenting, just pissed off. She shook her head, that wasn't him. She had felt it though, their anger. She understood why they did it.

Jude was still splayed across her. She didn't have enough arms to drag him so she needed compliancy. When he began to stir, she encouraged him to wake by adjusting him on her lap.

Half an hour after Jude had woken they had reached the path back down to the beach. Dominic had moved from the small stones next to the cliff to the large slabs of concrete mid-beach. He was crouched down over something. Shona went back to their original spot, in that irrational way on an empty beach, and set up her picnic.

When Dominic returned, he had had taken another step away from her. The skin around his eyes was wrinkled and he had thin sections of driftwood tied to his upper arms with seaweed. She knew him well enough by now that she wouldn't get an answer if she asked.

'I've received a message. I was told my true name. Kallu.' His eyes were focused just past Shona and she fought the urge to shake him back to sense, back to her.

In the end, she said, 'OK.'

'I have to think about leaving.'

'When?'

'Soon.'

Jude's eyes were as wide as his mouth. Shona nudged him and he put his hand over his mouth. Dominic did this kind of thing. She knew that from their meetings under the tree on Victoria Road. Shona had accepted him as he was and had to accept in return that he may need help at some point. Or she knew that in theory. While he was talking, while he was there, she absolutely believed him and in him. Afterwards, remembering, it wasn't so convincing.

'Do you know what that means?' she asked.

He shook his head. 'I don't think it has to mean anything.'

'You need to eat now, Dominic.'

'Kallu.'

'That's going to take a little while to get used to,' said Shona.

'I have time.'

Jude kept his eyes on Dominic as he ate, the bubbling questions making it hard to swallow.

The dark clouds pulled across their heads as they finished the crisps. The rain, welcome at first on their warm skin, soon became too heavy to be pleasant. Shona's faith in the strong wind faltered and she signalled their retreat. She wrapped up the rubbish inside her jacket and led the way up the cliff to the long field which led back to the café. She heard muffled music, and looked to see which of the boys was humming before realising it was her phone. She pulled it from her coat, dropping crisp packets which Jude chased down.

'Mariana, it's not a good time. We're getting soaked. Can I call you back?'

'Who's we? Isn't Jude at school?'

'We had a day off. Can I call you later?'

'I can hear rain. Are you in the rain with Jude?'

Jude ran back, waving the crisp packets, then tripped over and skidded on his knees across the gravel. There was a pause before he acknowledged he was injured and he wailed. Shona ran to him to grieve with him over the graze.

'Jude's hurt himself, so please can I call you back?'

'Tell me where you are and I will collect you.'

Shona sighed. She'd been putting off this meeting for months, years, had got it down to weekly phone calls, sporadic emails and Christmas cards. Now she couldn't argue; she needed to deal with Jude. She told Mariana and shoved the phone back in her pocket as the rain got harder and wetter.

The car pulled onto the gravel in front of the café so smoothly that there seemed to be no ripples in the pothole puddles. Mariana wound down the window to signal that they should come to her. The rain had stopped after they'd spoken, but Shona was painfully aware of the damp sand they all transferred into her manicured black saloon car. Jude still had his bribe in one hand, a half-melted Twix, but either Mariana hadn't noticed or was still traumatised by the screams.

After fastening Jude's seat belt, Shona sat in the front, her hair dripping onto her face, and braced herself for questions.

Mariana, self-consciously composed and beautifully tanned after her trip home to Portugal, raised one eyebrow. Shona could ignore eyebrows.

'It's been a while,' Shona started. 'You're looking radiant. How's the family?'

'Good.' Mariana's eyebrow didn't waver.

'I think you could probably start driving now.' Shona turned to the back seat. 'Do you remember me mentioning Mariana, Jude?'

'Of course he doesn't. We've never met.' Mariana gave words to his embarrassed wriggle. 'I haven't seen him since he wasn't baptised.'

Shona rolled her eyes. Mariana finally pressed on the accelerator and eased out of the car park.

'Isn't there someone else you need to introduce me to?'

'This is Dominic, Kallu, Dominic. I think I mentioned him, but he was called Dominic then.'

Mariana's eyebrow shot up again and she adjusted the rear view mirror. 'You're the boy who is staying? I thought you would be older.'

Kallu smiled. 'Sorry, I'll get older one day. It's my birthday today so I'm trying.'

Shona said, 'You never said it was your birthday.'

'And how are you finding the sofa?' asked Mariana.

Kallu said, 'I moved into the shed.'

The car slowed down. Shona was relieved he was fully back in the present and could hold his own with Mariana.

'You were Dominic who came to stay and now you're Kallu who lives in the shed.'

'Just for a while.'

The nails of Mariana's right hand tapped the steering wheel as she reset the mirror with her left. 'We really need to catch up properly, Shona.' She looked slyly at Shona while keeping her head forward, and muttered something in Portuguese.

Shona covered her smile as Mariana sped them away across the causeway. She always wanted to laugh when she felt awkward. But Dominic? Today was the first she'd heard of him thinking of leaving, even though they'd never really decided he was staying. She felt like Jude with his mouth full of crisps, unable to ask all the questions she had in case he answered them in front of Mariana. She looked to the side just as Mariana looked at her. She felt as if she'd been sent to the head teacher.

Mariana sniffed and reset the mirror again. 'Jude, normally this car does not carry chocolate, do you understand?'

Jude shook his head.

'Eat it up quickly,' Shona said.

'So when are you free for a nice long chat?' said Mariana. 'Now that Jude is at school it must be possible.'

Jude's eyes widened and he stopped chewing.

'She means me,' said Shona. 'How about next week?'

'I'll hold you to it.'

Shona smiled stiffly. Now she felt as if she'd been given detention.

After she'd put Jude to bed, Shona found Cerys sitting by the shed with Kallu, both leaning against the side with their legs bent up in front of them. Cerys had a pair of ridiculously brief shorts on and a top that Shona knew was from a pyjama set. She looked so happy and young and desperate, her studied hair twist learned from videos. Cerys stretched her hand towards Kallu's leg and stroked his ankle. Kallu looked confused, looked down at her hand and said something. Cerys blushed and Shona wanted to cry for her. Cerys stood up, and walked back to the house, her feet faltering when she saw Shona at the window.

She came in the back door and went to leave it before Shona could say anything, but she caught up with her.

'Cerys,' Shona said. 'Kallu isn't staying for ever. Don't get too used to him, OK?'

'I don't know what you mean.' Cerys was biting her lip, her cheeks still red.

'He's a good-looking boy, but he's not right for you. He's got things to work through.'

Cerys scowled. 'I'm not bothering him. I was just talking.'

'Cerys, I don't want you to spend time with him on your own.'

'In case I throw myself at him? He's made himself quite clear, thanks.' Her eyes filled and she ran upstairs. Shona didn't follow her. Humiliation was bad enough without someone watching.

3

She could hear Rob in his kitchen. Kettle boiling, bacon frying; breakfast at midday. The curtains were drawn and more than anything she wanted fresh air, a blowing breeze to strip the room of the smell of filthy socks and mouldy mugs. To get up, to allow the light in and fight with the stiff sash windows seemed too much trouble to go to, and she didn't really want to see her house through the window. Instead Shona picked her bra and T-shirt off the floor next to the bed and pulled on the smell of leaves and home. She lay back on the pillow and looked at his pile of books: eclectic bedtime reading, research for other people's essays and proof of other people's qualifications.

'Sarnie?' He held two mugs of tea in one hand and two hasty, dripping sandwiches flat on the other palm.

'Don't you have any plates?'

He shook his head. 'Why make more washing up?'

She took the tea and put it on the sisal drawers next to the bed, then took the sandwich in both hands. Rob got back on the bed next to her and they ate without speaking. He had brought up the smell of rancid, burnt oil with him from the kitchen. Rob wiped his hands on the duvet cover and folded his hands on his stomach.

'I needed that.' He looked at Shona from the corner of his eye. 'You look much better with no clothes on, Mrs Marks. What have you got dressed for?' He lifted her T-shirt up, but she held her arms by her sides. He slid his hand down her thigh. 'I think you should turn up to Parents' Evening like this. They're very, very dull.'

Shona placed the crusts next to her mug and smoothed the duvet back down. 'Don't you get tired of living like a student?' She had never seen a brush or a comb in his room, had never seen him clean-shaven. His forehead was beginning to retain a light crease when he was sleeping and his eyes were permanently shaded by exhaustion.

'Best years of my life,' he said.

'But you have to grow up one day.'

'Nah, you don't have to.' He imitated a teenager's intonation. 'It's a lifestyle choice to grow up. Or not. We don't all want to be like you, marriage, kids.'

'Still saving up for Thailand?'

'I'm going to live like a king.'

He waited until she put her mug down before putting his arm heavily across her breasts. He kissed her ear.

'I have to go.' She pushed him away.

'You don't have to.'

'I've got things to do.' She found her pants, still stuck inside a trouser leg, and pulled them on. She could see he was getting into work mode.

Shona had tried to imagine the kind of person who would rather pay for an essay than just write it themselves. Sometimes she saw a frail figure, oppressed by the expectations of those around them. Today she saw a hung-over rugby player, planning his advancement through the political hierarchy.

'I wanted to talk to you about some new order requests. I need to get my ratings up. Can you come back tomorrow?'

'I'm already doing the Apollo one. Let me think about it. Aren't you finishing temping this week?' Recently he was rarely here, less of a temptation. It was much easier when she didn't know where he was from one week to the next.

'I finish that maternity cover this week, thank God, and then next week I'm at some bloody school in Ipswich. That's why I need you to accept something so I don't look like I'm slacking.'

She did her special smile again. 'If you hate teaching so much, why don't you get a different job?'

'You're not quite old enough to be my mother.' He smiled. 'Are you? How old were you when I was born?'

She didn't have to work it out. 'Fourteen.' The same age as Cerys. And there was the same difference in age between him and Cerys, but she didn't mention that.

He lay back. 'So you could have been my mother. At a push. At some of the schools I've worked at you'd have been a late starter.'

She turned away and put her jeans on, standing to zip them. She knew she should break it off, that she'd crossed a line which should make a difference. She hadn't missed him over the summer holiday, hadn't even looked towards his house from her own, but she knew she would come back tomorrow or the next day. She needed this space. She dragged her fingers through her hair and smoothed down her top.

She pulled open the curtains and heaved up the sash window.

'That's better.'

'Christ, bit bright, Shona.' Rob got off the bed and sat down at his laptop. He pushed his sunglasses onto his face and began scrolling through the pages.

She looked out past his garden and looked for her house. She saw Dominic, Kallu, standing on her lawn looking back up at her. She shivered and moved away. By moving into her shed he'd put himself right between her and Rob. Did he mean that Rob had been watching her? She rubbed her arms.

'See, it's cold now, isn't it?' said Rob. 'Close it up, for fuck's sake.'

'In a minute. So what's on offer?' she asked. 'Work wise.'

'Ah.' Rob scrolled back up. 'A five-day twenty-page one on women in sport. Three hundred.'

Shona shook her head.

'I thought you'd like that.' He looked surprised. 'A pretty general one on Marx, boring.' He scrolled down. 'Dickens, the art of Benin, from modernism to post-structuralism, Heaney, Emmeline Pankhurst. Here's a list.' He handed her a print out. Shona sat back down on the bed. She had worked hard for her degree, had got a first and could have taken an easy path with it. She chose not to, but took a strange pleasure from imagining other people taking her expected route through life with her own work. She didn't like working towards other people's 2:1s or 2:2s. She suspected she might be a snob, but a well-paid one; there was more money in firsts so she didn't have to justify herself to Rob.

He tapped the page she was holding. 'I think I'll do a

couple of thousand on Harry Potter. I'll be up all night again.'

Shona wrinkled her nose. 'Try to have a shower, though.'

'Yes, Mum. And you could bring some milk next time. I'll probably have used it all.'

'What about your housemates? Don't they go to the shops either?'

'Whose milk do you think we've been drinking? Wasn't my bacon either—' he kissed her cheek '—or my bread.'

She put the paper, now folded twice, into her bag and shrugged her coat on.

'I'll try to remember.'

She left him at the computer, yawning and shaking empty cigarette packets. He shouted, 'Could you get me a packet of fags?' but she closed the door without acknowledging him. When she was on the stairs, he shouted, 'Come back and close the window!'

If he had to buy cigarettes, he might actually get some food as well, and he could close his own window.

On the way back home she knocked at her neighbour's house. She hadn't seen Amy for ages, but she had heard her crying in the night. There was no point knocking too early, but Amy didn't seem to want to answer.

She shouted through the letter box, 'Amy, it's just Shona!'

There was a shuffling noise and she let the letter box fall. Amy pulled the door slightly open, showing most of her face. She was wearing a dressing gown, one bare foot covering the other.

'Yeah?' Her eyes were heavy, her breath sour. Her long hair hung lifelessly and Shona thought she could see the edges of a black eye.

'Anything I can get you? I'm going to the shop later.'

'No.'

'OK. Let me know if I can help.'

Amy shut the door. As their houses joined, Shona knew when Amy had visitors and there hadn't been any for a while. Someone behind Shona cleared their throat and she turned, expecting to see her other neighbour, Lee. She was surprised to see Mariana waiting at her gate.

'Have you been waiting for me?'

'We did have plans, Shona.'

'Sorry, I got caught up with something.'

Mariana followed her around to the back door. She seemed jittery. She got jittery when she was angry. Her bracelets rattled as she dramatically illustrated her points in the air.

Shona said, 'Did you see Amy? She doesn't look as bad as before.'

'If I knew a woman like that one,' Mariana nodded her head towards the shared wall, 'I would force her to get help.'

'I can't.' Shona sat down heavily. 'I want to help her, but I can't force her.'

'Some people you can't help. But I would always say I'd tried.' She tutted. 'Before it was too late. She has a family, doesn't she?' She clamped her lips together and looked down at her mug.

'Maybe I just hear more because there's no firewall in the loft. There's just the bedroom wall and our ceilings are linked so the noise just jumps right over. Most of it is just her, falling over. Not all of it.' There was no point in lying to Mariana, or herself. Shona knew what she could hear wasn't right, but she had known Amy before she started drinking and didn't want to give up on her yet. Shona

34

had been in a similar place after Meghan and could easily have gone the same way. Mariana knew that, better than anyone. She made the coffee and watched Mariana wait for the next point to demolish.

They sat, challenging each other to change the subject first. Whoever blinked and did it would have lost this round. Shona usually won because Mariana became so infuriated she cracked and had to stand in the garden to have a cigarette. This time, though, she spoke. 'Nothing has changed, Shona. You're the one who would have to live with it. That woman next door can't look after herself. There's morally little difference between letting die and killing, even if some would argue a legal difference.'

Shona admired the way she elongated her vowels, as if partly to remind her listeners that she was Portuguese, not really one of them, and partly because it suited her languorous personality. Sometimes Shona mimicked her in response. Today she smoothed her hair around the back of her head. Her neighbour wasn't really what was making Mariana cross; she was just an excuse for an argument.

Shona said, 'That's not quite the situation, is it?'

'Depends what happens to her.' Mariana's face was stern but her tapping fingers betrayed her enjoyment of the discussion. Shona had often wondered why she was a solicitor and not a barrister.

Time passed. Neither of them drank any more coffee. Mariana's head twisted round towards the window. Shona became anxious that she was looking at Kallu, or Rob.

'I heard that Jimmy is getting out soon.' Shona took the mugs to the sink.

Mariana looked confused. 'Who?'

'My uncle, Jimmy. The one in Highpoint.'

'Oh, yes.' Mariana's eyes drifted away again. 'That's good.'

Shona could feel Mariana wanted to ask a question but would rather snip off her tongue before she did. She'd never had a silence like this with her before. Mariana was so full of words. There was clearly something she needed to say and couldn't.

'Are you OK?' Shona said.

Mariana snapped her head back. 'Of course. I should go.' She checked her watch and gasped. 'Shona, Jude!'

'He's having tea at a friend's. But I do need to collect him soon.'

Jude had eaten at Callum's and was settled in front of the TV when Shona arrived for him.

'Cup of tea?' asked Thea.

'Just a quick one. I haven't fed Cerys yet. I'll have to pick up some chips on the way home.' Shona looked at the bowl of celery and carrot sticks Thea had left for the boys to snack on. 'It won't hurt her to wait this once.' She couldn't remember when she'd last done a proper shop, had the cupboards full of more than lentils and ancient dried apricots. 'Do lentils get weevils, do you think?'

'No idea,' said Thea. 'Any reason you're asking?'

'No.' Shona smiled. Thea, unlike Mariana, didn't seem to need a full awareness of the thread of her thoughts. She was happy just to dip in and out. 'I have a confession.'

'Yeah?'

Thea sat down, her loose shirt sleeves rolled up to the elbow. Shona could see more of the tattoo than before, could make out a name.

36

'When I said Jude was sick—'

'I know, he told Callum all about the beach.'

'Oh. OK.'

'Sounded nice.' Thea raised her eyebrows. 'I wouldn't have said anything.'

'I know. Sorry. I don't know why I didn't just say.'

Thea reached for the ceramic pot in the centre of the table and pulled out a small packet of tobacco and papers. Shona watched her stretch out the tobacco and heat a small amount of resin, before crumbling it on top. She nimbly rolled the joint up and Shona watched her lick the paper shut. She wasn't sure what she felt about this. Thea tore a small oblong of cardboard from the ragged packet of papers and pushed the roach into place.

'Fancy some?'

'Yes, thanks. I would. It's been a really long day.'

They perched on the back doorstep, the door mostly closed, and Thea lit up. The sky was clear but the sun was long gone from this part of the garden and Thea rolled her sleeves back down.

'That name on your arm, is it a boyfriend?'

Thea nearly choked and blew the smoke out hard. 'No,' she croaked. 'Here, you'd better take this.'

She stood up until the coughing ended, her eyes streaming a little. Shona had a couple of puffs before handing it back.

Thea pointed at the tattoo. 'Jonathan was my name for a while.'

'You were a man?'

Thea shook her head but held the smoke in this time. 'I read Jonathan Livingstone Seagull at an impressionable age. What can I say?' She laughed. 'I quite liked it, being Jonathan. I liked the way it confused people. But when I had Callum it suddenly seemed really complicated for no good reason. Did you find that?'

'Yes, children make everything complicated.' Shona shook her head at the joint, feeling her legs going warm. Another mark against her, if Maynard ever found out. She'd not expected this of Thea, but then she'd never have guessed she used to be called Jonathan. That was a bit complicated, she supposed. 'At least you don't have a boy who lives in your shed.'

Thea, inhaling, got caught out again and coughed until she laughed.

Shona's mobile began to trill its annoying alarm. She got her phone out and felt confused, and then horrified.

'Oh, shit,' said Shona. 'I've got Parents' Evening.'

Cerys was waiting for Shona.

'You forgot.'

'You could have called, reminded me.' She pushed Jude in front of her and turned to go.

'I'm coming too,' said Cerys, closing the door behind her and pushing Jude back.

'But it's for parents.'

'It's about my GCSEs, Mum. I'm supposed to be there.'

Shona tried to think quickly how she could get out of it.

'Have you been crying?' asked Cerys.

'No, I think I have conjunctivitis. Maybe I should stay away from schools. It's catching.'

'I'm going.'

'Fine. We're all going. Fine.'

Cerys had the list of times and teachers, not that it meant much. They spent most of the evening standing in corridors waiting for their long-expired time to come up. Cerys did most of the talking. Shona tried to look unwell but interested. Why did you need parents when your children were as organised as her daughter? Cerys knew exactly what she was going to do. She hadn't even discussed it with Shona.

It was time to get up again. Shona followed Cerys, holding Jude's hand.

'Last one,' said Cerys. 'He won't be busy, he's only maternity cover.'

They walked into Mr Cartwright's History room. Rob smiled up at them and stood to shake their hands.

By the time she got home Shona could feel her eyes were still heavy. She put Jude to bed and made herself a sand- wich for dinner. Cerys was sitting at the table with a bowl of ice cream. She hadn't spoken while they were in the room with Rob, or after it. She was angry. Shona could see that.

Cerys glanced at her hand and looked back at the bowl. They both watched the consistency change from whipped to single cream.

'Can I change the time I am allowed to come in?'

Shona raised her eyebrows. A classic argument opener. 'No. Five o'clock on a school night.'

'So it's all right for me to spend time with pseudo mes- siahs in my own house, but I'm not allowed to spend time with actual friends outside the house?'

'Not after five, no. I need to know where you are and I need to know that you're safe. When you're older, I know we'll have to think about it, but not yet. I'm not ready yet. And I don't think you are either.'

Cerys looked at the door and then back to her mother.

'Do you think that you spend so much time with weirdoes that you see them everywhere?'

'I know that you like Kallu.'

'I did before, but even you don't trust him. You said I need to be supervised with him. You shouldn't have people in your house who you don't trust around your children.'

That was Maynard talking.

'So you've discussed this with your father too?'

'Oh, am I not supposed to talk to him either? Why don't you just get divorced?'

'We will, one day.'

'It's hardly a convincing pretence of a marriage.'

'I need to stay in this house. He doesn't want to, but I'm not selling it. That's all.'

It was the guilt of action which drove him away and the guilt of inaction which kept her there. Divorce was inevitable and would be a blessed relief. Sometimes she fantasised that Maynard already had a second family for his weekdays in London, a pretty young wife and a curly-haired toddler. Maybe a boy to play football with. She hadn't seen or heard any clues but she had never been to his flat in London and didn't really want to look too hard. Keeping two children safe was clearly all she could think about or manage.

Cerys spooned the melted ice cream and let it drip back into the bowl. 'Dad says it isn't up to you. He says we'll all be living somewhere else by Christmas.'

'What does that mean? He can't sell the house.'

Cerys kept her eyes fixed on the spoon, the final drip that hung there. 'He can. He paid for it and he can sell it.'

'It doesn't just belong to him. It's mine too. You don't want to move, do you? Cerys? I'll fight him.'

'You fight everyone.' Cerys dropped the spoon and shivered. 'I'm not going to keep to your rules any more. I'll be in when I like and you can say what you like.'

Shona's throat tightened. 'Stop it, Cerys.'

'You suffocate me. You're selfish and tarty, you drink too much and you only want to control what everyone does. You don't love any of us and you never have and I can't wait to leave.' She smirked. 'Where's your boyfriend? Keeping your bed warm?'

The only thing Shona could do was keep calm. She rested her arms on the table. 'There's nothing like that between me and Kallu.' She wasn't sure if that sounded convincing. She wasn't sure what to think of him, most of the time.

'You just picked up a teenage boy off the street and brought him home for no reason whatsoever? And this house is so fucked up that I didn't say anything because, in the scheme of things, it didn't seem that weird.'

'Why are you swearing at me?' Shona stopped pretending to finish her sandwich and folded her arms.

'It's only now, talking it through with my friends, that I realise you kept him away from me because you wanted him to yourself. Because you're a pervert.'

'He's a kid. Nothing has happened and it wouldn't.' Shona rubbed her eyes. She should have made coffee. Doing it now would look like an evasion. She rested her eyes behind her hand.

'What about my teacher?'

Shona looked up. 'What do you mean?'

Cerys shook her head. 'You want me to spell it out? The blushing, the flirting, the way his foot slid under the table towards your—'

'Stop!'

Cerys looked close to tears. 'In my school! Where I have to go! Didn't you hear them laughing in the corridor?'

So that's what this was about. Cerys had guessed. Rob had basically told her by the way he behaved and Shona hated him for that. 'Can we talk about that?'

'God, no!' Cerys rolled her eyes. 'Let's keep some kind of barriers in place. I really don't want to know the specifics.'

'I'm sorry. I've known Rob, Mr Cartwright, for a while. He was just being stupid.'

'You think that explains it?'

'Are you going to tell Dad? I'd just like to know.' What she wanted to say was, don't tell Daddy, darling, daughters always hold their mother's secrets. But she hadn't quite turned out to be that kind of mother, and Cerys wasn't that kind of daughter.

'Everyone else knows. Why shouldn't he?' Cerys pointed at Shona. 'Your boyfriend flirts with all the girls at school, he's all over them. Everyone knows to keep away from him. Only the desperate look twice.'

Shona hadn't ever wondered what Rob was like as a teacher but had to accept that this would fit with her own picture of him. Maybe it would be better if Cerys did tell her dad, maybe they could all go their separate ways, but she knew that Cerys would choose Daddy and the house would be sold. And that would be the end of that.

'So, don't tell Dad that you're a prostitute,' Cerys summarised. 'Is that it?'

'A prostitute? I'm not sleeping with anyone for money. And it's none of Maynard's business. I never ask you what he gets up to in London, do I?'

Cerys curled her lip.

'Right,' said Shona. 'It's not good, but this is how it

is. It's about time you just accepted the situation. Your father and I have a terrible relationship, you know that. We see other people but this was a bad choice and I'm sorry. I'm very, very sorry that I was seeing someone who worked in your school, but I met him before he got a job there. I do think you're exaggerating, and no-one noticed. If you don't say anything at school, it will blow over.'

Cerys crossed her arms.

'Next, I know you like Kallu.'

Cerys blushed and held her arms more tightly.

'I'm not trying to keep you apart to keep him for myself but because I don't think he's in a good place at the moment. What he's working through is a really difficult—' she struggled for a word to sum it all up and failed '—thing. A spiritual thing.'

'You're an atheist. You don't even believe in spirits.'

'But he does.'

'So why's he working in the Natural History Museum? Shouldn't he be on a retreat or something? A monastery?'

'It's not like that, it's complicated.'

'Why?'

Shona shifted in her chair. 'He needs a sign.'

'And you believe him?'

'I don't need to. That's not what he needs from me.'

Cerys stirred her melted ice cream round the bowl.

Shona placed her hand on the table. 'But I need you to believe me.'

'I don't believe you.' Cerys stood up. 'But none of it will matter because I'm not staying here any longer than I have to.'

Cerys left the room. Shona lowered her head to the table and closed her eyes. She'd run out of words. She had never managed to be the mother she thought she could be. All her life she'd been convinced that she would make up for her miserable parents by bettering them at everything, paying attention to what her children said and did and wanted to be. In the end, she had accumulated a few random people around her, most of whom didn't like her one little bit, and she could live with that as long as she had the house.

'Go then,' she said.

GRETA

It was only girls who had to worry about the devil. My brother, born two years after me, never believed any of the stories about the devil chasing us down across the counties. James would pull rough woollen blankets over his head and chase me around the room, making horse clopping noises and would make me laugh about it behind their backs. In bed I would rehear those hooves and pull my own blankets up. I never wondered if I believed. No-one ever asked me.

To their faces my brother was a dedicated advocate, devout to the point of ridicule. When he was twelve, he painted an icon for our grandmother's birthday, copied from the cover of one of her many religious books, and she adored him even more for it. She never asked him where he got the paint, the gold and blues, or the brushes with their fine spikes of hog's hair. She showed it off to the priest who was more interested than adoring of him. James began to be invited round for long nights of wine and books. The priest loaned him icons from the church or from the local cathedrals and offered him money to paint more. For the church, he said. We never saw them in our church. My brother bought a lot of clothes that year. No-one asked him where that money came from either, but I'd say it was straight from the collection plate. The flowers in the church were sparse in those years, even at my grandmother's funeral, and the candles were thin.

When my brother left school, only fourteen, he had enough money to travel to cathedrals and shrines all over the country, Canterbury, Durham and Walsingham, and came back with his sketch books full of humble mothers and serious babies framed by arching haloes and punctured with visible hearts. He became an expert on the lost icons of the Reformation, when Suffolk used to be the Virgin Mary's own country.

I'd been working for three years and James was fifteen, more than old enough to earn his keep. He was just back from Canterbury with a bag of apples for my mother and paper money for himself that he kept in an engraved copper tin with a large opal in the middle. He was eating a slice of the cake Mother had cooked for his return. I asked him when he was going to start working.

He brushed crumbs from his trousers and laughed at me. 'Only fools work, Greta, you know that.'

I hid my calloused hands under my apron. 'I do not.'

'Would you, given a choice? There's people who never work because they get given money, just sit there until they get it from other people who were given money. There are more worlds than this one, and I like them.'

'I don't know why you keep coming back, in that case. You never give Mother a penny and they could use your bedroom for their own instead of keeping it for you.'

He yawned and looked at me sideways. 'When she asks me to leave, I will.'

I rarely talked to him. I rarely saw him to talk to.

I had the box room, a small afterthought of a bedroom to play my records in, and my parents made up their bed in the front room every night and put it away every morning. My brother's bedroom, the largest room upstairs, became a studio to rival any artist. Deep dyed silks were nailed to the walls so he could absorb their colour and texture while he slept, slabs of wood held the traces of unique rainbows. I caught my mother, more than once, in his room with an exotic silk swathed around her shoulders, contrasting against the worn brown of her woollen skirt. She jumped when she saw me looking and threw the scarf away from her. It buckled in the air before it reached the bed but she left it on the floor, pushing past me to leave the room.

My brother started to use words like tincture and perspective, and it wasn't from the many books of illustrations that started to litter his floor that he got them, as his reading never improved. It was from people he crept out at night time to meet, taking my bicycle quietly from the shed and rattling away from the house. One night he never brought it back and I cried when I realised. A week later I had a brand-new bike resting by the back door.

No-one asked the question. Least asked, soonest mended was the thought on everyone's mind. The paintings started as smoothed planks, were decorated and dried and then were gone. My brother started to wear cravats and to come home less and less frequently until he wouldn't even spend one night at home in three months. At seventeen he had moved to London and my mother pined for him in a way which made me wish I had never spoken about him leaving her.

My mother cried when she saw his room was empty, and then moved her clothes from the front room to the bedroom. She caught me on the landing, watching her.

'Time to go to church,' she said.

Like her mother, mine spent as much time as she could in the church, on the cleaning rota, the flower rota and any other rota she could find. Churches were the only place I ever saw either of them not looking over their shoulders or jumping at the slightest noise. They stretched it out as long as they could. My mother would kneel and bend until her knees seized and she could barely walk. She often begged me to become a nun and put an end to the waiting. If I sacrificed myself, then the curse would be broken, this mother to daughter string of misery, expecting the devil at any moment. So she thought. And she spent so long waiting for the devil to find her that I couldn't believe it was going to happen. What did he intend to do with us when he got here?

With my brother gone my mother gave in, or gave up, and allowed me to marry, but not before telling me that she wished she'd left me at a convent in a basket. Even when it turned out that I should have listened and never, ever married I couldn't forgive her. Many years later my mother died waiting out in the cold, wrapped in her shawl, waiting for the devil to find her. I didn't discover her until the morning. James didn't come home for the funeral.

4

After a few weeks at school Jude was getting up just a little later and taking just a little longer to dress himself. Shona stood at the gate, shouting at him to hurry. That's how she noticed that Cerys hadn't gone the usual way, down the road to the right and then left, but straight down the road which ran up to their front door. When they moved in, people had talked a lot about feng shui and how bad it was to have a road coming straight at your door like that. They recommended that Shona buy some kind of octagonal mirror to ward off the bad energy. Shona had heard enough of that kind of thing as a child, and wasn't afraid to tell them so.

Now, as she watched Cerys walking along Audley Road, she wondered.

Mariana was waiting for Shona when she got back from dropping Jude off. They walked round to the back door.

'Were you late this morning?' she asked Shona.

'No. Of course not.' Five minutes didn't count. She

decided to change the subject. 'I think it's odd you still have Tuesdays off.'

'I am a creature of habit. Volunteering on Monday, my day on Tuesday, money slave for the rest of the week.'

Shona hesitated with her key in the lock. 'Coffee?'

'I thought you'd never ask.'

Mariana placed the ground coffee on the table with a flourish. The coffee was always made in a cafetière when Mariana used to call. Shona had found it in the back of the cupboard. Now she realised that she'd forgotten to clean it before putting it away.

It was so dusty it had turned sticky. She scrubbed at it while the kettle boiled but it didn't quite come clear, a misty glaze sticking fast to the surface. Shona's mobile rang.

'Can you finish up here? I have to take this.' She went into the back room and pulled the door closed behind her, feeling awkward about abandoning Mariana, but was not like she'd invited her. If Mariana wanted to pretend nothing had changed, then she'd had to accept Shona as she was and always had been. Rob wanted to talk business and Shona wanted to talk money.

'Tell me about the Tower one.' Shona turned away from Mariana, who had brought the coffee through to the back room and was making no secret of her interest in the conversation.

'Oh, that's a good one,' said Rob. 'Forty pages, ten thousand words. A twenty-day job.'

Shona lifted some papers and eventually a blue biro rolled out. 'What standard?'

'First class. It's nearly two grand, but you could get more than that doing three little next day ones.'

She scribbled the details on the back of an old envelope. 'No, I'll do that. Email it to me.'

'Do you know anything about the Tower of London?'

'No. And neither does the person who's going to get an MA. The difference is, by the time I've finished, I will. See you later.'

'Today?'

'Maybe, I'll have to see how things pan out.' She flipped her phone down. They never said goodbye. That was a total giveaway to Mariana she realised, all niceties abandoned.

'Is Maynard around this week?' asked Mariana. She sat with her back to the window at the side of the table and had piled up the books and papers to give herself space for her coffee. Behind her Shona could see that rain had speckled the window and obscured the detail of the garden. Shona switched all the lights on, giving the feel of the evening.

'No. He's working. I haven't heard when he'll be around.'

Shona folded the envelope over, put it on the mantelpiece and rearranged the photos in front of her. One showed a small, round roadside chapel in France and one of Jude and Kallu in the garden, both flexing their biceps and smiling.

Mariana put her head down and pushed the plunger of the coffee so it sat on the surface of the liquid. 'These trade fairs seem to be very frequent.'

'If he's even at them. He usually only comes back at the weekend now, if ever. Cerys barely sees him so, of course, she adores him.' Shona grimaced and sat down.

Mariana lifted her head. Shona conscientiously squinted out of the window to avoid Mariana's look. It didn't work, she could feel her gaze.

'I don't need a lecture,' said Shona. 'He's been talking

to Cerys about selling the house again. Apparently. I didn't hear it from him. I think he means it this time, but he won't say it to me, so I don't know. You know how things are. I don't know anything about anything.'

'You're right.' Mariana eyed up the coffee. 'Why am I here?'

'Love and devotion.'

'Coffee and not enough biscuits. Now you know that, at least. So, where is Maynard this week?'

'The last I heard was that he's just done some massively secret deal on a new Vermeer in Cologne, Cairo, wherever. Somewhere beginning with C. His mother phoned to tell me.'

'He didn't tell you?'

Shona stood up. 'I'll have a look for biscuits.'

'A really good look. Keep looking until you find some.'

Shona bent in a slight bow. 'I always liked our Tuesdays, Mariana.'

Mariana tried not to smile. 'They're OK.'

Shona found three soft ginger nuts and half a packet of Jaffa cakes in the cupboard. She arranged the Jaffa cakes on a plate for Mariana and carried them to the table.

They sat in silence for a while. The rain had stopped but the windows were still dotted with the memory. Mariana didn't say anything. Shona tried not to hold her breath, wondering what the question was finally going to be.

Finally, Mariana spoke. 'Has Jude asked who his father is yet?'

Shona held her hands steady. 'What's got into you recently? Who've you been arguing with?'

Mariana plunged and poured. 'I'm perfectly fine, just making conversation. I'm sure you'll make the right decision about everything. I'm going to go and do some shopping soon. I just wanted to call on you, in case you needed me.' She drank her coffee.

'I have missed you.'

Mariana looked confused. 'I don't know how you missed me as I was still there. All the time.'

'Things have been difficult. I wanted to make the most of Jude, while I could.'

'By keeping him to yourself? Children have to be shared around, Shona.'

'Jude is fine, happy. He's very happy.'

'And work? Writing about the Tower of London? That doesn't sound as if you've moved forward. You need to come back to me. I'll look after you. Jude's at school and you have untapped talents.' She smiled in the old way and drank her coffee.

Shona indicated the empty cafetière. 'Shall I make some more?'

'No, you have the pleasure of torture to write about. And lots of thinking to do. I'll see you soon. Phone me, maybe.'

'Thanks, Mariana. For coming.'

'As always. *Adeus*.'

Sometimes Shona wished that Mariana would just give her an opinion or advice. She spent so much time in the silence of disagreement or the silence of allowance, but Shona knew that Mariana would have an opinion on the outcome. She made Shona make her decision and then told her what she thought of it. The silence ended and the words spilled out; if she was angry, they were mostly Portuguese which cushioned Shona a little.

Shona heard the door slam and she relaxed. Drinking the last of her coffee, she turned off the ceiling light and put on the corner lamp instead. The tapping on the window reminded her that the gutter needed fixing. It was probably urgent. It should probably have been done when she first noticed in the spring. Sometimes she missed being able to delegate stupid little tasks like that to Maynard.

She thought about writing an essay plan but instead her eyes drifted to the photo of the roadside shrine she'd taken in France. Mariana had been asking for a copy of that photo. She'd do that first.

Mariana had been volunteering at the Citizens Advice Bureau for years when Shona started there, after Cerys was born. Mariana was doing it as penance for all the money she earned three days a week as a solicitor. Shona was there because she had been very publicly sacked. They met over biscuits when Shona found herself being scrutinised by a glamorous woman with dark eyes and darker lustrous hair.

'You're the Opium Wars fighter?' Mariana frowned.

'Not really.' Shona cringed. She had hoped it had faded in people's memories. 'Now I'm just a troublemaker.'

Mariana nodded. 'Well, we all need to be that, once in a while. But you went further than most trying to get drug smugglers acquitted.'

'Their defence had merit.'

'Their defence was the Opium Wars of the nineteenth century.'

'I wasn't even on the jury. I wasn't expecting it to be published until after the verdict.'

'But you persuaded the defence team to push for an appeal and many others that the argument of the smugglers was sound. That shows some skill in persuasion, if not in judgement.'

They looked at each other and Shona waited for what

she would say about the Mission, crumbled, folded and all funding removed. Mariana nodded.

'I'll be keeping an eye on you.'

In a way it was the threat that it sounded, but Shona enjoyed challenging people and within a year Meghan had been born and died and nothing was the same anyway. Shona clung to Mariana's brutal kindnesses in a way that surprised her and she enjoyed the way Mariana discomfited Maynard. She left the prayer cards and candles Mariana brought on the mantelpiece and in the centre of the table during meals so that Maynard had to look at them and be reminded and reminded and reminded. Mariana liked it and Maynard hated it and Shona didn't care because she couldn't forget for the length of a breath in any case. She'd left the Citizens Advice but Mariana didn't let her go. She came in, wanted or not, invited or not, and talked about the day Shona would return every Tuesday. She only drew the line at Mariana's attempts to take her to church. Mariana came to her, as no-one else did, and that was enough.

Mariana slowly persuaded her to let Cerys go back to nursery and to visit, 'just half an hour', at the Citizens Advice, until Cerys was doing a whole day and so was Shona. No matter how brittle and argumentative Mariana could be, Shona remembered how she coaxed her back into the world.

Shona spent a few minutes reading through the library books in her office, a few pages at a time, but put them back in the pile next to her computer. Apollo, Apollo, Apollo. 'Interventions of the gods in Greek tragedies.' She had to finish this by next week if she was going to have enough time for the Tower.

The office was accessed through the bedroom she shared with Jude. Their sharing was getting silly now. It was OK while he was little but he would only grow. They might have to get bunk beds. What other options did she have? Maybe she could install some fire escape so he could let himself in and out, but it was still a tiny room. She couldn't even consider displacing Cerys from her light, airy room at the front. That left going up into the loft. The mess and disruption made her shudder. The house was paid off but she'd never get a mortgage to make improvements.

She moved to the chair by the window and pushed up the bottom sash. The air was warm now and she leaned over the windowsill. The garden next door was empty apart from a couple of sparrows in the miniature apple tree.

She liked the back of houses, their hidden nature. Even in tightly packed Victorian streets you didn't expect to be looked at. A little four-foot fence did its symbolic job and directed the eyes upwards.

A quick movement in the window of a house opposite caught her eye; a young girl with long, brown hair stood holding both curtains open. Shona couldn't make out her features but she could see she was naked. The curtains closed.

There was a sense of familiarity, of something troubling. Gradually she realised that it looked like Cerys. This house had black guttering and an empty trellis against the back wall. The kitchen and third bedroom were on the left, the gate on the right.

Cerys walking a different way to school may have meant she wasn't actually going to school. Had they phoned? There were no messages on her mobile, but something didn't feel right about this. Cerys hadn't spoken to her since Parents' Evening. They'd fallen out before but this felt serious, like she was planning some kind of punishment for Shona.

She ran down the stairs, pulled her keys from her jacket pocket, and left the house. She ran round to Rob's house and banged on the door. There was no answer and she couldn't hear anything at the letterbox. She banged again and then walked around the side of his house. She couldn't open the gate, so pulled herself up using the small wall that marked the boundary with the next house. She could clearly see black guttering, but the far kitchen wall couldn't be seen. It was on the correct side and she could see into the kitchen when she jumped, but she'd only ever gone straight up to Rob's room so didn't recognise it.

She went back to the front door and banged again. She tried phoning his mobile but it went to answerphone. She tried her daughter too, but Cerys never answered her phone and she was at school, or supposed to be. She sat on the wall in front of his house and tried to think rationally. It probably wasn't Cerys; she had only an image of long hair to make her think so. It also probably wasn't Rob's bedroom, not that she had any misguided sense of loyalty, on his side or her own. She had no claim over Rob and no right to behave in this possessive odd way. Unless it was Cerys.

He knew she was married. She knew he had no desire for permanency in any area of his life. Neither of them had discussed their backgrounds, other than academic, or politics or beliefs. She liked having a space where she didn't have to be political and she doubted it even crossed his mind. In her real life, she was angry most of the time at every injustice and imbalance and unfairness. And she didn't need to write essays for the money. She took that because it was there. She liked his nihilistic arrogance and hated him for it. That's what made him attractive.

She returned to the door again and knocked more quietly, as if a different caller. There was still no response. She went back to her house wondering, should she wait on this corner, or this corner? She convinced herself that it was her own guilty conscience. There couldn't be a problem. The school would have phoned. Someone would have told her that her daughter wasn't where she should be. She decided to go home and wait for the panic to subside.

She went back in her front door and sat on the bottom of the stairs. A normal person might sit in the front room to see what was happening outside in the street, and she cursed the fact that she couldn't use her front room like a normal person, the door being locked to her and Jude.

She had had the occasional glimpse inside Maynard's room. There were paintings on the walls, ridiculously expensive, she assumed, none of which she liked, and imported hardwood cabinets with a minimalist display of glass and ceramics. She didn't like those either. His paperwork was kept in the antique bureau, all of the drawers painted with a delicate one-hair brush, so he'd said. As he made more and more money he asked her if they could move to a better house, a more appropriate house, but she refused. Instead he filled this medium-sized Victorian terrace with furniture for the house he wanted.

She needed this room, or another in the loft. She went back upstairs and lay down on the bed, trying to decide on how she could phrase it so that Maynard would see it as an investment for his house, rather than creating living space for her bastard cuckoo child.

The alarm on the phone woke her, reminding her to collect Jude. It was so warm. They could have gone to Mersea almost any day this month after the morning chill had lifted. As she cut across the grass on the way to school, daddy long legs lifted from the shudders of her feet, one after another, like tiny grey ghosts.

Shona heard Cerys pause at the bottom of the stairs, Jude shouting hello to her, before going up to her room. She was two hours late. She had ignored three phone calls and five texts. Shona heard the music go on in Cerys' room above her head and strained to listen for noises beyond that. Cerys refused to come down for dinner. Shona refused to have the argument in front of Jude. She could wait.

Shona took Jude to bed and lay down with him to read his story. When she woke up, it was dark and Jude's arm was sticky on her neck. She sat up, unsure whether it was morning or evening, her tongue thick in her mouth. There was a light underneath the door and she edged towards it, feeling her way. When she opened the door, her eyes ached with the strong hall light. She could hear talking in the kitchen and went through. Cerys was sitting at the table, her legs pulled up in front of her. Her chair was tipped backwards slightly as she turned to look at her father.

Shona filled the kettle. 'Why didn't anyone wake me?'

'We didn't know if you wanted to be woken,' said Maynard. He stirred the pasta in the saucepan.

'That isn't for you, is it, Cerys?' said Shona.

'You usually eat with Jude,' Cerys said. 'I didn't.'

'I left yours in the oven.'

Cerys didn't reply. Shona sat next to her but Cerys shifted away and kept her eyes on Maynard.

'How was your day, Cerys?' Shona asked.

'Fine.' Cerys yawned and left the room.

Maynard drained the pasta into the colander. 'I'll leave some for her, in case she comes back.'

Shona put her head in her hands.

'She's a teenager, you can't take it personally.'

'I'm not. I've got a headache.'

The kettle clicked off. Shona pushed her chair back but Maynard got the mugs from the cupboard and put the tea bags in.

'Why are you here?' she asked.

'The trade fair went well,' he said. 'I just thought I'd come home for a couple of days.'

'I know all about it. Your mother phoned.'

'Yes, about that. Could you at least pretend to know where I am when she calls you? Or care?'

Shona put her head back in her hands. She could hear him pouring the water, the snap of the jar and then the smell of the pesto as he spooned it on top the pasta.

'Have we got ham?'

'No.'

He went back to the mugs, took the bags out and added the milk. He pulled the cutlery drawer open and rattled through it. He stood next to her and waited until she raised her head before putting the mug down in front of her.

'Don't you want to know about the Bouts painting? This is going to make me.'

'Not us, then?'

'My reputation.' There was a look of the young

60

Maynard about him now, the swaggering tie-less student whose glasses were half as thick as those he now wore. His hair was fairly similar, no grey or baldness yet, just sensibly short with a slight quiff at the front. He used to laugh.

'It's not often that a new piece is discovered from the fifteenth century. It's a big deal. I'll show you.' His brief-case and travel bag were on the far chair at the table. He sat down, ate a mouthful of food and started to sort through the papers. He pulled out two laminated pictures, both of Madonna and child.

'I mean, he's notoriously problematic but just look at the similarities. The sleepy eyes, the fingers and the high foreheads, the use of perspective. The deep blue dress and red shawl, that's common. And of course it was found in Leuven. All these people who don't search their attics before they move, it's incredible, but it keeps them safe for centuries.'

Shona compared them. The babies were so old and young simultaneously, about six months, or a small nine months? The legs showed lines of plumpness, the feet were tensely pointing toes upright. The mothers' mouths were equally smug and indulgent but the eyes were full of long-lashed adoration.

Shona pushed the pictures back towards him. He wasn't going to say anything about the house. Either Cerys had been lying or he was waiting for Shona to ask.

'This really isn't working, Maynard. You can't come and go as you please. We need a clean break and we need more space. Either I have the front room as a bedroom or I need a loan for the loft. This is my home and it hasn't been yours for a long time. Cerys is old enough to visit you now and you've got your flat. Just give me the house.

That must be a fair split, or even in your favour. Whatever it is, we need to draw a line under everything.'

He sat back hard in his chair, looking ready to beat her down with reasoned negotiation of his needs and desires. 'We agreed, until Cerys was eighteen.'

Shona held onto the mug, her palms burning. 'That was before you got your own flat. I don't go into your flat. I don't even know where it is. I think we need to just split things down the middle and you don't come into my house any more.'

'It's not fair. You were never fair about this. It was just one of those things. I'm sorry it happened,' he whispered. 'Sorry. You have no idea. But you don't get the house.'

Shona blinked hard and looked at the table. 'Things have changed since we agreed. I'm divorcing you.'

'You?' Maynard's voice was artificially loud, as if he wanted Cerys to hear at the other end of the house. 'You're the one who brought someone's bastard into my home and made an exhibition of yourself in public, humiliating your daughter in her school. And don't think that no-one noticed. Everyone knows. You move some kind of Greek god into the shed—'

'What?'

'I'm talking from Cerys' perspective here, not mine. You're the one who poisoned everything we had.' He threw his chair back, emptied his dish into the bin and dropped the dish into the sink. 'You took our tragedy and made it into your own private philosophy where I'm the evil baddy and you're the poor wronged woman. It wasn't like that and you don't have more rights than me when it comes to Cerys.' He sighed and looked down at his hands. 'You've made it quite clear that we can't share the house, as we agreed. First the bastard, then the mad boy. You're intent on filling my house, which I let you live in with Cerys. Only Cerys. God knows you had trouble looking after one, but three? Look at this shit hole.' He pointed at the sink, the clothes falling out of the dryer, the bin so full it didn't close. 'So I'll have to sell.'

'You've done it again! You've made it look like I forced you to make a decision you'd already made. I belong and Cerys belongs. She is at school, she has friends. She can visit you.'

'Who says she wants to stay with you? Who do you think she'd choose? She hates you. She thinks you're a slut. I think you're a slut.'

The door to the back room banged open and Jude leapt into the kitchen with his space gun. He aimed it at Maynard and mimed shooting him repeatedly in the head. Maynard stepped towards him, grimacing.

'Get out!'

Jude kicked at Maynard's legs and Maynard raised his hand.

'Stop!' Shona pulled Jude towards her and hid his head with her arms. 'You were going to hit him!'

'He deserves it.'

'Did Meghan?'

He gasped. 'Shona!'

'Just fuck off, Maynard.'

He slammed the kitchen door behind him, then the back room door, then the front room door.

Shona held onto Jude until he stopped shaking.

'Shall I make you some milk?'

He nodded and wiped his nose on his sleeve.

'You're very brave, Jude. We'll look after each other, won't we?'

'I've got the gun though.' He held it to his chest.

Shona poured the milk into a mug and heated it in the microwave. She watched Jude drink it, his body tensed for Maynard's return. Cerys loved Jude, Shona was sure she did. She'd seen them cuddle on the sofa and, for every complaint that Jude had been in her room, there was a secret chat under her duvet. Cerys wouldn't leave him, even if she had nothing to say to Shona. And Maynard had clearly forgotten that Shona had something on him that meant he couldn't do this to her. She'd kept the clippings about the cyclist.

5

OCTOBER

The gatehouse was always cold and she hadn't had any time to adjust, autumn having suddenly arrived over the weekend. She didn't usually have to spend too long there. She had all of her identification checked and, after the first six visits, had remembered to leave her mobile outside. Today it was in the glove compartment of Mariana's car which didn't have gloves in it, or anything else. The entire car was so clean and bare that Shona felt she had dirtied it just by being in there and had decided she would take it through the car wash before returning it. It was a nice change from trains and taxis.

Now, with her presence checked and noted, she sat on a cold chair in a colder room to wait for an escort. Her canvas bag warmed her lap a little. Officers pressed the buzzer on one door and, if the other was closed, it would open. If it was open, they would hesitate self-consciously in front of the camera.

At the glass-enclosed office they would slip coloured discs into the hole and get a set of keys, or return the keys and clip the discs back on a key ring hanging off their belt. The men tended to be older than the women but there wasn't a uniform look to the build or faces of the stream of people. That had always surprised Shona, expecting to be able to recognise a physical sense of 'them' and 'us'. It was only the clothes which signalled who belonged where, and the guilty verdict.

'When the gods intervene, it is love that wins, not justice.' Shona had sent the essay on Apollo to Rob the day before, but she hadn't stopped thinking about it. The more she discovered the more she recognised him: the bearer of prophecy, healing, truth and light, the classic beardless athletic youth, lover of men and women. It felt as if she was reading about Kallu. It was stupid, but she couldn't shake the ways they linked. The bringer of life, and death too. Murderer of Achilles, the god who cursed Cassandra, who, together with his hunter twin, Artemis, had slaughtered Niobe's children.

Shona shivered, rubbed her gloved hands together and stood up again. She had to wait until one of the three women and two men decided to talk to her, even though they saw her straight away. The older woman, long grey hair strung back, lifted her eyebrows.

'I was wondering when my escort will be here,' said Shona.

'I'll check.'

Shona sat down again. This was the third time of checking but this was part of being in prison, for visitors as well as inmates.

She'd worried about leaving the house empty. She'd kept the front door bolted and taken the back door key, hoping Maynard didn't have a copy. Every time she left the house to take Jude to and from school she wondered whether she would get back in or would Maynard have changed the locks. She would rather not have come today but it wasn't an appointment that was easy to change.

The far door opened: 'Marks!'

She responded to her name and followed the officer through the door. He didn't look at her. There were a lot of officers here that seemed to believe that a prisoner should be isolated from the world for the duration of their punishment. His hair was clipped short, greying around the ears. His jacket stretched slightly across the back as he unlocked and locked each gate and door they passed through. Shona thought about the stress on his wrists of such repetitive movement, rubbing her own wrists in sympathy.

The high fences were topped with old-fashioned and unnecessary-looking tumbling razor wire, each building with enough space around it for the wind to carve circles in the dust; so much air out there and so little in the over-heated buildings.

He opened the large outer door, locked it, opened the smaller inner door, locked it. Shona was left in her usual room. She knew where the panic button was, the nearest prison officer, the procedures for all types of crisis. What scared her was not what might happen to her but the possibility that she wouldn't ever leave. With relief that she was finally in, she emptied her bag onto the table.

Jimmy strutted past the officer, scrapbook and note-book under his arm. A recent haircut revealed his heavily lined forehead as well as the pattern of hairless scars, but he looked relaxed and happy. The blue jogging suit was clean, which was always a good sign. The officer closed the door.

He looked at his watch. 'Morning.'

'It's not my fault I'm late.' Shona smiled. 'You're looking better.'

'New mattress.' Jimmy stretched his arms in a cartoon fashion above his head. 'I've been moved to the new block they built. My own TV, toilet, it's brilliant.' He leaned over the table and lowered his voice. 'Built like a piece of shit for that kind of money, though. If they asked us, we could give them a list of hundreds of faults. It won't even be standing in ten years. I could be out and away in less than an hour.' He sat up again. 'But why would I want to?'

Shona fiddled with her pen. 'You sound quite settled for someone who's nearly out.'

He shook his head. 'I'm just enjoying the last few weeks of being fed and clothed. Parole is never certain until you're running out the gate.' He pulled at the jogging top. 'Can't wait to wear something without zips. Anyway, you're nearly sacked as my solicitor, my girl, so what is your parting gift?' He opened his notebook and took one of the spare pens she had put on the table.

'They're all for you.' She pushed the books towards him. 'Two on della Francesca, one on Van der Goes.'

'No Reni?' he said.

'Those weighed a ton, and they're expensive too,' she said. 'I think you mean thanks.'

He grinned. 'Thanks, Shona. You're my favourite niece. Only, but favourite all the same.'

'How are you going to carry them all out? You'll need a trunk.'

'Ah, ask and you shall receive.'

He lifted his hand to the scars on his head as he flicked through the plates. Shona sat back, watching him. Considering he'd been sentenced for ripping off little old ladies by undervaluing their family art works, she had never been surprised that he only asked for books on painters. If she'd known what weights she'd shift over the years, she might not have agreed so readily. She hadn't been involved in his defence, hadn't even attended his trial, it being when it was. But it hadn't been the first. The last time she had been in a room with her mother, her uncle and Maynard was at her own wedding reception. Jimmy had kept a low profile after that and since this last sentence her mother had disowned him, for good this time apparently. Maynard refused to hear his name spoken. Shona had missed him, her funny, complicated uncle.

At seventy-two he looked at least fifteen years younger, his eyes bright and hair still thick and dark. His mouth drooped a little at the sides when he was concentrating, but in conversation he always looked a little amused.

Shona checked her watch. 'Really, are you all sorted for when you leave? Do you need somewhere to live, or need a lift?'

He waved his hand. 'All sorted.'

'I can pick you up.'

He shook his head. 'I'll get my address to you when I'm settled.' He kept his head down but she was sure he was grinning. The smile faded. 'Your mum never visited.'

Shona adjusted her bag on the table. 'No. She still doesn't go out much.' She opened a book and flicked through it.

'No.' He looked up. 'Do you think she'd like to hear from me?'

Shona looked up from the open book. 'Yes. Write to her. It can't hurt.'

He looked down again but Shona guessed he wasn't concentrating any more.

'Do you have a favourite?'

'So many. There is so much art in the world that I would kill to hold in my hands and just breathe it in. And then, I've seen so many paintings of things that the painter didn't believe in. You can tell in every stroke.' He narrowed his hand as if it was holding a paintbrush. 'Art is fantasy, life is fantasy and politics is the biggest fantastical invention of all. I'll stick with art, I think, where I can see the lies.'

'Is this research?' she asked quietly. 'Are you going back into the same kind of business?'

'Business?' He laughed. 'Shona, such euphemisms.'

'My mother—'

His eyes flickered. 'Don't. Some things can wait.'

Shona picked up her papers and pens and slowly started to put them back in her bag. 'So you definitely have somewhere to go? They're not going to find an excuse to keep you in here?'

'Six weeks and I'm out, don't you worry about that.' He smiled. It nearly reached his eyes. 'How's Maynard?'

Shona shrugged. 'Same as ever.'

'He's got a lot going for him, but you're right not to trust him.'

'You know why I don't.'

'But that's not what I mean. It's not about the baby. You need to get a divorce and move as far away as you can.'

'Why? It's my house. I'm staying, whatever he thinks, and he can leave me whenever he likes.'

'And he won't. You're the one who has to take control of this, Shona. He'll still have to see Cerys and all of that stuff but you need to put some distance between him and you for your own good.'

'Emotionally?'

'Don't be stupid. He'll drag you down when he falls, and he's got a long way to plummet.'

'I'm not going, and he's not dragging me anywhere.'

'There's something he's still after from you, Shona. I know more than you think.' Jimmy frowned. 'Sometimes being stubborn is the most fucking stupid thing you can be. You should know that, you've had enough practice.'

Shona snapped, 'You're the one who's locked up!'

Jimmy gathered his books together. 'I'm ready to go back to my cell now.'

'Sorry.'

'It's OK. It's true, but not for long.' He winked at her. 'See you on the outside.'

Shona checked her phone when she got home; three missed calls from Rob. She still had thirteen days to complete the Tower for him but he liked to keep an eye on her progress. She reminded him that he wasn't her teacher but it was his name on the contract and he did it anyway. She texted him a reassuring, and made-up, word count.

There was also text message from Kallu: 'Are you free?' Since Maynard had called him a Greek god it had got stuck in her head. 'My little Apollo,' she murmured, and laughed, embarrassed by herself. She'd check on him later.

The phone started to beep and she left it to charge on top of the bread bin.

It was time that she got started on the Tower essay, she supposed. Forty pages was over three pages a day, quite achievable unless she found that she actually wasn't interested in the subject after all. That had happened before and she had forced out an essay on Icelandic sagas in two solid nights of writing. Freud too proved to be a great disappointment, but luckily that had only been ten pages.

She pushed the books on Apollo to one side to take back to the library. Shona had used her three usual places for research. The Internet had enough to give her an initial overview of her title: 'Entertainment at the Tower of London: The Oldest Pleasure Park'. The library had the usual books, the standard texts and all for free. Greyfriars Bookshop on East Hill had second-hand oddities, the kind of books that would be impressive and indicative of a first. It also had the pungent smell of age and ideas and time and little chairs in which to absorb all of this tactile knowledge. She had bought three books on London and one on torture. She had only managed to read half of the tortures so far, although she knew she shouldn't be reading about anywhere other than London but she felt attracted, in a perverse way, to the suffering of others. Even those long dead. It angered her and she thrived on this energy. All her achievements, she felt, came from this dark space.

Mariana rang to let Shona know she was coming in the back door, and came upstairs to the office off the bedroom.

'Hey. I left your keys on the kitchen table.'

'I got them. Thought I'd just ask how it went.'

'He'll be out in six weeks. All set, apparently.'

Mariana nodded. 'Good. It will be tough, but it's good.'

She migrated to the table and began reading the Tower web page, open on the computer.

Shona thought about telling her she was busy and changed her mind. 'I'll get some coffee.'

'Even better.'

When she returned, Mariana had scrolled through the page on torture. Shona put the biscuits down and handed Mariana her mug.

'I'd like to squeeze the Kray twins in, but I don't think it's going to work.'

'Are they important?'

'No, just interesting in a tabloid kind of way.'

Mariana looked through the A4 pad in which Shona had been making notes and began to read aloud.

'"The Scavenger's daughter, A-frame metal device, forced the head down and the knees up to compress the body making blood spurt from the nose and ears."'

Shona shrugged and dipped a ginger nut in her tea.

Mariana kept reading. '"The rack was also known as the Duke of Exeter's Daughter. The body was stretched until the joints dislocated and muscles were often rendered useless." Were they named after someone's actual daughter?'

'I haven't got that far, but I don't think so.'

'Why daughters then?'

'No real reason. The dukes created them or used them so they were named their offspring. I suppose daughter sounds spookier than son.'

'It's disgusting. But isn't your title about pleasure?'

'I got a bit distracted. Do you want to help me get back on track?'

Mariana shook her head. 'No. I don't do torture. I will have nightmares and you've given me enough of those.'

Mariana did look tired, her eyes darkly sunken. She should have given her the option to stay away, dropped the car back at Mariana's house. As it was, she had forgotten to wash it like she promised herself.

'Here, let's finish the coffee and you can drop me in town on the way home.'

'Haven't you got to pick up Jude?' Mariana picked up her mug and folded her fingers around it.

73

'He's having tea with a friend. I have a couple of hours to myself.'

Mariana shook her head. 'That's when the devil makes work for you. You have to make your own work.'

Mariana dropped her off as it started raining. Town wasn't busy, just a few school children making their way home with little enthusiasm but no money to extend their meandering. Cerys would be home soon too with her new key. Shona had always been there to make sure she arrived safely, but since her conversation with Maynard she was trying to give her a little more space, a little more responsibility, without changing the time that Cerys was expected home. It hadn't been discussed again but Cerys was always there, always sullen, always with a slight sneer when Shona spoke to her. Maynard kept out of it in front of Shona, but sometimes she could hear Cerys complaining to him at length on the mobile before asking for more credit. She wondered why Maynard hadn't given her a key.

She sent Cerys a text message, letting her know what time she'd be back.

Shona pushed open the door to the Natural History Museum. Kallu was sitting cross legged on the floor with a selection of necklaces in front of him. She sat down next to him.

He smiled. 'If you're here, then you must need to solve a problem too.'

'Do I?'

'Look. There are forty-eight necklaces here, each one linked to the others. It's an exercise in patience and simplicity, removing the knots and seeing the situation clearly. It called you.'

Shona smiled. She didn't understand his thought

74

processes, how everything could link together in life, how situations and objects could call to her. Kallu could see the threads between everything and, while she was with him, it did seem possible. She watched his long fingers teasing and unravelling. His eyebrows were lowered over his eyes, his lips slightly pouting. His hair was curling across his cheek. Shona ran her fingers through it, pinning it more firmly behind his ear.

A clump of necklaces fell loose to the floor and he passed it to Shona. 'However many there are is your answer.'

She felt responsible for him, what he ate and where he lived. He felt responsible for her soul.

'You only have one shadow,' he had said early on. 'You've lost one. You can get it back but you need to spot it when it's around. Maynard has lost one too, but it's gone for ever.'

And so Kallu cared for her, protected her because of this lost shadow she never expected to have. She would take him out to woods and the seaside. He would create circles around her with sticks and flowers or sit silently. He didn't mind that she sat with a book, that she didn't believe any of it. She had enjoyed the space, the silence and being celebrated for being there.

Shona nodded to Kallu and began to undo the problem she didn't know she had. The answer turned out to be seven.

'Goddess of the seven stars,' said Kallu.

Shona carefully lined up the separated necklaces. 'Who's that?'

'Questions, questions.' He was still hunched over his tangle.

'Well, what does it mean?'

He smiled at her. 'I don't know. It's your answer.'

Sometimes Shona wanted to shake him. Her voice rose, 'Answer to what?'

'Your question.'

Shona tried to jump to her feet for a dramatic exit but her right foot had gone to sleep and she stood, holding onto a display cabinet, waiting for the pins and needles to pass.

'It would be quicker if you walked on it,' he said.

'I know.' She placed her foot down but knew there was too little sensation to shift any weight onto it.

Kallu watched her, raised his eyebrows and nodded. 'Ah.'

She refused to ask this time, absolutely refused.

She checked her phone on the way to collect Jude. There was no reply from Cerys. She rang her while she waited for the bus, and then she rang the house. Nothing. She comforted herself that Cerys was just continuing her silence. Dumb insolence, Shona wanted to call it. She hadn't said a word to Shona since Maynard had last been at the house. Shona accused her of being childish, being selfish, being ignorant but all she got in return was a haughty toss of the head or a yawn. She was strong-willed, Shona had to concede that. But every day it was getting harder not to say something, however dreadful, to get a word of reaction from her. She started to imagine it was a plan she'd concocted with Maynard to punish Shona or to force Shona into inviting Maynard back into the family home and marital bed. But Shona didn't believe that was really what Maynard wanted, however downcast he could look about it in front of Cerys.

No, it was just Cerys showing Shona how much she

hated her and how little she needed anything to do with her.

She left a message anyway.

When she got home with Jude at half past five, Cerys was sitting at the kitchen table in her slippery dressing gown, talking into her mobile. Shona waved at her.

'Speak to you later,' Cerys said into the phone. She hung up and moved around to face Shona. Her gown fell open to show an ornate bra Shona hadn't bought for her.

'Hello,' said Jude.

Cerys didn't look at him. 'Is Kallu coming round?'

'You know Kallu. He comes, he goes. He'll probably be around. Why?'

'Didn't you see him today?'

Shona frowned. 'Yes, but I never mentioned that. I wasn't expecting him to come over for tea or anything.'

Cerys shrugged and left the room.

'Cerys didn't say hello,' said Jude.

'I know. What a dope,' said Shona. 'I'll make my dinner, you watch TV, OK?'

She thought about whether she'd been wrong, and maybe had mentioned something that Cerys may have overheard. She certainly hadn't told her directly as Cerys was still having her silent protest. She must have read Shona's phone messages. Shona checked them, wondering whether she had invited Kallu round and forgotten, but there was nothing like that, just him asking if she was free. Cerys must have assumed that he would be coming. So why had she been wearing a loosely gathered dressing gown? Shona groaned and left the pasta to boil. Her first conversation with Cerys in weeks and she couldn't just try to be normal and be nice. She'd promised herself she would. She would let Cerys know that she loved her.

Shona knocked on Cerys' door and walked in. Cerys glared at her and the planned reconciliation disappeared again.

'Were you planning to throw yourself at him again? You have to have more respect for yourself, Cerys.'

Cerys turned away and Shona noticed the sports bag open on the floor. There were some T-shirts on top and a bundle of underwear.

'Are you going to Dad's this weekend?'

Cerys stared at the window and settled down against her pillows.

Shona sat on the end of the bed. 'Cerys, Kallu is nineteen. He's too old for you.'

Cerys turned away to the wardrobe and snorted. 'But you're not too old for him.'

'I'm not chasing him in my pants!'

Cerys turned. 'I'm not talking to you, you bitch! I hate you more than anyone in the world. You don't trust me because you know what you're thinking and what you're doing. You have destroyed Dad and made him leave and you're making me leave too.'

Shona stood. 'Oh, grow up. Not everything your dad says is true.'

'But he loves me and knows exactly what you're like. You're such a slag that you're rotten inside.'

Shona closed the door behind her and pressed the heels of her hands into her eye sockets.

6

Cerys wasn't home.

Shona had called the house phone to let her know she would be late, in the hope that Cerys would answer if she didn't know it was her. Instead Maynard answered and he said he'd tell her. She hadn't worried about not being there when Cerys got back from school because Maynard would be there to collect some things and eat with her, but then Shona got home and Maynard was there and Cerys was not. And there was a secret, something hidden behind his words, that she couldn't get an answer to, so she hid in the kitchen and cooked for herself and Jude.

Maynard wasn't concerned, not at five or half five, that she wasn't back. He said she'd been back after school, changed her clothes and headed out again. He was working at home, he said, nothing strange in that, as if he'd ever done it before. He never spent any time in the house if Cerys wasn't there.

It wasn't until six o'clock that Cerys' absence became somehow real.

Shona left Jude in front of the TV and let herself into Maynard's room. If he was staying the night, he normally had the sofa bed made up by now, but he was sitting on the sofa with a pile of papers which he placed face down beside him. He raised his eyebrows.

Shona said, 'She's not answering her phone, now where exactly did she go?'

Maynard stood up. 'Can you get out, please? I'll talk to you in the hall.'

'This is my house. You have no right to keep me out of this room, lock me out. Tell me where my daughter is.'

Maynard took a step until their feet were nearly touching and spoke slowly. 'She went out.'

'You were here. You were responsible for finding out where she was going, if you couldn't say no to her. It's dark and she's fourteen. I'm going to have to call the police if you don't help find her.'

'Call them then,' he sighed. 'They'll quickly have you pegged for what you are, a mental case. I'm busy.'

Shona looked around at the antiques, the glass display cases full of tiny breakables, the walls full of paintings and spaces that used to hold them. There were boxes on the floor, the large one holding bubble-wrapped painting-sized squares, the smaller one holding files. Where had they been hidden?

'She's not in here,' he said, as he returned to the sofa.

'Why are you packing up?' she asked.

'Oh, first you want me to move out and now you want to know why I'm packing.' He picked up the papers again and held them to his chest.

She felt butterflies, as if excited and slightly panicked. 'Are you leaving?' This is what she had waited for and yet, now, with Cerys missing, it seemed overwhelming.

'I am just moving some of my things from one place to another.'

'Why today?'

'Because they are mine.' He held the papers out and started to pretend to read them, and then changed his mind. 'There's not as much work at the moment, because of the recession. I'll have to sell some things.'

'Are you selling the London flat?'

'No. That belongs to the business in any case, and I need a London address for work.'

His money had always been filtered through the business, which consisted of only him: a trendy tax ploy he'd explained to her at length one night after too much wine. She'd never understood it. 'A tiny bolt hole, not a flat really, more of a bedsit. Just somewhere to sleep.' That had been his reason for not moving out properly, that and Cerys. The cyclist had been her main hold over Maynard, enabling her to stay in the house, but Shona had always suspected that his mother wouldn't allow him to leave before Cerys was eighteen. She didn't want the shame, and Maynard didn't want to risk his inheritance.

'Will I still get the housekeeping money?'

He smiled and looked back at the papers. 'Cerys will never go without.'

Cerys. It was so late now.

She left the door open to take Jude to bed, but when they walked past it was shut again. Jude brushed his teeth and noticed Cerys' door was open and her room was dark.

'Where's Cerys?'

'She's just out. She'll be back later.' Shona kissed his head. 'What book do you want?'

Jude found his favourite three books and, as usual,

whittled it down to one without explaining how he arrived there.

'This one.' He jumped into their bed and switched the lamp on while she switched the main light off.

Shona planned what she would say to Cerys when she finally returned, and went over the rules that she had agreed to stick by, however reluctantly. At half past seven she realised that she didn't have any numbers for Cerys' friends. They were all on the mobile she had with her. Neither did she know more than a couple of surnames, which weren't in the phone book. No-one she knew was in the phone book any more.

At eight she set out. Maynard agreed to stay with Jude until she got back. It made her angry. This is what it should have been like with Cerys, two parents who could trust each other to care for their children. A husband she wouldn't ever doubt would still be there when she got back from a night out with friends, or a late-night trip to the shop. Instead she'd gone without people and food because there was no-one to trust and nothing to believe in.

She walked through the alley to the fields by the school. The lights were on in a couple of downstairs rooms and she remembered that Cerys had gone to Guides here for a term. Guides was Tuesday, piano on Wednesday, swimming on Fridays; the days when she always knew exactly where Cerys was because they went and came back together. When had that ended, when she was twelve, nearly thirteen? It was so hard to let go, to see her walk away and not walk back. The parents were arriving to pick up their daughters in the hooded jacket and baseball caps that Cerys had worn, but Shona didn't recognise any from her days as a Guide's mother.

Shona walked away from the school. She walked down to the main road, scanning benches next to phone boxes and driveways. She knew that she wouldn't find her but the looking became the point, the thing that Maynard was not doing. She walked rather than face the emptiness, rather than acknowledge that even Maynard might be getting concerned.

She found herself in front of Rob's house and knocked on the door. A man, slightly older than Rob and a beer in one hand, opened the door.

'Is Rob in?' she asked.

'No.'

'Do you know where he is?'

'No.' He looked at his beer. 'Do you want to leave a message?'

'No, thanks.'

She waited until he had closed the door before leaving and sat back on the wall outside the house.

That morning Rob had left a message about the paper due in on Monday. Shona had reassured him that she had written twelve thousand words and was preparing to edit it down to ten and check the references. What she hadn't told him was that she didn't think it was going to get a first. It was too dry, too derivative. She'd found no angle to make it her own work, which it wasn't in any case. If she didn't deliver, the organisation might blacklist him, but there were thousands of others that would pay. He hadn't arranged to see her for fun, he was just chasing his investment and that bored her. She didn't care enough about him to pull something brilliant together and she certainly didn't care about the student who was waiting for their work to be completed. There wasn't much that she did care about any more.

She checked her watch. Quarter to nine. If Cerys wasn't back by nine, something terrible had definitely happened. She slowly walked back, not stepping on the cracks in the pavements just in case. She paused outside Amy's house. She would check on her later. When Cerys was back.

She went around the alley and in through the back door. She had gone past anger now. She clasped her hands together and sat at the table facing the clock. The movement of the fake French hands on the crackle-faked old clock, which Maynard hated, became visible as she stilled herself. The clock showed nine o'clock and she pushed her body away from the chair with both hands. She felt her head start to pound as she made her way to the front room. She almost knocked on the door, and then turned the handle.

Maynard was sitting at his desk, his back to the door. He didn't move but stayed with his head lowered towards his lap.

'What haven't you told me?' she asked him.

He sighed and looked at her from the corner of his eye. 'She left in a car.'

Shona's hands flew to her stomach, squeezed the flesh between her fingers. 'A car.'

'I thought it was just an older boy from school. She doesn't have any chance to breathe, Shona. I thought she deserved to have a bit of freedom.'

'A car.' Shona started to register the pain her fingers were causing and tried to relax her grip a little. 'You let her go off in someone's, some random person's car?'

Maynard turned, one hand on the back of the desk chair. 'She can't talk to you about boys, can she? I didn't know he had a car but she said, as you were going to be late, would it be all right, just for half an hour. That's all.'

He was so calm. He was enjoying this chance to tell her how awful she was.

'So why aren't you worried?'

'I am worried, just not hysterical.'

Shona leaned back against the door jamb, and placed her hands behind her hips. Maynard stared with his eyebrows lowered but she knew that look. It was guilt masquerading as fury.

'It's all your fault.' His voice was getting louder. 'If you'd just let her out now and then, she wouldn't have to creep around behind your back, would she? If it was any kind of normal relationship, she could have asked you. You won't even let her dye her hair.'

'She's fourteen.' Shona's whisper stopped him. 'You have been conniving behind my back, letting her sneak out, and what else? Buying her the odd bottle of vodka or a packet of fags?'

'Don't be stupid.'

'Oh, sorry. Just letting your fourteen-year-old daughter go off with a complete stranger who's old enough to drive, that's entirely different. Of course. Have you got any idea what people are capable of?'

'Yes, of course I do. You're obsessed with dangerous people prowling the streets. Some boys are just boys who might be interested in your daughter. It's completely normal.'

Shona had stopped listening. What if it really was her fault?

'Have you phoned the police?' she asked.

He seemed to register the fear in her voice, seemed to spot a suggestion that the guilt may be hers after all. He shook his head. 'I'll do that now.'

'I'm going out to look for her again. Did you see him at all? Any idea of his age, what kind of car?'

He shook his head again and pressed the buttons on the phone, calling one of those directory numbers instead of just looking in the phone book. Not an emergency, then, just a normal enquiry. She slammed the front door behind her. Jude was there but she forced herself to run away, back towards the school.

Now that the school was closed there was no light to allow her to judge distances. She started to shout Cerys' name, trying to identify any shifting in the darkness, her ears alert for any reluctant reply. She headed towards the other two local schools. The path became narrower as she passed between the schools and then widened out into dimly lit car parks. She went on towards the houses and then turned left. Bluebottle Grove. She had never ventured further into it than a dirt path between steep banks, but there was more to it than that.

She took a few steps down the path but couldn't see anything. The feeble orange lights from the streets around didn't penetrate further than fifty metres. She called again and again. Someone in a neighbouring house shouted at her to shut up so she shouted louder. She was shaking and her voice was starting to crack. She wasn't going to find anything down there and she was scared to be proved both wrong and right. She had to go back to Maynard but didn't want to be proved wrong or right there either. She walked back to the car park and through the fields surrounding and dividing the schools. By the time she had turned back into her street she could see the police car parked outside. She felt her knees go and she scraped her hand on a wall trying to hold herself up. When she hit the ground, she stayed there, one knee raised and the other growing a painful bruise where it rested on the pavement.

They could have found her and brought her home. She would be angry, humiliated and sorry.

They could be asking Maynard for all the details of the car, what she had said, finding the best photo to take with them.

They could have found her. They could have not been able to bring her home. They could be telling him right now and asking if they could phone anybody. She pushed herself up from the ground and turned back towards the main road. She arrived at Rob's house without really thinking about it.

She knocked again. The same man as before answered, now in his dressing gown and without the bottle.

'He's still out,' he said, before she asked. 'He doesn't always come back, you know, if he gets lucky.' He smiled nastily at her.

She turned away and this time wouldn't turn back.

She used her key to open the front door and one of the two police officers guided her into the front room. She remembered thinking that they weren't wearing their hats and this was probably a bad sign. Maynard was sitting on the Victorian sofa, arm over the back of it. Someone had made him a cup of coffee and placed it on his £3,000 occasional table without a coaster. A second one appeared for her and she was pleased that it would have two marks on it, seared into the delicate rosewood as sharply as a brand. Maynard was far too busy talking to notice.

The policewoman sat and the policeman stood behind her.

'So, even though it's completely out of character, you don't see any reason for concern.'

'No.' Maynard made a half-laugh. 'She's fourteen, it seems quite normal to me after there have been so many arguments.'

'What did you argue about?'

'I didn't.' Maynard turned to Shona.

'It was a few weeks ago,' she said. 'Cerys wanted to be allowed out later but I refused.'

'And what time should she be back?'

'Five.'

'And at the weekend?'

'Half five.'

The policewoman raised her eyebrows before scribbling her notes.

Maynard said, 'There was another bigger argument, wasn't there? About you sleeping around.'

Shona flushed. 'Not exactly. She—'

'That's what she told me. It's no wonder she wanted to leave after what she's been through.'

The policewoman said, 'So, if you're not worried, sir, why did you phone us?'

'My wife insisted.' He shrugged apologetically and reached for his coffee. 'Oh, for fuck's sake!' He lifted both mugs up and examined the blanched wood. 'You are going to have to make a record of this, officer. This is criminal damage and I will be requiring compensation.'

'But, you didn't mention—'

He stood up, looking for somewhere else to put them. 'Only a total moron would put a hot drink on a wooden table.'

'Sir, I don't think your tone is appropriate.'

The policewoman was standing now too, the policeman fingering his radio. Shona kept her eyes on the table. There was something wrong with this situation. The only emotion he'd shown all evening was about the table. He had to know something else, know where she was.

When they had finished, Shona stood up. Her stomach

felt as if her fingers were still pinching, but much deeper inside now. Her breathing was quick and shallow but it was familiar. She looked away from the serious faces in front of her.

'Is there anyone we can call for you?'

Shona was sure that the woman had already said that but she wasn't thinking about anyone else. She didn't care who else knew or how they found out.

She wasn't shaking any more, she thought, as she picked up the precious items from the shelves, the tiny fragile antiques acquired by fleecing ignorant traders, and hurled them at Maynard's bowed head. The Elizabethan wine glass smashed on the wall behind him and he turned his head to the noise. The seventeenth-century waffle maker, for pressing designs into the communion bread, caught him solidly on the temple. He looked at her then, all right.

'Where is she?' she shouted.

The policeman held one of Shona's arms behind her while the policewoman prised her fingers away from a silver wine taster in the shape of a vine leaf. Shona could see her determined face grow in frustration as Shona's fingers were peeled off and clamped back on again. Finally free, the policewoman threw the silver to the ground.

'What the fuck do you think you're doing?' shouted Maynard, picking it up. 'Just because she's gone crazy doesn't mean that you can be disrespectful too!'

The police officers, clearly only prepared to sympathise and leave, looked at each other in disbelief.

'We appreciate that, sir. Can you calm down?'

'You let her attack me!' Maynard pointed at Shona and started shouting at her. 'I don't know where she is, you stupid cow! You're the one who's driven her away!'

The policewoman stood in front of Maynard to prevent

him advancing, fists raised and blood dribbling from the wound on his temple.

Shona spat at him. 'You've killed her! I had two daughters and you killed both of them, you fucking bastard!'

The policeman kept his hold on Shona who stood perfectly still, waiting for him to release her so she could kick over the Jacobean cabinet.

'You're not leaving her here,' said Maynard. 'I want her arrested for assault.'

'Tonight?' gasped the policewoman. 'I think we all need to calm down. You're both in shock.' She appealed to them both with an expression of pity. 'I'm sure that explains a lot of what's just gone on.'

'I'm serious,' Maynard said. 'Arrest her or I'll have your fucking badges.'

She looked at her partner. Shona could feel the tension increase on her arms as he shrugged.

'Let's go outside, Madam,' he said.

Shona opened the front door and sat on the wall outside the front room window. She could hear murmurs from within, Maynard louder than the police officer. He was pointing at the table.

'Can you describe your daughter for me?'

Shona took a breath and focused on him. 'Fourteen, brown hair, quite long now. She's slim, hates her knees. I can get you a photo when I'm allowed back in.'

'Why do you think she might have run away?'

'We have argued,' Shona said. 'But it wasn't anything major. Teenagers push the boundaries. That's what they're there for.'

'And is it just you and Mr Marks that live here?'

'No, my son as well. Jude. He's five. He's not Maynard's child.'

'But you are the parents of—' he checked his notes '— Cerys?'

Shona nodded. He raised his eyebrows and scribbled for a minute.

'Christ,' Shona said. 'She's gone. I waited to see who she would choose and it wasn't me.'

'We'll find her, Mrs Marks. Teenagers quite often haven't gone far. We'll get a list of friends and talk to the school.'

Shona looked back through the window. Maynard was calmer now, showing the policewoman something on his phone. Now she was the one who looked angry.

She came to the front door and the policeman followed her into the hall. Shona watched Maynard. He was listening to them, his mobile in one hand and on his face a smile he couldn't quite suppress.

They both came outside.

The policewoman said, 'This is a legal matter, not a police one, Mrs Marks. Your husband has shown me evidence that Cerys left of her own volition and has every right to do so.'

'Where is she?'

'He doesn't think she's in any danger and we are going to send someone round to talk to her now.'

'But she's my daughter. I don't know where she is.'

'You need to speak to your husband. This has become a custody matter and we need to talk to your daughter.'

Shona, wide-eyed, took a step back towards the house.

'You're not going to be talking tonight, though. I'm afraid you need to come with us. It will let everyone calm down, won't it? Maybe a solicitor would be a good idea.'

Shona tried to move away and realised that the woman had hold of her arm. 'My son. I can't leave him on his own.'

'He isn't on his own.'

'You don't understand. I can't leave Jude with him.' She turned back to the window. Maynard was smiling out at her. He pulled the curtains and she heard him lock his door. 'He won't look after him, he hates him. It isn't his child.'

'Are you saying he isn't a fit guardian?'

'Not for Jude. He's locked himself in his room. Maynard has, I mean. Go and check. We have to bring Jude with us.'

The officers exchanged a look and the man went back to the house and knocked on the door. Shona felt her head pushed down as she got into the back seat and she waited. Jude would see her arrested, in a police car. Jude would be taken away from her. Maynard had the best of reasons to keep her away from the house now that she'd attacked him in front of the police. She would lose the house, but she couldn't lose Jude.

GRETA

My brother made it to the wedding, which I never expected. Within a year he had started his first prison sentence, but that was after.

He got on well with Larry. He got on very well with Larry. They were always hiding out in the backyard, smoking and talking – London art, London artists, London parties, London men.

In the pub, after the wedding, I watched them standing at the bar, laughing loudly, just them two, not looking at me at all. My brother's glass was always empty, and Larry's always full.

Larry wasn't shy any more. He didn't stutter.

I smoothed down my dress, sat with my mother and wondered why none of his family could travel for the wedding. 11th of January 1962. In later years, I would discover that, thirteen minutes into that date, in Peru, an avalanche buried a village and killed four thousand people. Sounds like a coincidence to most people, I expect.

Our honeymoon was abroad, the only time I've ever needed a passport although I've always kept one ready, for running. It's like a talisman now, despite where it took me then.

Larry arranged the trip with my mother. She adored him, even though she never wanted me to marry, and even though he insisted on a registry office wedding which she had always said didn't count. She wanted to wave us off at the airport, she had never seen a plane, but he borrowed a car and drove us himself.

I felt so sophisticated, just one of twenty people privileged to board the plane with its giant silver propellers. I was wearing clothes I'd bought specially. Well, the cerise fitted jacket with three large matching buttons was bought. My mother had made the buttercup knee-length pencil skirt and matching blouse. I had the same hairstyle as for the wedding, a chin-length contour cut which swept up either side of my face into two large curls. I was happier having my hair done than I was standing next to Larry, but the plane distracted me and I resolved to be a good wife and enjoy what he had arranged.

We arrived in Paris on the 18th of January and Larry seemed happy, if slightly tense. He looked around a lot and fidgeted with his buttons. I had the impression he was waiting for something, and it wasn't me. Our hotel was in Montmartre, and I'd have happily stayed in those cool, tight streets but he was always heading down to the wide boulevards, the open squares and the people.

We sat in cafés and bars outside Saint-Chappelle and Notre Dame, but never went inside them. He barely spoke but watched the drift of airy, composed women who never looked quite straight at him, and echoed the ever watchful men posed with one hand holding a cigarette and the other in their pocket. Larry looked like a local, carnivorous, with one eye closed against the smoke from his cigarette.

I tried to copy the women, dispassionately flinging their wrists to the sky but I felt stiff. Larry laughed at me and I stopped. I discovered he could speak French, picking up foul slang I supposed, guessing from the reactions of the women he tried his statements out on.

He drank strong coffee in tiny cups. I always seemed to end up with soup bowls of milky coffee that I was too scared to pick up. I had my going away suit and one spare blouse to rinse in the sink with my stockings. Larry took me by the elbow, directed me into shops but I was bewildered by the handwritten Francs. Their uncommonly fashioned sevens I read as ones, the comma which marked some kind of division of numbers. I couldn't translate it into pounds, never mind shillings. He picked up one item after another and I shook my head. I was starting to feel that everything, this honeymoon, my clothes, was a debt to be repaid.

Outside Notre Dame he said, 'I have to make a visit about half an hour away, a bidonville. Do you want to visit some of these churches you've been so desperate to see while I'm busy?'

I did want to go to them. The Sacré-Cœur was about three streets away from our hotel, but I didn't trust his smile.

'I'll come with you,' I said.

'In those shoes?' He pointed to my feet.

I looked at them, oxblood leather with an oversized buckle. I hadn't had time to save for them before the wedding and I had a good few months until I could pay them off.

'Yes, in these shoes,' I said, lifting my chin. 'They're good enough for anywhere in Paris.'

He smirked. When we arrived, he explained that

bidonville wasn't the name of a place but a translation. It was a slum, full of bright, clever, filthy children and shoeless, hollow-cheeked adults. They looked at his feet, rather than his face. They knew him and he scared them. All of the anxiety that had built since our arrival began to feel justified.

I couldn't understand any of what he said to them or them to him, but I could tell enough. He owned them in some way. I felt as if my wedding and my honeymoon had been some kind of excuse to let him finish his deal. What kind of business he had with poor immigrants living in half-sheds outside Paris I never knew. The next day I had a pretty good idea but I didn't ask. After all this time I had freed myself from parents who I couldn't ask about anything, and a brother I couldn't talk about, and nailed myself to a man I could neither ask nor talk about. I couldn't look at him either, only at the mud stains around the sides of my shoes. They never came out, no matter how much I polished them.

The women sat me on a stool while the men raised their voices. One gestured to me, her right hand tapping her left ring finger. I nodded. She turned to a woman next to her and said something to which the second woman tutted repeatedly and shook her head.

I agreed with her. I wanted to slap myself. I knew I'd never get away.

When we just missed being blown up the next day, the 22nd, outside the Foreign Office at the Quai d'Orsay, I just wanted to go home. Larry was thoroughly enjoying it, the dead and the injured. He revelled in describing to me the details of how the bomb on the truck killed a postman, how others were injured by the shattering glass which had nearly pierced us, looked slightly disappointed by the safe return of the abducted MP.

He didn't show a single flicker of surprise. The bomb was close enough so we could witness it but not so close that we'd be hurt. I knew in one way he intended to protect me, he didn't want me dead, but I didn't understand what else he wanted from me. I thought back to the quick-eyed men of the bidonville and the slow-eyed women. I thought I would faint as he explained what had happened and I asked him to stop translating.

'You look pale,' he said, his voice flat. 'What a delicate little flower you turned out to be.'

He sat in the bars, listening to the outrage and gossip, the rumours and condemnations, flexing his fingers, one at a time. It was then that I noticed he could move each finger quite independently. First I couldn't breathe at all and then I couldn't stop breathing, shuddering and faint. I couldn't focus on anything else.

He eventually saw me watching and turned to me with a grin which showed his teeth.

'Second thoughts, Greta?'

I shook my head. I was onto my fourth, fifth and sixth thoughts.

'Good.' He loosened his tie and winked. 'For better or worse.'

At home my mother asked me about Paris but Larry answered for me.

'The Eiffel Tower was the best bit, wasn't it?'

I nodded.

We hadn't been anywhere near it. I had seen it from a few distant places, like Montmartre, but I just smiled as he told my mother all about the incredible views.

'You got Greta to go up the top of that tower?' My mother was astonished. 'She can't climb a ladder.'

97

'She loved every minute. She was like a different woman. That's the effect Paris has, I suppose,' he mused.

My mother giggled. She didn't read the papers or watch the news, knew nothing about the fighting for and against Algerian independence. She noticed nothing different about me whatsoever. I said nothing that whole afternoon and she didn't even look at me. I began to wonder if she'd ever looked at me properly. She started to talk about my brother's descriptions of Paris to Larry, as if they'd never met. Larry cut her off in mid-flow and she didn't mind a bit.

There had always been a girl and then a boy. My grandmother had one daughter and then one son; my mother had one daughter and then one son. But when I had a son (and in my twenties too, not my forties) I could see the stress lift from my mother's brow. Things had altered. The order of things had changed. Her movements became larger. She even smiled, now and again. She would leave her house, once without her shawl, and come to our new-built house.

'A brand-new bath that's never been used.' She shook her head. 'It's beyond anything I ever imagined for you, Greta.' The inside toilet she didn't mention, because she didn't talk about them, but she meant that too. She still had to walk to the bottom of the garden to empty the pot she kept under the bed.

Sean was born on the 22nd of November 1962. For years I told people that he was born on the day that Kennedy was assassinated, but it was a whole year earlier. I'd said it so many times that I started to believe that they'd recorded Kennedy's death wrongly. I was always looking for links, even then, even when they were wrong.

Sean was exactly a month old when the winds brought the winter properly and, on Boxing Day, the snow which froze the country. I was convinced he would die, and shut us up in the back room with a fire going day and night. Larry always found coal and wood and I didn't ask how or where.

My mother was happy and left her house every day, and not to visit the church.

She said, 'When there's snow, you can see if there have been hoof prints. It's the only way to be sure if he's here.'

I hated her coming, opening the doors to let the heat out. She adored Sean, although she couldn't understand why I'd allowed his father to give him such a foreign-looking name. She would come round in the daytime and leave after I'd prepared tea in the icy kitchen. When it thawed in March, I didn't see her for months. I missed her then and didn't like the thought of her keeping a watchful eye for the devil by herself.

7

After seven mornings waking in a strange room, she still wasn't used to it. Shona lay on the unfamiliar bed, her eyes swollen through tears and exhaustion. At the foot of the bed was a large picture accented with gold-leaf-effect halos. The Madonna was placid and almost sleepy, allowing Jesus to rest against her relaxed left arm. He raised two fingers of his left hand and smiled like a condescending adult.

Shona wanted to close her eyes but hadn't slept all night. The dawn prompted the same scene to run behind her eyelids, the last time she could have killed Maynard.

It was three o'clock when he finally took the baby from her. Meghan had been crying since the ten o'clock news, had been fed and changed multiple times. Shona was exhausted. Although the baby did sleep in the morning and early afternoon, two-year-old Cerys did not. Shona was blurrily certain that she'd got through the last five nights on blinking alone. Eventually, reluctantly, she gave up and passed over the writhing baby. Maynard went downstairs.

Lying in bed Shona had followed the vibrating, furious sound of the cries, from the kitchen to the dining room, the kitchen to the front room again. She heard the sound of the laptop booting up and a sudden increase in the volume of misery as Maynard must have put the baby down on the sofa. She heard Cerys stirring in her bedroom at the front, a half-murmur, and raised her head. But Cerys quietened down again and Shona rested her head back on the pillow and closed her eyes.

She felt shivery with tiredness and drew the duvet around her shoulders, her legs bent up to her chest. Her eyes ached, even though they were closed, and she breathed deeply to stop herself from crying. That's when she realised that the other crying had stopped. She tried to feel relief, to consciously relax every muscle but she couldn't. It felt wrong, a dangerous, potent silence. She knew she should go downstairs and check but she was too tired. She knew that she should trust Maynard but she didn't. Her eyes opened and she waited.

There was a glimmer outside in the gap where the curtains didn't quite meet at the top. She had seen more dawns in the last three months than ever before and each one was like a secret she wished she didn't know.

She heard the laptop shut down and the lid close. His feet were silent but she visualised him approaching the sofa. There was no noise. Cerys mumbled in her sleep.

Eventually, much later, she heard Maynard come up the stairs. His dark outline walked through their back bedroom and into the third bedroom where the baby's crib and clothes were. He was holding the baby, now wrapped in the green cellular blanket. They intended to swap the arrangement around; they would have the front bedroom and the children would have the connecting bedrooms at the back. They would grow up to be close, to argue and fight and support each other. They would side against their parents and whisper secrets through doors left slightly ajar.

The door was always left ajar.

Maynard put the baby in the crib and quietly pulled the door closed with a tiny click. That was when she knew, the quiet closing of the door.

Now it had stopped pretending to be night. The bedside light had faded as the sun rose and the room, the painting, was cast in a red light through the thin guest room curtains. Jimmy said that Maynard was after something from me, she thought. He must have it all now.

When she didn't have Jude, she thought she could live without the house. She hated Maynard for making her think she had to make a choice – her son or her house, and her daughter with it.

She listened to Mariana getting Jude ready for school, gently teasing him. Jude asked for Shona but Mariana distracted him. She was good to Jude. She was kind. Hearing them together made Shona twinge with guilt for being so useless and for lots of other things. She should have let them get to know each other and not withheld him from other people just because Cerys' father was so awful. She should have been a much better person, but she couldn't un-wish Jude.

The bed felt large and empty. Shona couldn't get used to not having Jude in the bed alongside her, but this was a single and there were other bedrooms. She'd been in this room before, over five years' ago, and wished that she had been given a different room.

A door closed somewhere in the house and the sound of running water became masked by a radio. There were noises next door too. People were going to get up and get clean and go to work, regardless. They would eat and think about sex and worry about exams, look both ways before crossing the road and come home. People would survive today, despite all of the reasons why they should not.

Mariana opened the door and then knocked. 'Breakfast, Shona.'

Shona turned over and faced the blood red window.

'If you're not up in ten minutes, I'll come and get you.'

'I don't want to get up.' Her voice sounded as if she was speaking through scarves tied around her mouth. Her throat was scarred and she could taste metal in the back of her throat. She didn't want to argue all day again for the right to go home.

'Ten minutes.' Mariana shut the door.

She heard someone call, 'Imaculada!'

Fernando was here. Shona pulled the duvet over her head. What couldn't have got worse was much, much worse.

Shona had met Fernando once. She had never intended to stay over, never intended to leave Maynard in charge of Cerys for a whole night, but the amount of sweet wine and food, endless courses of Mariana's Portuguese back catalogue, had floored her.

Mariana had invited her over on the pretext than it was some important saint's day. Shona had no idea which one. They had spoken at length a number of times but Shona found this sudden elevation to dinner guest peculiar. But she had had no other offers for years. She had no other friends. She had Cerys, now eight years old, and a husband who lived in the same house. 'Mariana' turned out to be a middle name chosen for the English. She had brothers and sisters. Many of her nieces and nephews were godchildren, and the way she showed Shona their photos was touching. She had no children of her own to show off in silver frames. Mariana turned out to be a whole person rather than just a stout, pushy solicitor who rubbed people up the wrong way.

They had sat at the table in the dining room for the entire evening. Usually in any room, Mariana would be the centre of attention, provoking and angering whoever was in there with her. In this room she didn't stand a chance of domination. Fernando, balding and bearded, nothing to shout about on paper, was even more captivating than his wife. Shona's eyes flicked towards her, to see how she handled this coup, but Mariana seemed to willingly abdicate the floor, leaning back in her chair and talking over him when she wanted to correct or rebuke him.

Fernando had much less of an accent than Mariana but more of the hand gestures and sly sidelong looks. The more Shona looked at him the more she became convinced that he had just come into his looks, that he had been quite ordinary until he started to lose his hair. Some men did only suit age and he was one of them. And he knew it. Mariana wouldn't have married someone who would challenge her dominance. Shona suspected that he had found a sense of virility in maturity and something had shifted between them.

He had spent the first hour claiming to have been raised to hunt wolves around Lisbon, while his wife calmly repeated that there were only wolves in the very north, above Porto. She said that, far from being a goat herder,

Fernando's father was the main driving force fighting for nuclear power plants in Portugal.

'He's a scientist,' said Fernando.

Mariana tutted. 'He's a moron.'

Fernando rolled his eyes and smiled at Shona. Shona smiled at him, and then Mariana, unwilling to be allocated a side in their civilised altercation.

After two bottles of wine and most of a bottle of port, the conversation turned to Mariana herself.

Fernando leaned forward. 'Has she told you about her weeping statue?'

'Fernando—'

Mariana's tone would have stopped anyone but him.

'She was twelve, the age of greatest delusion, when her statue of the Virgin Mary started to weep blood.'

Shona covered her mouth to suppress a laugh. She didn't dare look at Mariana, but she could tell that she had become very still and could just see her clenched fist resting by her wine glass.

'Can you imagine her, in her nightdress with two little plaited pigtails, on her knees? Her eyes are squeezed shut and she's praying, praying, praying for a horse. And she opens her eyes and Mary is crying ruby tears, dripping down her face and off her cheeks. And what does little Mariana do? Does she pray even harder, does she collect the tears in a little bottle with a cork stopper? Does she phone the Vatican? Or does she run to her parents and demand that they come, immediately to see how much the mother of Christ wants her to have a horse?'

He laughed, throwing his head back as if it was the first time he'd told such a well-rehearsed story. He didn't look at Mariana when he'd finished but rested his head on one hand and gazed at Shona.

'You don't believe that, Shona?'

Shona lowered her hand and frowned. 'That a statue can cry or that Mariana wanted a horse?'

'That a statue can cry tears of blood, of course. Mariana is clearly the kind of woman that came from the kind of child who desperately needed a horse.'

'I don't know.' Shona hoped she could tread between them. She had a feeling that when they got going there was little chance of escaping. 'I've heard of weeping statues and ones that drink milk from spoons. Who knows?'

'So you do believe her?' Fernando raised his eyebrows dramatically and then focused his eyes and hands on his glass. 'She'll be pleased. She invited you tonight because, even though you have no feelings left for your husband, or no good ones, you refuse to break the covenant of marriage.'

Shona heard Mariana inhale.

'She thinks she can make a good Catholic out of you, Shona. Get you in the Mother's Union, take you to Walsingham and Lourdes. There are heavy-duty pilgrimages where you have to stay up all night with no shoes on and walk around on stones all night. Not somewhere warm – Ireland.' He faked a shiver. 'That kind of experience can get anyone seeing a statue weep. Ah, you think I'm joking.'

Shona turned to look at Mariana, for reassurance that this was another of Fernando's teasing statements. Mariana, quite composed now, held her gaze quite steadily. It was true.

Shona cleared her throat. 'I don't think that's very likely.'

'We'll see,' Mariana said. 'Would you like some Medronho? Think of it as strawberry schnapps.'

Shona felt very sober all of a sudden. 'I've had wine and port. I think I should get a taxi.'

'No,' said Mariana. 'You must stay here tonight. A nightcap, just one.' She pushed the dish of fat, brown olives towards Shona and left the room with some empty dishes. Shona looked at the doorway after she'd left. She'd expected – what had she expected? Not some strange conversion over rosemary and lemon pork stew.

'I can't stay,' Shona said to Fernando. 'I have to get home to Cerys.'

He ran his finger along the top of his glass before finishing his port. 'She'll make you stay. I wouldn't fight it, if I were you.' He placed the glass down carefully. 'I'd like you to stay.'

Why, Shona wanted to ask, but she knew. He raised one eyebrow.

'It's a big house,' he shrugged. 'And I'm not as Catholic as Mariana.'

'I noticed.'

He slid over one hand towards her. 'What else have you noticed?'

'A few things.'

She couldn't sleep with Mariana's husband. But then she couldn't believe that Mariana brought her here to awaken a non-existent Catholic faith. It wasn't religion or marriage that kept her with Maynard, but pure anger and fear.

Mariana, coming back in now with more glasses and a different bottle, was so smug, and why? She had a husband who didn't look at her without sneering and a house that was too big without children to fill it. Mariana poured the drinks and set one in front of Shona and another in front of Fernando.

Shona picked up her glass. 'I'd love to stay.' Fernando clinked his glass against hers.

The light brightened momentarily behind the curtains and then faded. The sound of the voices carried from downstairs but left the words behind. Shona tried, again, to close her eyes, but it was too painful. Lack of sleep had left her eyes too dry.

Mariana came back into the room and pulled open the curtains. Shona squinted and covered her head with the duvet.

'No, no, no,' Mariana murmured. 'We never stop fighting, Shona. Not if it's important. Up.' This time she left the door open.

Shona dressed and walked down the two flights of stairs to the kitchen sat down on a heavy kitchen chair and placed her left cheek on the solid table.

'I don't care if you don't talk,' said Mariana. 'But you are going to eat today. One week of sulking, that's all you get. Jude's at school, quite safe.'

Shona felt a tear run from her eye across the bridge of her nose, across the eyelid and run onto the table. She hadn't even wondered where he was. Every day she'd just assumed Mariana would do everything. 'Thanks for taking him.'

Mariana looked away. 'Fernando took him.'

Shona felt sick. She had no reason to think Fernando suspected anything, but it felt wrong for them to be together. He could suspect. He would have had time to ask questions and count the months.

'Are you all right?' asked Mariana.

Shona nodded.

The kitchen had large terracotta floor tiles and a black

slate worktop. There were no religious icons in here, just rows and rows of jars containing pickled vegetables and large bunches of herbs in oil. Not decorative, their levels varied.

She watched Mariana as she made toast, made tea, fiddled with the radio and cut up the toast into tiny bite-size squares. The plate was placed just out of her eyeline, the tea a bit closer. Shona watched the steam rise from the mug.

'I have news. Fernando talked to Maynard last night about you going back home.' Mariana sat down next to Shona. 'Not that there is any rush.'

'He won't let me. He's got actual reasons now. I've lost it.' Shona lifted her head to look at Mariana and turned to the kitchen window. The sun had come out again, lighting the wine glasses on the windowsill.

'We need to work out what happens next. Do you want to sell the house?'

Shona shook her head and cleared her throat. 'I will never leave that house.'

'Do you want to stay with Maynard?'

'No.' Shona took a sip of tea.

Mariana sat down. 'You do realise that it isn't his fault. She has gone, but sometimes teenagers do. And usually they come back.'

'He knows, he knows something. He's hidden her away somewhere.'

'He's abroad. Bulgaria. He says he's working and the police say she has not been abducted. She's in Britain.'

'He's got her, somehow. Why would he work if he didn't know where Cerys was? He killed one of my daughters and now he has stolen the other. How can he not be responsible for all of it?'

109

Mariana took a breath. 'It's just a terrible, terrible thing, but babies sometimes die for no reason.'

Shona shook her head again. 'It wasn't cot death.'

'The coroner...' Mariana changed her mind. 'Have one bit of toast. It's just a tiny bit.' She pushed the plate towards Shona.

Shona counted them. Sixteen pieces of wholemeal toast, lightly buttered. Cut as if for a child.

'Think about what you want and what you need, Shona. Why do you want to go back to the house?'

Mariana picked up a square of toast and held it out.

'My baby died in that house. I hid her things so he couldn't touch them, but she's still there. I feel her there, and I'm not leaving her.'

Mariana put the toast down. 'It's like a shrine?'

'Not one of your shrines. A living shrine. My office was her bedroom. That's where it happened and there's no way I'm going anywhere. It was all for Meghan. That's why I stayed. And now Cerys...' Shona pushed the plate away and put her hands to her eyes.

'You think you need the house and that means you have to deal with Maynard.' Mariana pushed the plate back. 'The police are content that Cerys is making decisions of her own free will. Leave that aside. We can look into that, I know how. We need to think about your legal position and then we can worry about what is and isn't known. And you need to eat.'

Shona looked at Mariana's serious expression. She knew that she was saying anything, absolutely anything to get her to eat that bloody toast. She picked up the nearest piece of toast and chewed it slowly. When she couldn't feel any solidity, she swallowed it with a sip of tea.

'Good girl,' said Mariana.

'Don't the police have to tell me where she is?'

'They're investigating. I think there are stories being told, Shona. They are stories which mean things are going to get very hard. At the moment they are waiting.' Mariana sighed.

'Who is telling the stories?'

'Cerys.' Mariana put her hand on Shona's. 'But they aren't her words. Fernando thinks that Maynard will allow you to go back until the house is sold. It will take a few days, but it will give you time to come to terms with everything. And the deal is Cerys' silence for yours, it seems. Does that make sense?'

Shona nodded. 'She's saying things that might endanger me and Jude?'

Mariana nodded. 'My advice is to agree.'

Shona opened her mouth to speak but Mariana gripped her hand.

'Think about whether you want to tell me what it is he doesn't want you to say. Don't say anything now. Eat and think.'

Shona obeyed. All this time she'd thought she was playing her game but Maynard had always been in charge, slowly taking Cerys from her. He'd taken charge of Meghan's funeral too. All Shona had done was turn up, Cerys in her arms, and stand dry-eyed as the vicar praised a baby he hadn't known and hadn't done anything and would, now, never do anything.

Shona had attended the coroner's court too and listened to all the sympathy and all the lies. The statistics on sudden infant death (which exonerated everyone), the possible genetic links (which gently led the blame back to her) and the painful impossibility of ever knowing (because she didn't speak). She refused to speak, keeping

111

her lips pressed tightly together and her arms wrapped around a wriggling Cerys. She wouldn't let Maynard take her, or anyone else. She listened to all of them, at the court and at the funeral, but all she really heard was the final cries of Meghan that she hadn't gone to.

Mariana cleared away the plate. 'What do you think about what I said?'

'You're right. Tell him I agree. I won't chase Cerys and I won't say anything about what he did.' She waited for Mariana to ask what it was, but she didn't. 'He would have Jude taken away, wouldn't he?'

Mariana raised her eyebrows. 'I think Jude isn't his concern. Destroying you is.'

'I want my house too.'

Mariana nodded. 'I know. But one step at a time. And just remember that you don't need the house. It's a symbol and we can create those anywhere. It's become something he can use against you. You need to behave in a certain way to get what you want. And Jude needs his home, even if it's just for a while. I can take him to school and I can give him dinner, but he needs you back.'

Mariana looked stern. Shona realised that this was her work face. She had become a client. Mariana storming into the police station had been a wonderful sight, fully made-up and suited at two in the morning; arms open and the full weight of the law in her voice.

'I know what you've done for me,' said Shona. 'I know you're the only reason why I wasn't arrested the other night, or committed.'

'I just want you to be safe, from yourself as well as him. You will find a way through this, even if you don't get exactly what you want.'

Mariana played with the silver crucifix that nestled against her breastbone.

Shona snapped a warning. 'Don't you dare mention God to me.'

She let the cross fall. 'I wasn't going to. It's just habit.' She folded her hands together. 'A bad thing has happened, I know, but you have a purpose now and it's probably best to draw a line and have nothing to do with Maynard. You will have to deal with him when you're strong enough, but keep your focus.'

'Mariana, all this means that she chose to leave. My daughter chose to go and didn't even tell me. They've both gone.'

Mariana bit her lower lip and then got up from the table and stood behind Shona, her arms wrapped around her. She felt the whisper before she heard the sound.

'Do you want me to take you to the cemetery?'

'Yes.' Shona pushed herself up from the chair.

The cemetery was set out like formal Victorian gardens with wide, sweeping driveways and mature trees. Of course, they'd need to swap the chapel for a bandstand, and the gravestones for feral clumps of daisies.

Shona directed Mariana through the lanes and they parked. Shona led the way to the grave. She'd never taken Mariana there before. She realised that she didn't really know anything much beyond their working relationship and the past few days she had lingered on the top floor of her house.

The gravestone was clean and the carving still starkly cut: *Meghan – Taken*. Shona ran her hand across the curved marble top. There was a small posy in the vase at the foot of the grave, not that Meghan's feet would have reached to the bottom. She was tiny, in the middle of a double bed of space. Mariana crossed herself.

'I never wanted her buried in the ground. Or cremated. I wanted to build a shrine, to keep her out of the earth but Maynard just organised everything while I was,' Shona exhaled, 'wherever I was. I heard him arranging for her things to be collected so I got my mum to take them first. He was so angry with me I thought he might kill me too. When I got the call from the stonemason, I didn't tell him.' Shona pointed. 'Maynard hated the inscription.'

'It's individual.'

Shona looked up. 'That just sounds rude.'

'Sorry.' Mariana didn't sound sorry.

'You should have seen what I wanted to have.'

'Gravestones should be a comfort, not an accusation.'

Shona didn't look away. Mariana had the look of someone familiar with graves, with the look and tending of them, with the importance of tradition and the right words in the right order.

'Have you lost someone?'

Mariana shrugged. 'That's not for today.' She crossed her arms and rubbed both shoulders. 'Sometimes you have to think about one death at a time or ...' She threw her arms up and recrossed them. She closed her eyes. Shona wished she could pray as well. She thought of Mariana's large home, bought for children but holding none.

'Mariana, Kallu says he has a message from Meghan.'

Mariana didn't move. There was no wind, no clouds. It was one of those trick days in the middle of October where the ozone gets blown in from the coast and the summer seems coarsely imminent.

'Is that why he stays with you?'

Shona had forgotten she said anything. 'I suppose, yes.'

114

'And has he given you a message?'

'Not yet.'

'Six, seven weeks and no message? Throw him out, Shona, if that's why he's staying. I know about people like that. You don't need parasites around you.'

Shona sat down with her legs beneath her and, eyes closed, lifted her face to the sun. Maynard may have already done that, she thought.

Mariana said, 'He's a fraud, and you're a fool for believing him.'

Shona stared at Mariana who didn't look away, but held her gaze with the absolute certainty only she could convey. As relieved as she was to have her house back and as guilty as she felt about the way she'd betrayed her, sometimes Shona felt Mariana was the most toxic person she knew.

8

Mariana drove away after checking that Maynard really had left as he promised. Gone straight from Bulgaria to Berlin for work, he'd told Fernando. He wouldn't speak to Shona any more and Mariana had become an unofficial legal representative, but he preferred to deal with Fernando. He reported back that he would only use the flat from now on, but he wanted the house sold. If she agreed, Shona could use it until then. Shona didn't agree but Mariana managed, over the days, to phrase it in a way which sounded acceptable to him.

However marvellous she was, Shona was glad to be shot of Mariana, who had continued to be rude about Kallu for the rest of their stay. Every comment she made felt to Shona like a personal insult. Finally she was gone and Shona relaxed.

Shona stood by the front door clutching the brown bag which Maynard had let Mariana pack for her and Jude. All the clothes needed washing. Toothbrush and hairbrush needed to be replaced upstairs. There was nothing else in there. Shona let the bag fall to the floor where it made a reluctant thump. Jude sat on the stairs.

'Do you want to watch TV while I do some washing?'

He shrugged and then shook his head. 'Is Cerys on half-term too?'

'Yes, I expect so.'

'Is she upstairs?'

'No.'

His head sank into his hands. 'I'm bored.'

'No, you're sad. I'm sad too, but we're home now.'

'He'll make us go again.'

Shona sat next to him and drew him to her. There was occasional noise from beyond the door, slamming, clanging, cars pulling away. From inside the house there was no noise at all. She'd been waiting for half-term since he'd started school, time to spend with him recovering the relationship they'd had before. Now she couldn't even think about leaving the house with him. What if Cerys came back? What if Maynard sold the house from underneath them? At least, if she was here, she could stop people viewing the house.

She thought of all the time Maynard had alone in the house.

'I just need to check something. Do you want to come up with me?'

Jude nodded and followed her to the bedroom. It looked tidier than usual.

'Do you want to get changed, Jude? I'll put a wash on in a minute.'

She left him in the bedroom and went through to the office. Something prompted her to check the file of small browned press clippings. She looked through the bottom shelf where it always was, tucked in amongst A4 files and her encyclopaedia. It wasn't there. The information on the cyclist, his name and age and where he'd died, all gone. Maybe she could find his trace on the Internet, but it was going to be hard. Cyclists got killed and forgotten all the time, and the fact that she'd saved the clippings had always seemed evidence in itself. No wonder Maynard felt confident enough to break their agreement and put the house on the market.

She went back through to the bedroom. Maybe they'd just been moved. She had to search the house for them, but she didn't want to unsettle Jude.

'I'll phone Callum's mum and see what they're up to.'

'Can't we go out? Just us.'

She held him tighter. 'Not today.'

He nodded. She looked at him. She'd been putting off the question, but now they were on their own she had to ask.

'Jude, what did you think of Fernando?'

He shrugged.

'Did you talk about anything?'

'No.'

'OK. He didn't ask how old you were?'

'Everyone asks that.'

'True. I'll call Thea.'

She opened the door to Cerys' room. The clothes had been pulled from the wardrobe and drawers, the mattress had been pushed from the bed. It was as if Maynard had been searching for something. Something big, as the little things, the books and files hadn't been moved. Or Cerys had been back and made a statement. She couldn't hear Jude downstairs and she didn't want him to come up and find this. In any case, she wasn't ready to look at anything yet, to acknowledge the last music Cerys listened to, or that she'd left the top off her cleansing lotion.

There was a knock downstairs and she opened the door to Thea.

'This is really kind, thank you,' she said.

Thea said, 'No problem at all. It's only a couple of hours, I'm afraid. We've got plans later.'

'Two hours in a play centre deserves some gratitude.' Shona pressed a ten pound note into Jude's hand. 'Bring me back the change, OK?'

He thought about it for a moment before nodding.

She watched them drive away and thought about going back to Cerys' room. Not yet. She fetched her mobile from the bag and took it to the kitchen to recharge it. The kettle boiled three times before she remembered to make a cup of tea.

She sat at the kitchen table and leafed through the letters and papers Maynard had left there. He may have left them there for her to look at, but she didn't read any of them. She was only interested in what he was hiding. She went back to the front room and pulled down the handle. The door didn't move. She banged against it with her hip. It was locked.

Back in the kitchen she switched the mobile on. It sang to her and then registered its search for a signal. Twenty-two messages. Voicemail started to ring. The first message was Rob, and the second. She only listened until the sixth message, by which time the swearing and insults had become incoherent. She put the phone down on the table and held her head with both hands. The deadline for the Tower of London paper had expired at some point in the last couple of weeks.

'Fuck.' Her voice sounded dull in the empty room. She knew she should phone, explain, apologise. She also knew he wouldn't answer. She could barely face him again, seeing only Cerys' embarrassment and shock whenever she thought of him.

The crying started next door. She hadn't given Amy a single thought either. She should have told Mariana to watch out for her, to check on her. Kallu would have been waiting for her to help him out at the museum. She wasn't sure how she felt about Kallu any more, but she knew that would change when she saw him. She had failed everyone she had promised to help.

She flicked through the papers again. End-of-service contracts with the utilities. Maynard wasn't going to pay the bills any more. She'd have to set up direct debits and all that stuff.

There were three envelopes addressed to her which he hadn't opened. She put the bank statement to one side and ripped open the next, a card from Kallu with some weird stone pagan symbol. That was one less thing to worry about then. He must be all right, wherever he was. The second wasn't a card but a photo. She turned it over. A photo of Cerys, hair suddenly and strikingly blonde, smiling at someone behind the camera. She'd wanted to dye her hair for years. She looked happier than Shona ever remembered. She was safe, happy and someone wanted her to know it. The envelope had been printed, the stamp had no postmark.

Shona decided to think about that later. She needed to try to make amends first.

She knocked at the familiar door and Rob opened it, his face stiffening as he recognised her. His worn, towelling dressing gown was loosely gathered to one side in his left hand.

'Can I come in?'

He mumbled, as if he'd just woken up. 'I've lost my contract with that company, thanks to you.'

'Can I come in and explain?'

'You know I relied on that, I was good at it.'

Shona stopped herself saying that she was better. 'You've got the work at the school.'

'That's cover, there's no certainty of work.'

'There are plenty of other companies who want to rip off students.'

'Oh, you developed a conscience.' He nodded. 'So you can't be here wanting more work like that then. Can you?'

Shona tried to push past him. 'Just let me in for a minute, please.' Before he pushed her out again she saw a school tie hanging on his banister, Cerys' school. 'Screwing mothers is one thing, but schoolgirls?'

He gathered his dressing gown together again, smiled at her, all teeth, and tried to slam the door. It hit the side of her foot.

'I'm sorry, I'm sure it's all a mistake. I didn't mean to let you down.'

'Sign up yourself. You know how it works. I can't rely on you.'

Shona walked away. She didn't want to sign up herself. She didn't want her name on any of the paperwork. It was shitty work and she couldn't justify it to herself. It had only ever been fun, and then a case of just one more. Now she had bills and no money coming in from Maynard to cover them. She would have to open the bank statement at some point. Not yet.

Shona lay down on her side of the bed. She could see the book Maynard had left on the bedside table, his place still marked. He had slept in her bed, her and Jude's bed. The sheets smelled of him. She picked up the book, a history of Renaissance art, and flicked through the illustrations. Same, same, same. He would have to come back for that, or she could hide it, pretend he'd lost it somewhere else. His marker fell out and she unfolded the sheet of paper: 'gross incompetence'. She sat up and read it through properly. Maynard had been sacked, not made redundant. She smiled and then laughed quietly.

She opened all three of the drawers on the side that used to be his. Some change, earplugs, she emptied everything into the bin. There was nothing else incriminating. It would all be in the locked front room.

She didn't care about the money. He could have paid this house off four times over, so he said, and he could keep it as far as she was concerned. All she wanted was to be here and, if she couldn't have all her children, to at least be here without him.

A pain grew from the centre of her chest and spread up to the base of her neck. It felt that if she didn't cry her throat would slit itself from the inside out. She found herself gasping for air, not letting the sound escape.

She went back to Cerys' room. The more she looked the more she saw that had been left. She began to push the large wardrobe back against the wall, first checking behind it to see whether something had been hidden there. There were fingerprints in the dust, but nothing else. Had Maynard been looking, or had it been someone else? He said he'd been away but the letter, she realised, meant that was a lie. If he was in Bulgaria and Berlin, it wasn't for work. Not paid work.

The clothes back in the drawers, she checked under the mattress and then put it back on the bed. She stripped off the sheet and duvet cover and then hesitated. Cerys' smell. She wasn't ready to wash it out, just like she'd kept Meghan's things in boxes at her mother's house.

Her mother. It was a long shot, but worth a try.

She went back downstairs, found the house phone and took it back to Cerys' room.

'Shona? How lovely to hear from you.'

'Hi, Mum.'

'Are you going to come over?'

'Soon. Listen, Mum, Cerys is missing.'

'When did that happen?'

'A couple of weeks ago.'

'A couple of weeks? Shona—'

'So, she's not with you? You haven't seen her?'

'A couple of weeks.' Her mother was breathing heavily. 'No, no, I haven't seen her. You didn't think to tell me?' Her voice was cracking.

'I'm sorry, it's been really difficult. I have to go. Jude's going to be back in a minute.'

'OK. Thank you for phoning, Shona.'

Shona grimaced and rang off. She took another look around. Most of the clothes were packed away and she was no nearer guessing what might have happened. She heard a female voice and turned, but it was next door. Amy.

Amy had been screaming at someone for twenty minutes when Thea came back with Jude.

'Wait out there, Jude,' said Shona. 'We're going into town.'

Jude grinned and looked to Callum to see if he was jealous.

'What's going on next door?' whispered Thea.

'She has a drinking problem. I don't know what's

happening, but she sometimes brings people back and then there's trouble.' Shona noticed Jude listening. 'Come on, nosey.'

'Should we call someone?'

'I don't think that would help.'

They walked to the end of the road together before separating.

'Shall we go to the library?' said Shona, regretting not thinking this before they left. She still had a pile of books that she was probably collecting fines on.

'And the toy shop?'

'Maybe the toy shop, but definitely the library.'

The walk into town was, other than when they got back, the first time she'd been alone with Jude since Cerys left. Jude held her hand and then, remembering his age, let go to scuff the leaves which rested against walls. The streets were quiet as they walked past the old cinema. Someone had told her it was full of dead pigeons. She remembered a cinema in Sidmouth she'd taken Cerys to where they could hear seagulls all through the film. The house they'd rented was down the road and the lights from the street and the garage across the road made sure the seagulls were awake all night. So much fighting over the territory of a cinema. The roof must have been disgusting and she wondered if the wind ever dropped enough for everyone to smell it.

That was before Jude. He had rarely been to the cinema in town as it was so much easier to buy films on the TV and make their own popcorn. She should take him. Half-term wasn't even halfway through.

They cut past buses and into the small lanes which ran up to the library. As Jude looked at the books Shona caught up on the newspapers. She always used to know exactly what was happening in the world, and where. She'd stopped buying papers a while ago, just catching up on the laptop or her mobile. She'd forgotten how nice it was to flick the pages backwards and forwards, to zoom in by moving her head rather than swiping her finger.

There was a lot on Occupy. St Paul's had been turned into a protest camp, people were resigning and civilisation was being remade. She felt the pull of jealousy. She wanted to be there too. She had become boring, obsessed with physical things, a house, while other people fought for big, abstract hope.

Jude brought his books over. She smiled. They were all old favourites. One of them he even had at home, but she checked them out with the automatic machines and they left. She tried to renew the books she had out but the machine kept telling her to talk to someone at the desk, and she gave up.

In the toyshop Jude couldn't choose. Everything looked so plastic and cheap to Shona that she didn't try to force a decision. Even the wooden toys looked plastic.

'Let's go to the museum,' she said. 'Sometimes they have things on in the holidays and they have good things to buy.'

Jude agreed and they walked up towards the castle and turned right, Jude pointing out the unicorn above the door, as usual. There was no lunch sign on the door, but Shona couldn't remember if this was one of Kallu's days to work. There was a rota, but it ran, unwieldy, over a fortnight. She'd lost track.

She pushed the door open and let Jude run in before her. The tape of bird calls was playing. As he lifted the stones and geodes and flashing pens, she looked around for Kallu. She couldn't see him and walked over to look at the massive cast of megalodon jaws suspended from the ceiling. Past the stuffed Brent geese, the seaweed display, birds that used to walk around the dunes and saltings, to the fossils. She liked the elephant found at East Mersea, maybe exactly where she'd been with Jude and Kallu. She knew the giant elk by the office had come from Clacton, and the stuffed parrot was supposed to look like the local parrot fifty million years ago. The thought made her want to laugh. This place had been so tropical and look at it now.

From the back of the display Shona could see into the office where the phone and kettle were. She could see Kallu standing, looking down at someone sitting in the chair, very short hair and stocky. Shona thought it must be his boss. Shona couldn't see Kallu's expression but he stood like a child being told off, hands clasped in front of him. Maybe he'd finally been caught one too many times. Maybe he was in trouble. Maybe it was even Kallu's dad. The man stood and rubbed his head with his hand. He picked up a hat, like a trilby, and placed it on his head, then put an overcoat on. He left the office and Kallu watched him go. So did Shona. It was Jimmy.

Kallu looked concerned. He turned slowly and flinched as he noticed Jude, rooting through the boxes. His eyes searched for Shona and when he spotted her he smiled. She nodded and walked towards them.

'Have you finished, Jude?'

He held up a geode in one hand and a pen microscope in the other.

'Have you got the change from earlier?'

'Yes,' He put the things down on the counter and pulled the coins from his pocket. 'Is it enough?' he asked Kallu.

Kallu hadn't taken his eyes off Shona but now he clicked

back into place and rang them through. 'Fifty-eight pence more, sir.'

Shona got her purse out and handed it to Jude to find the change. She didn't trust her fingers.

'Who was that?' she asked, nodding towards the door.

'I don't know.'

'He was in your office. You were talking to him.'

'I know. But I still don't know who it was.' There was something slipping in his gaze. It wasn't one of his episodes but, Shona thought, lies. He was lying to her for the first time. Although most of what he'd said could have been evasion or gibberish, he'd never lied.

'Do you want to eat with us later?' she asked.

'Are you back home?' There was something funny about the way he said that too, like he knew.

'Just back today.'

'I might, thanks.'

'You have to,' said Jude. 'I haven't seen you for ages.'

Kallu's lips moved, but it was an echo of a smile.

Shona took Jude outside and immediately felt sick.

'Are you OK, Mum?' asked Jude.

'Yes. Let's take a bus back.'

Shona sat on the stairs. It was half past one in the morning. Jude had finally grasped something like sleep but she couldn't. Kallu had eaten with them, been normal and chatty and yet there was something odd underneath it all. Something had given way. Shona wanted to blame Mariana. Maybe Kallu's thing, whatever it was, only worked with an open mind. And now he was back in the shed like everything was normal, but she knew it wasn't. There were noises coming from the shed. She'd heard noises before, but these sounded different.

She went back into her bedroom and inched the curtains across. The houses which backed onto hers had open curtains too, shadowy figures trying to identify the sound.

She would have to go out.

She unlocked the back door and crept out in the dark. She stubbed her toe on the concrete and gasped. He was making such a weird, guttural noise that she was scared. She'd heard things like this from the shed before, but this was louder and made her feel sick with anticipation.

A foot from the door, she called. 'Kallu?'

The noise stopped.

'Kallu, are you all right? Shall I get someone?'

Silence. She knew she should check and reassure herself. She knew (with Mariana's voice in her head) that there was nothing to it except attention seeking. How could he be so mad and so functioning simultaneously? It made no sense. She knew that. But she also knew how people did believe the most insane things and incorporate them into their reality. Just look at her mother.

Shona hesitated once more and looked around the windows. All quiet now, but she half expected a police car to pull up and paint everything blue. But as she never called about Amy as she tore herself apart, no-one had called about the sounds of a boy being murdered in a shed.

The cold had worked its way through all of Shona's toes now and she locked herself back in the house. As she rubbed warmth back into her feet she knew she should have done more for everyone. It was Shona who had driven Cerys away and Shona who had talked about Amy without doing anything to make it better. She should have checked on her more often. She should have asked for professional help and stepped aside. And poor Jude. He was the only person she had left, and what was she doing to him? He was having nightmares. She knew he was suffering and didn't know where he lived any more. And didn't know who his father was. She had created that too, so he only had her because that's how she wanted it. How could he make a choice and favour his father, like Cerys had? But to tell him now, or ever?

And now Jimmy, who must know Kallu. Or was it Jimmy who had placed Kallu here, knowing how gullible Shona was, how much she wanted to save the world? Kallu had even told her she was being watched, and if he was the one watching then he'd be the one to know. They both wanted something from her, as did Maynard, as did everyone.

So she clung to the bricks and the scraped paint of her house with its memories of skin and bone. That was all she could offer Jude, other than herself. At three o'clock, not knowing if her eyes hurt more from crying or exhaustion, she lay down, wide-eyed, beside Jude.

9

NOVEMBER

The phone rang and Shona glanced at it ready to cancel the call in case it was Marianna. She kept asking about Kallu and Shona didn't know what to say, and she definitely didn't want to be lectured again on her own stupidity.

It wasn't Marianna. It was Sean.

'Hello?'

'Hello, Shona.' Her brother spoke slowly, as if he was humouring her.

'Are you OK?'

'Yes. Of course.' He paused. She could imagine him fiddling with a pencil, trying to think of words. 'Mum phoned.'

'She told you about Cerys?'

'Yes. I thought I'd ring.'

'Thanks.'

Shona heard a noise and looked behind her. Kallu was coming in, closing the door behind him.

'I didn't speak to her. She left a message.'

'Right.' Shona sat at the kitchen table next to Kallu

and rested her forehead on her free hand. 'We still don't know where Cerys is.' The face on the leaflets on the table smiled up at her.

'No. It must be hard.'

Shona closed her eyes and thought about the accent he was developing, or putting on. Every part of his skinny childhood self was being stripped off. He sounded breathy.

He finally spoke again. 'I thought I'd ask if there was anything I could do.'

Shona smiled. 'No. Thanks, though.'

'You don't want me to come down?'

'No, we just have to wait. I'll let you know if I hear anything.'

'All right then.'

Shona could hear something being tapped. 'Thanks for ringing, Sean.'

'That's all right. Bye, Shona.'

He clicked off and she put the phone down. Shona had the feeling Sean's wife had pushed him to call, to offer to come. Maybe she'd wanted a little holiday from his solid, sensible self. Maybe she wanted a little time on her own, their sons having left home, to go to the bingo.

Shona rubbed her eyes with her fingertips and tried to ignore the lump in her throat.

'Isn't Sean your brother?' said Kallu.

Shona swallowed hard. 'Yes. Mum rang him. I don't know when they last spoke. That could be something good to come out of it, I suppose, if they are back in contact.'

'Everything is for a reason, Shona.'

Shona glared at him. 'No, it isn't. The world is full of pointless misery all made for no reason at all. Just because people find a way through it does not make it for a reason.'

Kallu nodded and opened his mouth.

131

'Don't!' she shouted. 'Don't say pebbles or wind or something like that.'

'I was going to ask if you wanted to do the leaflets.'

'Oh. Sorry.' She flipped through the images of Cerys, the words overlapping. Have you seen her, you seen her, seen her, her? 'I don't know. If the police have already spoken to her friends and she's probably not even here, it won't achieve much.'

'They're for her, the posters and the fliers. Isn't that what you said?'

'I know. If she sees them, she'll know I haven't given up on her. I don't know where she is but I know that she'll be wanting me to look for her. But, honestly, I think I just wanted something to do.'

Her mobile trilled. A message from Marianna. She turned the phone on its face.

Kallu pulled the chair out and sat next to her. 'Something has changed in you. You don't think she's gone now, not properly?'

'I think she's making a statement, that she doesn't love me or need me.'

'So by sending out the leaflets you're allowing your daughter to emotionally blackmail you? To prove how much you love her before she makes contact?' Kallu put his hand out and held a flyer up. 'That's mad, Shona.'

'That's motherhood.'

'Something has changed.' Kallu looked into Cerys' flat paper eyes.

The phone rang and she looked at the display. The number was withheld. It was probably Marianna, but maybe not. Maybe.

'Hello?'

An almost silent static and the call was ended.

'Wrong number,' she said.

'Do you think it was Cerys?'

She shrugged and placed the phone face down on the table.

'Something has shifted.' Kallu was talking to Cerys. 'What has moved?'

Shona threw her head back at looked at the ceiling. She wasn't in the mood for Kallu today. There were real things happening. She had to do something real. And where was Maynard? Maynard didn't care, he wasn't bothered. He was going to get his money from the house. He said Cerys could look after herself. He said Shona was overreacting. The police said she was somewhere safe, and there of her own volition and didn't want Shona to be given the address. Everyone said she would just have to wait. She wanted them to trawl the river, to dig up gardens, to get the helicopters out and turn the town over. She had the clear feeling that everyone knew something except her. Especially Kallu.

She was trying to be open with him, but the idea that she was a fool believing in a fraud hadn't left her. Even, she thought back, that he'd had his episode the very day she began to truly doubt him, that was suspicious, like he was proving himself.

At some point during the night she'd decided that she wasn't going to tell him anything. If he was for real, whatever he was, he could convince her.

'It's you,' Kallu said. 'You've shifted.'

'What?' She swung her head down and her neck cricked.

'Tell me about the last time you saw Sean.'

'Why?'

'It's important.'

'We argued.'

'Tell me.'

'No. I can't remember, it was a long time ago.'

Shona went to the cupboard and took out two mugs, slamming them down with such force in front of the kettle that one bounced off and smashed on the floor. They stared at it. Kallu went to fetch the dustpan. Shona sat back down at the table.

'Now you can remember,' he said.

Shona didn't recall much of her brother during their childhood. The nine-year gap meant that they had little in common apart from their parents, and they rarely wanted to talk about them.

When their father died, no-one went back to the house after the funeral. There were a couple of people who had worked with their father who turned up at the crematorium, but no-one had been invited. They tried to sympathise with the family, angled for an invitation onwards. Their mother, dressed in a yellow polyester dress which stuck to the back of her legs in the heat, flapped the order of service.

'No, we're not going on anywhere. I have shopping to do.' She put the pamphlet down and smoothed out the creases behind her knees. 'Lovely to meet you.'

Shona heard her on the way out asking when she could pick up the ashes.

Sean had taken Shona's hand and reluctantly led the old workmates to the local pub. Shona tried to drink a glass of Coke but it made her feel uncomfortably bubbly. The men exchanged looks before making their excuses. Sean drank the two pints people put behind the bar for him and began to talk about leaving.

Sean left home the year after the accident, found lodgings and began work as an electrician's apprentice. He wrote home every week and Shona was in awe of this giant brother who scaled pylons and danced along the wires, or so she believed.

By 1988, when Shona was sixteen, Sean was twenty-five and had a house and baby of his own. He came back to show Greta the baby, already fifteen months old.

Shona stayed for as long as she thought was polite and then went up to her bedroom. Sean knocked on her door.

'Hey,' he said. Shona put her book down on the bed and watched him look around her room.

'You never moved into my room.'

'No.'

'It's bigger.'

'I know.'

He looked at the bookshelves. 'Law and religion. A strange combination.'

'They're not on religion really. Spirituality.'

'What's the difference?'

Shona hesitated.

'You're going to have to be quicker than that in the court room.'

'I don't want to do that kind of law. I want to investigate bad convictions.'

'Ha,' he said. 'Same old Shona. You always knew more than everyone else, didn't you? I think, if someone's convicted, there's a bloody good reason. But you? No, you wouldn't accept that, would you? If someone tells you something, they must be wrong.'

Shona sneered at him. 'If laws were truly right, they would never be changed.'

'You always were a smartarse.' He pulled a book from the shelf and flicked through it. 'The precious, favourite child.'

'Oh, shut up.'

'Had a better time of it then me, though, didn't you?'

Shona stiffened. 'You weren't the only one. Dad hit me too.'

'Oh, yeah. Once.'

Once. He'd hit her once and then he died. It was then, aged six, she decided that her life would be dedicated to punishing the wrongdoer, to looking at them until they admitted their actions were wrong and changed. If they wouldn't change of their own accord, then she would force them.

Sean looked at her. 'You still think you did something magical that night, don't you?'

Shona flushed. 'No.'

'Something spiritual?' He laughed. 'Jesus.'

'Just a strange coincidence, was it?'

'You need all the evidence. You should know that.' He pushed the book back onto the shelf. 'You've had a gift for making people look at you, Shona, and that's your only talent. There's nothing special about you. You were a girl and your mother took pity on you.'

'Mum never did anything.'

'Didn't she?' Sean looked at her posters. 'Someone was looking after you, Shona, but there was nothing mystical about it.'

Shona thought of her mother, thin and so breakable, fighting the muscular delivery man, the man who humped around boxes and wielded sharp tools. But then, she'd seen the look in her mother's eye the morning after he died as her lips pressed against each other.

'I don't think she could have done anything.' Shona shook her head. 'Not after all that time. She was more scared of him than anyone.'

'Oh, yes, she could. You were worth protecting,' said Sean. 'You had everyone standing up for you, you always have had.'

In his face there was a glimpse of the boy she remembered in the lumbering man. He looked as if he might cry and turned away. Something had been transgressed and she knew he could feel it too. He looked relieved that memory had been pricked like a bubble and dispersed. There was nothing left between them.

'I'm sorry, Sean.'

He pulled the door closed behind him.

Shona had never said anything to Greta about it. The idea of her struggling with her father was too ridiculous. Both she and Sean had created their own versions of what happened. In her version, she was the victor. In his, he was the victim.

Since returning to Essex Shona had forced herself to visit her mother twice a year, on her birthday and Boxing Day. They never spoke about her father. His presence had never really been felt in the ornaments and books, but Shona suspected that the house had been cleared of anything that had been his. Still the space where his chair had been felt occupied.

On her third visit as an adult, as she lounged in the armchair, her belly swollen, there was a phone call. On the verge of sleep, as she had seemed to be for the whole pregnancy, she could hear her mother's voice becoming more strident and angry. Shona opened her eyes and considered rearranging her limbs, placing her feet on the floor, but couldn't bear to raise her head from the soft purple cushion. She caught the flow of her mother's anger and then let it float past her. There were so many colours in the room now, primary and secondary, it hurt her eyes to try to process it all at once. There were no sugary pastels, just the pure colour of flags.

Her mother's present was still unopened, Shona's card next to Sean's on the mantelpiece. There were two photos at either end: one of Shona, aged about ten, serious and pale in her school uniform; one of Sean in his cowboy costume, aged about six, with sad, shadowed eyes.

Her mother slammed the phone down and came back into the room. She settled herself back on the sofa and picked up the knitting. A small luminous orange cardigan. Shona would never put it on the baby.

'Who was it?'

'Patricia.'

'Auntie Patricia? Does she want to visit?'

'Yes, it's a bloody nuisance.' Greta turned the needles around for a new row. 'She wants to stay for a few days, or a week, and fill it with talk about what a fabulous brother he was. I couldn't be bothered with it then and I certainly can't be bothered now. She said I said I'd call her eighteen months ago. Fancy waiting all that time for me to contact her.' She frowned. 'Is this a purl or a knit?'

Shona closed her eyes again. After a while the ticking of the needles resumed, slowly with an unpractised skill.

'Can you give it a couple of weeks and write to her? Say I've died or emigrated or something,' Greta said.

'How about, you've been sectioned?'

The ticking stopped. 'If you like. Anything to stop her calling.'

Shona opened her eyes and her mother resumed the row. She had started dyeing her hair, back to the dark brown Shona remembered from childhood. The way it fell forward onto her face reminded Shona of being put to bed, gently tucked in and lying perfectly still while the shouting escalated in the front room underneath her bed.

'I'll change my phone number too.'

Shona nodded and closed her eyes again. She would have a sandwich and a slice of birthday cake and then she could leave.

Shona looked at Kallu. There was something else she needed to know. Jimmy had said Maynard wanted something. The more she thought about it the more she thought this could be her way out. Somewhere in her mind she must know what it was, but she was sure that she'd seen Jimmy with Kallu and until she knew why she wasn't saying anything. Just maybe Maynard wasn't the only one who wanted it.

Kallu was watching her face carefully. 'Is there anything you need to ask?'

'I need to see my mother.'

'Give me her address,' Kallu said.

Shona wrote it on the back of an envelope. 'You're not going to visit her, are you?'

'No. I want to meditate on it. There's something else there and it's easier if I can place her in the world. But you, Shona, will find answers with her.'

He stood up.

'It was Halloween last night,' Shona said.

'I know.'

She wanted to say, what about the veil between the worlds thinning, isn't it supposed to mean something? Make messages between the worlds easier? Instead she said, 'Happy All Saints Day.'

He smiled and went to the shed. She shivered as he let the cold air into the house. She lay down on the sofa and then made herself sit up. She was so tired, but resisted having a nap because she was bound to oversleep and be late for Jude. Since they came back from Mariana's she had started a habit of wandering the rooms in the night, rushing to every noise outside the house or downstairs. That's if Kallu wasn't making a weird scene and covering every noise. What if it was Cerys knocking lightly so she didn't wake Jude? What if she couldn't get in? She could barely close her eyes despite knowing that the sounds she heard were fantasies, little fabricated hopes and disappointments. All the fireworks going off in the dark made her jump, and it hadn't reached its peak yet. She needed to get tickets for the display for Jude, but she wasn't sure she wanted to walk around in the dark.

The letterbox snapped shut and there was a thud almost simultaneously. She forced herself from the sofa, expecting the image of someone, maybe Cerys, behind the patterned dips of glass. Something had changed, he said. It could be her. There was no-one there, just a small package on top of the local paper, no address or stamp.

She picked both up with her fingertips and took them to the kitchen. With a knife she sliced the brown paper underneath the Sellotape on the package, thinking all the time about where fingerprints were most likely to be found. Loosened, she teased the paper away from the contents. Bubble wrap surrounded something hard and silver. She tried to slice underneath the Sellotape again but had to give up and use her fingers to rip a hole in the wrap. It was a photo frame with a picture of a still blonde Cerys, underneath an umbrella, laughing. She was looking up at something or someone; it had to be someone, the way she was looking so engaged. It was dark, the flash having whitened Cerys' skin and the shine on the umbrella. Shona scrutinised the details: the clothes were all new, she hadn't seen any of them before, and they were shorter and tighter than anything Cerys had worn at home. Neither did she recognise any buildings in the background. It looked like any town centre; a Costa café, a phone shop and WHSmith. Not abroad, then.

Shona pulled out the back support and stood it on the table. She was less angry than before, but much less scared. She realised that mostly she was angry that Cerys was well and cared for, free to come back, and angry with Cerys for being happy without her. She dialled Cerys' mobile again. Sometimes it went straight to voicemail and sometimes it rang first. It must mean something. She didn't know what. This time it was voicemail.

She couldn't talk to Mariana about this. She wanted to phone Thea, she wanted her lightness of presence. Thea was like Kallu, she realised, but accessible and with no answers beyond common sense. But sometimes common sense was quite enough and being stoned would be better than getting drunk again. Or different, at least.

She picked up the pile of leaflets, all with Cerys' smiling face on. She was going to put one through every door between here and Jude's school. One of her friends was bound to see it, if she put them through enough doors. She was probably still talking to them on Facebook or FaceTime or something like that. Shona had never got the hang of them, but Cerys' friends would know how to tell her that her mum was still hoping. Still thinking about her.

GRETA

I think Sean was four, just about to start school, when my mother took him upstairs to change his top. He'd bitten off the bottom of the square cone and dripped yellow ice cream right down to his waist. She never mentioned the bruises on his back. She never came back to the house either. She could finally see Larry for what he was, the devil she'd always anticipated.

She blamed me, of course. After all the stories and warnings, I hadn't been vigilant. I'd forgotten the rules and married him. I'd allowed him into the family. As far as she was concerned, I'd married the devil that was chasing us. It was just us three against him.

I watched my daughter alter and grow as my son, nine years older, shrank into himself and begin to disappear. His back curved and the skin at the sides of his fingernails was ragged. He developed a habit of looking over his shoulder at the slightest noise and he often complained to me of a stiff neck. The same monster which fed her was killing him but I saw my son sitting next to the baby, stroking her hand and passing back the toys she would throw to make herself laugh.

I thought, maybe, it would be good for him in a way, make him stronger and more self-sufficient. It didn't.

He begged to be allowed to stay with his granny, but I wouldn't allow him in her house in case my husband killed her while fetching him back. I thought of running but didn't even know where to start. He had the money and all I could have gathered would have taken us to the end of the road before he caught up with us, his work van stinking with its faulty exhaust.

I knew I should have done something to protect him but, if I'm honest, I wanted Sean to save me. My little boy. Smaller than average even when he wasn't cowering, he was sweet and affectionate as a toddler. His father saw this and called him a pansy, a mummy's boy because he didn't follow him into the garden and demand to play football or cricket or learn boxing. And I thought, what if he's right? What if I'm encouraging Sean in traits that will get him bullied and beaten up at school and at work? Instead I allowed him to be bullied and beaten up at home.

My daughter had an entirely different father, smiling and indulgent. She smiled, she pouted, she shut her ears to everything she shouldn't hear and she had absolute confidence in the world and its infinite fairness. Her father took her side against me or her brother, and she would never have disagreed with him, brought forward that frown. And so she was saved from his anger, and gave herself the credit. My son was sacrificed in the process but she didn't seem to notice that. We see what we want, and the rest creeps around our peripheral vision.

Larry's apparent affection for her made her grow confident and assertive. Whatever she wanted she got.

Whatever he said, she would do because she believed she wanted to do it. Then when she was six she disagreed with him. He looked at her as he looked at my son and raised his hand and slapped her hard on the face. Her adoring face. She looked stunned and then furious. She wasn't upset but appalled. It was as if every slap and punch she'd seen her brother receive were suddenly revealed to her in that single action. She looked at him, as if daring him to do it again and then turned away.

Looking back, I should have seen the signs in the world around us. I hadn't started to notice patterns at that point, not like I do now. Now I know that at this point there were three serial killers active in America. Three murders in less than three weeks by three serial killers, as January turned to February. I could feel the gap where real time was suspended and evil could dominate but I wouldn't have been able to explain it then. Sometimes there are moments where evil bursts through the seams of normality, and now I can see how my decision to act took place in this gap between worlds.

In the lonely empty years after Meghan, I drew up timelines and saw the links emerge. We are all bound by synchronicity. I became obsessed with ley lines and the way Coggeshall sat in the middle of so many. Where too many meet it's the sure sign of a devil's path. I know that now. I know the track my great-grandparents followed was one of those paths. I know wherever I travel I won't be able to avoid one. There was no path I could take back then and I could see no other way out. Yet I had to act.

Every Friday night Larry asked me to drive the van into the garage he'd rented near our house. It was one of a long line of brand new, wooden gated buildings behind the back of our garden, a two-minute walk. That was the only way that the Isinglass Factory would allow him to keep it over the weekends. He would stand at the end of the garage and solemnly guide me forward, there being a matter of two legs' give on either side of the length of the garage. The van had to be slightly more to the left in order to allow someone in and out of the door as well. That Friday after he'd hit my daughter I kept my eyes down as I carefully put the puttering van in gear.

When I first thought about doing it, I didn't think about it as attempted murder. I thought of it as killing the beast. I sat at the wheel and he stood at the back of the garage. He waved me forward. I placed my feet on the accelerator and the clutch, found the biting point, released the handbrake and shot forward.

I heard the crunch against his legs and felt sick when I saw the shock on his face. I left it a couple of minutes before I put the car into reverse and inched out of the garage. I parked up carefully in front of the neighbouring garage. No-one came.

I turned the engine off, locked it and walked up to him. He was lying on the oil-stained concrete, his hands bent up to his chest. My heart was beating so loudly that I couldn't hear his moans until I was right on top of him.

'If you ever raise your hand to either of my children again, I will kill you, no question about it. You're not as quick or as clever as you believe. I will be there before you even realise it. I'll leave you to have a think.'

I stood by the open door, next to his body and listened to his stuttering breaths, waiting for them to fail him. He kept breathing.

I walked back to face him. One of his hands shot out

and grabbed my left ankle. I dropped the keys in fright, then I raised my right foot and stamped on his wrist until he let go. I stepped out of reach and crouched down.

'Can you walk?' I said. 'Only it would be easy enough for me to close the garage door and leave you here all night. There won't be anyone around until the morning and it's going to be very, very cold tonight. So what do you think?'

I folded my coat around me and tried to make out his expression in the dark.

'I'm quite cold,' I said. 'You have thirty seconds to apologise and promise to keep your hands to yourself.'

I started counting to myself; I got to thirty and stood up.

'Yes,' he said. 'I agree.'

'To what?'

'To being sorry and never doing it again.'

'Right,' I said. 'Put your hand out.'

He did and I dragged him from the garage to the side of the house and realised I'd left the keys on the garage floor.

I could have run back to the garage and grabbed the keys but the thought of someone seeing and calling an ambulance stopped me. I had to call Sean. I knocked, quietly at first, but he didn't respond so I shouted through the letter box and finally saw his feet on the stairs.

He opened the door and saw his father lying on the ground. The relief on his face nearly made me cry. Then Larry moaned. I could tell from Sean's face that he was upset he wasn't dead. He helped me drag Larry to the front room and we left him to die on the floor.

I should have left him in the garage. It was difficult for the post-mortem to explain his injuries, but they concluded he'd dragged himself home after being hit by a

146

car. I cleaned the blood from his work van before it was collected and ran it into the back of the garage to disguise the dent. No-one wanted to blame the dead man or his widow.

I still thought things would improve from that point, but they didn't. I'd left it too late for Sean to believe that my actions had anything to do with him. I'd hidden it from Shona so well that she somehow gave herself the credit for the monstrous silence that dominated our relief. She built in weeks of fatherly penitence and appeared to believe that he'd died of shame. It's strange what makes us happy. She was right that she did change people, although she changed me, not Larry. But what had I become?

I would lie awake remembering him in the garage. He didn't look like a demon or a devil. He was just a man with crushed legs fighting for each breath. No spirits came up from the earth to drag me to hell, or fix him. He would never walk again but no demons revenged him. We were all glad he was dead, but what if he wasn't the devil at all? I couldn't kill the devil. No-one could. If I had killed Larry, then that only proved that he was a man and nothing else.

All three of us crept about as if he was still alive, hunched in his chair, waiting for him to erupt into violence again. Even dead he occupied the same space, haunting the house between his chair and the downstairs bathroom and the bedroom, back and forth over the ever-thinning lino, an angry, quiet spectre.

After the post-mortem, after the funeral, after we believed we'd packed him away, I realised that he hadn't gone anywhere. He was there in an even more determined way than before, when his arms swung and his voice belted us. We tried to ignore him, but we could think of nothing but him. Even Shona, who had never been afraid of him and claimed his defeat as her victory, would sit and anxiously observe his chair. She may, like me, have been wishing him to say something, anything, to show he was still there somehow. I hadn't killed the devil. I'd just made him harder to see.

10

Finally paid up at the library, Shona felt as if she was on the right path again. She popped in to the museum see Kallu, her shopping bags full and her purse nearly empty. The money she'd saved up from essay writing was running out but they still needed to eat.

She could hear the persistent beep before she pushed the door open. Kallu was having problems working the till again. He looked round at Shona. The woman waiting sighed.

'Let me help you,' Shona said.

Shona reached across him and pressed void. He kissed her on the cheek as she passed back behind him. She could smell the sea in his hair, darkly curled like seaweed.

'Where have you been?' Kallu started to type in the codes again. 'I've been waiting. I thought you'd know.'

'I was busy. I'll make you some tea.' She went into the tiny office behind the till and hid until the woman had left.

Kallu came to find her.

'You know to press void. You were just being awkward.'

Kallu smiled. 'That woman needed time to think. It was for her. And I knew you needed to remember there's always a void button.' His deep blue eyes looked black today. That meant he was feeling separated from himself. He would talk and talk and all of a sudden ...

'And I thought you needed me.' Shona smiled awkwardly. He looked away and rubbed both upper arms, absently. She could see a single small piece of driftwood tied onto each bicep.

'Yeah, I know.' Kallu was slipping away, she could see his eyes becoming unfocused. She had to be quick.

'Is there anything, any message for me?'

He'd gone. It often happened when she arrived. He said it meant he could relax, knowing Shona would protect him, cover for him. And she always would.

She watched him leave the office, walk slowly around the stuffed animals. He found the fox, curled up in its pretend hole. He sat down by the glass case, cross-legged and eyes closed. Shona could see the fox and his reflection merge. She sighed. Ever since she'd come back to the house he'd seemed to do this more and more often. She wanted it to mean that the message was on its way but suspected that the phone call to some authoritative body was becoming inevitable.

No messages. She knew it sounded ridiculous, would never dream of telling or trying to explain it to anyone else, especially not after Mariana's reaction. Shona didn't even believe in spirits. But something deep within her stomach did and stopped her picking up the phone.

She put the lunch sign on the door and locked it, posting the keys back through the letter box. There were other people who worked there and it surprised her that he never seemed to get in trouble. The place was never packed or anything, but people must have noticed these absences. That's why, when large groups were booked in, Shona had offered to be on-site, just in case.

'Shall I make some tea?'

Shona had tried to tidy before she arrived, but hadn't got very far. Now that Thea was here, the papers she thought were fairly hidden under the sofa looked an obvious last-minute shove. The plates and mugs she had piled up ready to take to the kitchen were still on the table next to a bowl containing a couple of wrinkled apples. She hadn't even thought of sweeping the floor.

Thea picked Cerys' photo off the windowsill and sat down.

'Is this her?'

'This is Cerys,' Shona said. 'She's fourteen. Long, brown hair, blue eyes, five foot one. She's blonde now, actually. Slim build, a scar on her left shoulder from a dog bite when she was four. She works hard at school and wants to be an art teacher. She likes music and films and lying-in at the weekend.'

'You sound like a newspaper report.'

'You can't try to sum anyone up without sounding like one.'

'So, let's get the food on table and talk,' said Thea. She moved to the table and emptied the shopping as Shona took the dirty plates to the kitchen and came back with clean ones. Thea pulled from her bag tortillas, breadsticks, humus and guacamole.

'This was supposed to be a thank-you for looking after Jude so much. There's loads here.'

'But a thank-you is not necessary and it doubles as dinner for Jude too.' Thea sat down. 'You need to spill, so just spill. Katya always said I was the best listener, right up until she dumped me.' Thea faked a sad face and smiled. 'And I have wine, unless you want tea.'

'You're a bad influence.'

'Yes, Katya mentioned that too.'

Shona went back for glasses. Thea poured and they both drank a good mouthful.

'Have you had a bit of a day too?' asked Shona.

'Too right.' Thea prised open the hummus. 'Had to do a birthday party for a dozen toddlers.'

'That's your job? I thought you said you weren't completely mad.'

Thea ran her hands through her hair, making it stand up. 'Only for money. There's very little that is too mad if you get paid for it. Haven't you seen my van? Seven Stars Parties.'

'Seven Stars?'

'I used to live at Seven Stars Green, just past Eight Ash Green.'

'Are you making this up?'

Thea looked confused. 'No.'

Shona thought back to Kallu and his necklaces. The goddess of the seven stars.

'So?' asked Thea. 'Spill.'

'I have no idea where to start.'

'Start with Cerys, of course.'

'Cerys is somewhere. She says she doesn't want me to know where. Not to me, she's said it to other people. Maynard apparently knows, but he won't tell me either.'

Thea cut the cheese to place on her bread. 'So, there's no other way you can find out?'

'Not that I can think of.'

'Oh, and what's Maynard's problem?'

152

'I blame him for our other daughter dying. He says it wasn't him. The court says it was cot death. Cots. That's all he talked about after we buried her, wanting to know where I'd put the crib.'

'Why was he so interested in that?'

'It was an antique. He loves antiques and paintings more than people. To me it wasn't worth anything because of that. It was Cerys' and I knew he'd sell it or something, so I packed up all of her stuff and hid it from him. I told him I'd taken it to the tip. He never believed that, but he never forgave me for taking it from him.'

'And you've been living together with all that hatred hanging over you?'

Shona nodded. 'For Cerys.'

'I'm sorry, Shona, but I'm amazed she stayed as long as she did.'

Shona froze.

'I'm not blaming you, but that's bloody horrible.'

It was true. What a waste.

'All so you could stay in this house?' Thea asked.

Shona nodded. 'Sounds stupid, I know. And now I have to accept that Cerys might have chosen her father over me. That she wants me to lie awake and wonder where she is and what she's doing. That she hates me enough to just leave without saying a thing.' Shona drank the rest of her wine. 'It's barely bearable. If it wasn't for Jude, I don't know.' She looked at Thea.

'Go on.'

'When Meghan died, I wanted to die too. I had Cerys but I saw how much she adored Maynard. I thought, I hoped, that Meghan would be my child, would love me instead. But she died. She was killed. And nothing was enough to mark her going, nothing was big enough to hold the thought of her. I wanted to build something. Have you seen those roadside shrines in Europe, in France and Belgium?'

Thea nodded. 'For the farmworkers.'

'Yes. I ordered the bricks, even, but Maynard took one look and persuaded the building yard to collect them. I could have beaten him to death with just one of them. I dreamed I did, one night. I woke up in the morning and felt so happy, so relieved and there he was, sleeping next to me.' Shona shuddered. 'But there was always Cerys to think about. She never even remembered Meghan. She doesn't talk about her at all, probably because she doesn't want to upset Maynard. But this house is where I had them both, for a little while. I can't leave it because that is leaving Meghan behind. And Cerys needs a safe place too. If she ever comes back, that is.'

'So it doesn't feel ended? You feel that no-one was punished for Meghan's death.'

'No. Maynard killed her and now it looks like he's taken Cerys.' Shona felt the wine and carried on. 'If I couldn't mark her with a shrine, then I had to keep the house. And then Jude came along, and that complicated it.'

'Who's his father?'

'Some guy. No-one.' Shona shook her head. 'And now Kallu is here.'

'What's the deal with him?'

'My friend, Mariana, thinks he's scamming me, pretending to have access to messages from Meghan. I don't know what I think any more.'

'Anything else?'

'Cerys found out I was having an affair with her teacher. That didn't help.'

'OK. That's enough to start with. Who do you know who knows Maynard?'

154

'I don't know any of his friends. There's his mother, but she doesn't like me.'

'That doesn't matter, it's still worth a go. Phone her.'

'Maybe.'

'No, now. Phone her now.'

Shona fetched the phone and dialled Maynard's mother.

'Sylvie, I need Maynard's address in London.'

'You don't have it? You're his wife, in name at least.'

'Can I have his address, please?'

'Have you once phoned me to talk? Have you kept me informed about your daughter, my granddaughter? There could be a perfectly good reason why Maynard has not given you his address and I, at least, am loyal to him.'

'Please. I think he may have Cerys.'

Sylvie barked a short laugh. 'I will be so pleased when he divorces you. I have no idea why he has supported you and your bastard for so long. Ask Maynard for his own address.'

The line was dead.

'Did you hear any of that?'

'I saw your face.' Thea grimaced. 'It needed to be done, just to cross it off.' Thea ate a couple of olives. 'Can you remember any clue about where he is, what area?'

Shona fetched the photos which had been posted and went back to the table.

'These are the only clue I have.'

'Who sent them?'

'Maynard, I suppose.'

'That's pretty vindictive.'

She had the photograph of Cerys which could have been taken in London. She had Maynard's lack of concern and the fact that the police hadn't done more that issue a short statement after the first report. No press interviews, no posters other than Shona's own. She had never been to Maynard's flat and only knew that it was in Edgware, maybe, or somewhere like that. She tried to remember him talking to other people about places he'd been or had visited, but she had clearly paid no attention at all.

'So, where in the house did Maynard keep his stuff?'

'In the front room.'

'So what's in there?'

'Furniture, stuff. The address is bound to be in there, on some bill or scrap of paper.'

Thea said, 'Let's have a look.'

'It's locked.' Shona led her to the door.

Thea tested the handle. Locked, as usual. Half-heartedly, she banged her hip against the panels but they didn't shift. They were those 'quality Edwardian doors' Maynard had been so proud of when they moved in.

'Have you lost the key?' Thea said as they went back to the table.

'Kind of.' Shona dipped a tortilla chip in the humus. 'When Maynard left, he must have accidentally locked me out, like he accidentally locked me out for the previous five years.'

'When Jude was born?'

Shona nodded.

'OK, I'm going to have a think. Tell me about this legal thing that happened. I keep hearing half-stories about it but I don't understand what went on.'

'People are talking about it?'

'Shona, if people are talking about you they're thinking about Cerys. Just go with it.'

'I worked at the university for this department called the Scrutiny Mission. It was a cold-case review thing, something which gets a lot of press. The university asked me to do an interview about our work, about miscarriages of justice, because there was a grant review coming up and they thought it would help. Stupidly, as it turns out.'

Thea nodded.

'So I thought we were chatting and I was asked about this drug-smuggling case and I said that I thought their defence had moral weight. That's not quite what got printed because their defence was the opium wars. We didn't get the grant and we lost other funding. The Mission ended up being disbanded in a reorganisation of the department. Jobs were lost, research money was removed.'

Thea nodded. 'Unfortunate.'

'Sometimes I feel cursed, Thea. Nothing ever works out the way it should.'

Thea shook her head. 'Welcome to the world. Everyone feels that.'

'No, they don't. And then I'm supposed to go and see my mother next week,' said Shona. 'I've made and cancelled three appointments.'

'Why do you have to make an appointment?'

'It feels like one.'

'But it's hardly a curse.'

'I have to ask her if she murdered my father.'

'Oh. That's more like an appointment, yes.'

Shona laughed at Thea's serious reply. 'Are you ever surprised by anything?'

Thea dipped another breadstick into the guacamole, while putting on an expression of intense thoughtfulness. 'I'm sure if I thought hard enough there must be something that would do it.' Thea ate the whole breadstick before she spoke again. 'Are you really OK? I know you're making light of it, but I can do serious if you need serious.'

'I'm not OK. Everything's crumbling. I have no idea what will happen next.'

Thea pushed herself up from the chair and hugged Shona. Shona felt awkward, her shoulders stiff, until she realised it was the first time since Rob that anyone, anyone adult, had held her. Thea moved away.

'Time for a cup of tea?'

Shona nodded. She had nothing to say that would be more useful although her head was full of things she wanted to say, had no-one else to say them to. Her mother had tried to kill her father. Maybe she had brought on his death after his silence and stillness. Shona herself, it turned, out was nothing special at all, just quite academic and particularly annoying when it came to right and wrong. And Maynard, who she'd married knowing that he was a deceitful and arrogant person, had turned out to be deceitful and arrogant. She had herself to blame for that, for believing that she could change him, as she thought she'd changed her father. She had no effect on people around her other than the change they wanted for themselves.

When she felt Thea's hand on her shoulder, she realised she'd been crying again.

'We've got twenty minutes until the boys need collecting,' said Thea. 'I'm not going to offer to pick them up because you need the fresh air, quite frankly. That's the end of serious for today, but I can be back tomorrow.' She hesitated. 'Well, just one more bit of serious. You need to feel like this house is your house. Get a locksmith to change the locks. Start taking control and stop just reacting to other people. Time to drink up.'

Shona nodded and gasped as Thea drank the tea in one go. She wiped her mouth with the back of her hand.

'Don't look so freaked out. I put some cold water in it.' She jangled the keys in her pocket. 'And yours. Hurry up, coat on, please.'

'There's loads of time.'

'There's loads of time if we want to be late, but not much time if we want to be early. It's all a matter of perspective, smarty-pants.'

They walked slowly across the field. Shona could feel the soles of her socks becoming sodden. She needed new shoes.

'So, what needs to happen is that you need to break in,' Thea said.

'To where?'

'The front room. I wouldn't advise going through the wall. It's probably a supporting one. But the door, they're designed to move.'

'Just bash it in? I've tried forcing it. It's pretty solid.'

'If you don't want to damage it or the surround, just get the locksmith to do it.'

Shona stopped and stared at Thea.

'But that's so obvious.'

'Doesn't mean that it's not the right answer.'

11

When the door closed, the stinging smell of burnt hair grew stronger. Shona cleared her throat again but it still felt tight.

'Shall I put the kettle on?' her mother asked.

'If you like.'

Greta was looking dishevelled, a just-got-up-air clinging to her. Clearly surprised by this visit even though it had been arranged, not her birthday and not Boxing Day, she must have thought Shona would cancel again. Shona could see her watching from the corner of her eye as she went into the kitchen and filled the kettle.

'Is everything all right?'

Shona shifted her feet. 'No, not really.' She went into the front room and moved a half-formed pile of wool from one end of the sofa and put it on a pile of books at the other. She saw the title on top, *Exploring Leys*, and didn't want to know what else her mother was reading. She took her coat off and dropped it over the arm of the sofa, then stared out of the window until her mother came in and handed her a mug of black tea.

'No milk, I forgot to get any.'

'Right,' said Shona. 'Do you want me to?'

'Not on my account.'

Greta sat down carefully in the armchair and shifted more books on the coffee table to make room for her mug. 'It's good to see you. And it's not even my birthday.' She raised her eyebrows. Shona sat on the sofa and looked around the room, looking for changes that weren't there, and her mother picked up a section of knitting, unravelled the wool holding the needles together and began clicking. Shona watched her, *over, click, through*, as the ball appeared to undo itself. It never quite fell from her side.

'Why does it smell strange in here? Did you burn something?'

'I don't think so.'

Over, click, through.

There were few noises: the occasional car, the sound of the TV next door smudged through the wall, a clunk from the clock as it turned the hour. Her mother had turned off the chime but it still tried to mark the change.

Greta paused her knitting. 'What have you been up to?'

Shona took a breath. 'After I spoke to you about Cerys, Sean phoned me.'

Greta nodded. 'Is he well?'

'I think so. He said to say hello.' Shona looked away, across the room. 'We didn't have much to say.'

'As usual.'

'We don't have many nice memories to talk about.'

They looked at each other, both avoiding looking at the space that had held the armchair. Now it formed a gap in the circle around the fireplace. The emptiness of the place where the chair had been that had held the man that had been.

Greta cleared her throat. 'Is there anything I can do? Are you putting up posters and things like that?'

'No, I put some leaflets around, hoping she'd hear from a friend and get in touch. Her friends, if they know where she is, wouldn't tell me. Whatever she's been saying, I don't think I come out of it well.' Shona realised that what she was saying about her daughter, her mother could have said about her. As a child, a teenager and an adult, Shona couldn't remember saying a single good, or even neutral, thing about her. She looked at her mother, saw the stiffness of her pose and the eager way she looked for answers from Shona. She was desperate for Shona to like her. Shona hoped that she wouldn't be treated like this: two grudging visits a year and a total lack of interest in Cerys' eyes.

'It will all turn out for the best, Shona.' No matter what her mother said, Shona always ended up wishing she hadn't come. And now, here, trying to see some silent vengeful goddess where her mother sat, she found the whole idea suddenly ridiculous. Why had she ever believed Sean? 'Did you ever run my father over?'

Her mother's face fell and Shona started to laugh in breathless bursts.

'That's what he said, ages ago. He said you just got in the work's van and ran him down!'

Greta wasn't laughing. She looked slowly from Shona to the door and back again.

'You didn't tell him that, did you?' Shona wiped her eyes. 'He believes it, you know.'

'I don't want to talk about him today. You're still not ready.'

Shona put her tea down by her feet and leaned forward. 'Is this to do with that stupid hoof print thing?'

Greta clasped her hands in her lap and looked straight back at Shona. Shona knew that look of dumb insolence. She used to practice it in the mirror to see if she could do it as well. Silence was the most powerful tool her mother had ever had and had kept them distant when they should have united against the monster downstairs.

Shona said, 'Right, don't talk to me then. But I know that you would never have had the guts to do it. All you ever did was watch and I was the one who did something about it. You can't stand that, can you?'

Her mother stayed perfectly still.

'So I think you're cruel for saying that to Sean and I think it's an extension of this devil story too. You chose a shitty husband, but, no, it wouldn't be your fault, would it? The devil made you, like he personally intervened to ruin your mum's life and your gran's life, and so on and so forth. You couldn't take responsibility for your mistakes and now you're taking the credit for something you could never have done. You need to tell Sean the truth. You're pathetic.' Shona stood up. 'He thinks I'm a liar, but I remember what happened. You must have told him that to make up for doing nothing all that time. You just don't have the capacity to care about anyone. Just demons and ley lines and dowsing and whatever other stupid distraction you can pick up along the way.'

Shona picked up her coat and walked away.

'I didn't tell him,' Greta said quietly.

Shona stopped and turned round.

'Sean had to help me. I couldn't get him inside.'

'You really did do it? You can't have.'

Greta closed her eyes. 'It wasn't you.'

Shona blinked. 'Why would you let me believe it for all those years?'

'It made you, Shona. You were nothing before you believed that you had the power to change people. It was the only bit of power you ever had over his memory.'

'I was nothing?' Shona walked back to stand in front of her. 'You bitch. I was six. I built my whole life on something I made up when I was six. Because you let me. I would have found something else, I would have been all right. But just imagine how stupid and empty I feel now. The choices I made were because I believed I could change people. One child dead, one child gone, a husband I hate and a crazy mother who wants me to believe that the devil is after her and, when she's gone, will be after me too. It's all I had left, that if I tried hard enough I could make a change.'

Greta kept her eyes closed and her hands still.

'Nothing here is going to help me, is it? If it's true, then my life may as well be over.'

Greta's voice was quiet but steady. 'It's not over. It may not be easy but it isn't over.'

Shona stood and walked to the door.

'See you later,' said Greta.

Shona didn't leave straight away. If she wasn't ever going to come back them, she wanted to see her bedroom one last time. She stumbled on the landing, thinking that there was still one step to go, and looked down in surprise. Her feet were solidly placed, but she felt unstable somehow. Her bedroom door was the first, the box room for the second child, so small that the door slid on a runner to save a little space. Her brother had been given the larger second bedroom next to their parents', but he'd asked her a few times if they could swap. She never asked what he could hear through the thin, papered walls.

She gripped the key-shaped catch and pulled the door

along the wall. It stuck before it was fully opened. The bed was still made, headboard against the window. She lay down and looked backwards at the sky. It could have been the same sky she had seen on her last morning here, bright and cloudless. The streetlight outside had meant she could read for as long as she liked without alerting anyone with a strip under her door. She had gloated, she shivered to remember, over the silent husk of her father. And it was no victory after all.

She turned her head to one side to see the books she had left behind. Periods of her life in piles and marked with tickets or strips of notebook paper. Once she'd settled on law she had forgotten these other thoughts. She sat up and then lowered herself to the floor. There were books on symbols and magic, from when she'd believed that that might be how she had defeated the monster. There were earlier books on religion from when she'd decided that she might be a saint in training, that it was the power of a fair and just God that had aided her.

She picked up a thin local book on the long-lost Maria shrines of Suffolk that Jimmy had posted for her birthday, or got someone else to post. Her mother must have told him she was interested. He had taken all of the religious paintings from his mother's house when she died but Shona had never seen him as a religious person. Maybe she should give the book to Mariana, but then she would have to tell her where she'd got it. She put it back. There were no novels, just early feminist writings and socialist discussions of moral government. Everything that concerned the law had moved out with her in one suitcase and a backpack. And she had nothing to show for it. No career, just a lapsed financial dependency on a husband who she would happily slaughter in his sleep. Her marriage had been no happier or healthier than her mother's, just two people waiting to see how far the other could be pushed.

The books, the cutesy ornaments, the cassettes could all stay. She checked the runner to see what was jamming the door, but couldn't see anything. Greta was waiting at the bottom of the stairs.

'I did it to save you from what Sean went through.'

'What, he wasn't worth saving?'

'I did things wrong, like you have.' Greta folded her hands together. 'Can I see Jude sometime?'

'Jude really doesn't need to see you. Jimmy would like to though. He's out any day now.'

Greta opened her mouth to reply, and then changed her mind. She opened the door for Shona, and Shona felt the ghost of a hand on her arm as she left.

'You do have people who care about you, Shona. Don't let them leave without telling them that you care too.'

Shona stopped but her mother had already closed the door. Was she talking about Kallu? She almost knocked to ask and then turned away. She knew what would happen once she'd got on her bike and was out of sight. Her mother would get the salt from the box by the front door and cover the footprints so the next set were visible.

Shona lingered on the driveway, looking at the garage behind her mother's house. Everything that Meghan ever touched was still in there, quietly waiting. When she was rid of Maynard, she could finally clear it out and take it back home.

There were two letters from the bank on the mat when she got back with Jude, with a solicitor's letter and one addressed to Maynard from an estate agent.

'Go up and get changed while I make dinner.'

'Do I have to? Can't I watch TV?'

'Look at your trousers, Jude. I need to get the washing machine on or they won't be dry.'

Jude looked at his muddied knees, kicked his shoes into the middle of the hall and slid his trousers off. 'Now?'

'Go and get changed.' Shona bent down to pick up the trousers. 'See if—'

She'd forgotten again that Cerys wasn't there. Jude looked at her.

'Nothing,' she said. 'Just clean trousers.'

There was a knock on the door. She turned to open it.

'Are you busy?' asked Mariana.

'You can come in but I have to make dinner.'

Shona put Jude's shoes next to Cerys' under the coat rack and took the post to the kitchen. Mariana sat down and took her coat off, hanging it on the back of the chair behind her. She could wait. The back door unlocked and kettle on, Shona opened the post with her finger before deciding which one to read first. The estate agent confirmed the contract, the asking price and included photos to use in the advert. The solicitor confirmed divorce proceedings and asked for the details of her solicitor. The bank statement showed that his payments to her had stopped in October. It wasn't surprising. Everything else had stopped in October. Shona made the coffee and sat down.

'So,' she said. 'I guess you're here to give me another lecture about Kallu?'

Mariana sipped her coffee. 'I just want us to be friends again.'

'We are friends.'

The back door opened and Kallu walked in. Shona waved at him and carried on.

'I just need a little space to make my own choices.'

Shona waited for Mariana to reply, but she just stared at Kallu.

'You remember Kallu?' Shona said.

'I was hoping for a private conversation.'

Shona looked at Kallu. He was standing by the sink with his eyes closed, his fingers flickering as if remembering a tune.

Mariana said, 'What exactly is wrong with you?'

Shona turned back, but Mariana was talking to him.

'The world talks to me,' he said.

Shona closed her eyes.

'What does it say?'

'It says you have known death. You are haunted by a spirit. Your soul hurts for what you did and what you saw and what you know. He cries for you. He tried to show you that.'

'Tell me more. Tell me facts, not this he, she stuff.'

Shona hissed, 'Mariana!'

'What?' Mariana looked pleased. 'He won't break, he wants to say it.'

'Stop it! Kallu?'

He opened his eyes.

'Jude's watching TV if you want to go through.'

He stretched his arms and closed the door behind him.

'What are you doing?' she asked Mariana.

'Me? I'm watching out for you, Shona. Your life is complicated enough without your shed god. For God's sake, focus on what's real.'

'Kallu is my friend. He needs me.'

'I've known people like that, Shona. Messiahs, gurus, all liars. When you press them for specifics, it falls apart. Everyone has lost someone. Everyone has made someone

168

cry. It's a cold reading, that's all. I guess he's made you dependent on him, feeds you a little information now and then, a whole lot of promises?'

'It's not like that at all. He's not like that.'

Mariana waited, tapping one finger on her mug.

'What can you offer me, Mariana? As far as you and religion are concerned, my beautiful, blameless baby is stuck in some limbo for the unloved and the unwanted.'

'What does he offer you?'

'Hope.'

'There is no hope.' Mariana looked away. 'That's how you should know that he is lying, your little shed god.'

Shona laughed and looked towards the back room door. She wished he hadn't come in. What he said only made sense when it was him and her. When it was questioned, it slipped away.

'Hold on, why am I being asked to explain? He's my guest in my house. You're happy enough to believe in invisible gods and crying statues, aren't you? You're here because you like to talk at people and show them how clever you are. Apologise or leave.'

Mariana pressed her lips together, centred her mug on the table, put her coat back on and left by the back door.

Shona slumped on the table and put her head in her hands. The door to the back room opened and she jumped up.

Kallu put his hands up. 'Sorry, I didn't mean to scare you. I saw her go.'

'Don't worry. I've haven't started dinner yet, but you can eat with us.'

'I'll cook.'

She thought of refusing, but couldn't bear to be polite. That was fine by her. If someone could just walk in at five-minute intervals and assign themselves a piece of her life, that would be perfect. Cooking, someone could do that, someone else could look after Jude and someone else could think about Cerys. Another could work out her finances and, finally, Shona would be free to sit in a corner and close her eyes. That would be more than enough to occupy her.

She nodded and he smiled. She rested her head on the table. She didn't think she and Mariana could ever go back to how they were, which was more her fault than Mariana's. She didn't open her eyes when she heard Jude come in.

'Shhh, your mum's sleeping.'

Kallu organised Jude and asked him about school. Jude sang a carol they'd been rehearsing, even though there were weeks to go until the carol concert.

'You sing that very well.'

'I get shouted at for not being loud enough. I have to practise my big voice. I don't like my big voice, I like my small one.'

'I like your small one too. Teachers are idiots sometimes. Like Mariana.'

Jude sniggered and whispered something and then laughed his full-bellied laugh that Shona realised had stopped in October too. She wished she could disappear from the room and let them be naughty boys without a witness, but any movement would stop them. Maybe him being there was a prompt for Jude, to release his annoyance and frustration at Shona for being so preoccupied and crap. He had Kallu. But not enough. Shona needed to be more like Kallu. Shona needed to be more like her mother and act when it was necessary. Shona needed to be a lot less like Shona.

When she opened her eyes, she found a cooling bowl of pasta with tomato sauce and grated cheese. She hadn't eaten lunch, and possibly not breakfast, and finished the bowl without heating it up. She heard the boys in the next room, their voices rising above the TV to comment on it. Shona put the kettle on and switched on the laptop.

She wasn't expecting an email from Jimmy but hoped there might be something. The prison had released him but she still hadn't heard anything about an address. She felt that she should chase him, check he was OK but she also didn't want to find him right now and have to deal with whatever hole he had managed to end up in. She couldn't imagine him in a bed and breakfast, a halfway house. She hadn't seen him much as a child, but what she remembered was smart and slick. He could have lost his shine in prison and be more comfortable in track suits after such a long time, but she wanted to see him in a shirt again.

She heard the TV go off and the noise of feet going upstairs. A little while later Kallu came down to the kitchen.

'All sorted,' he said. 'I left the light on.'

'That's fine. Thanks.'

Kallu picked his coat up from the back of the chair.

'Don't you want a cup of tea?' asked Shona.

'No, I'm just off to the shed. If that's OK.'

'Of course it is, but it's really cold. I know it's your thing, but you can stay inside.'

Kallu was looking past her to the dark window. 'I'm fine.'

'Sorry. I don't get it. Feel free to use the shed. Do you need anything else?'

'No.'

He kissed her on the forehead and closed the back door quietly behind him. She would keep the door unlocked, just in case.

12

Kallu emerged from the shed and stretched. Her shed god, Mariana had said. My little Apollo, she thought. His top rode up and Shona looked away from his slender belly. He knocked on the kitchen door and then walked in.

'Hungry?' she asked.

'Starving.'

Jude had wanted to see him before he went to school but she knew better than to try to disturb him. She certainly didn't want to see him in one of those trances again. She'd gone out to him in the garden last night after seeing him kneeling on the grass. It was so cold that she could see her breath streaming from her mouth, but she couldn't see any cloud from his. He was, as usual, in a T-shirt, his arms extended out at his sides. He had looked at her as if he hated no-one and nothing more. Scared, she backed away. Back inside, she didn't stop shivering for an hour. He wouldn't remember, he never did, but a weird episode always meant that he was more lucid than usual for a few days and she had a list of questions for him. But food came first.

'Eggs? Scrambled, fried?'

'Both.'

'Let's try one at a time.'

He selected an apple, not the first or second he picked up, but the third. He sank his teeth into it with his eyes closed. Shona broke four eggs into a bowl with milk and cheese and, once that was cooking, put two slices of bread in to toast. He'd finished one apple and had started another. Five rejected apples sat on the table. She put them back in the bowl. The toast popped. She buttered it and poured the eggs on top. He had started eating with his fingers before she fetched the cutlery.

She collected the post while he ate. Jimmy had finally made contact. He had somewhere to live and was asking for visitors, as if he was still in prison. If he knew she'd seen him with Kallu, he hadn't said anything. Or Jimmy was just going to deny it.

Lexden Road seemed a strange address for a halfway house. The letter was beautifully written, even the envelope had flourishes. She checked her phone for messages. Mariana had clearly decided that Shona should have forgiven her, and left a message asking her to call back. She sounded very polite, which made Shona nervous.

Kallu slowed down once he got to the soggy toast and tore pieces off with his fingers to eat without biting.

'Did you get any messages last night?' she asked.

He nodded, glanced up at her and then down again. Her stomach clenched and her hands started to feel clammy as she tried to interpret the look. His face was smooth but he looked older than nineteen. It was all in the eyes. Sometimes Shona found it difficult to keep eye contact, especially when whatever he saw seemed to amuse him.

With one piece of toast left he pushed the plate away.

That would be his offering. Shona didn't shift uncomfortably when he mentioned this any more, and simultaneously he stopped mentioning it. She waited and he raised his head.

'And?'

'It's Greenland,' he said.

She sighed and it was her turn to lower her eyes. She put one elbow on the table and rested her head on her hand.

'That's definitely where you're going?'

'That's where I'll find my mentor. There's a shaman waiting for me. And it's soon.'

Soon meant little when Kallu said it, but it was going to happen. Her urge as a mother was to immediately warn his parents of this plan. Her desire for it to be what was right for Kallu had to be stronger.

'A shaman.' She tried to believe it. 'Does that mean that you're a shaman?'

'Would you believe me if I said yes?'

Shona said, 'Maybe. I've read about Greenland. It's not an easy place to get to, even if you have money. Especially now, in the winter. I know the cold doesn't affect you much, but it's nearly December. There won't be any sun at all for months.'

'It will happen.' He waved his hand. 'I don't have to work out how.'

Shona slid her hand from her cheek in front of her mouth. 'When?'

'When it's time.'

'Did you ...' She moved her hand to the table. 'Did you get any message for me?'

As he looked at her his face became young again, his eyes clouded with the doubt of wanting to say the right thing.

'It's just, Maynard's trying to get me out of the house and I can't buy him out, or get a mortgage. I want Cerys to come back, and it's Jude's home, the only one he's known.' She took a breath. 'And Meghan died here. I want to stay with Meghan.'

He spoke gently. 'Meghan's not here.'

'So where is she?'

He held her stare but something inside him had moved back within himself.

She stood, trying not to shout. 'You promised me—'

'Nothing.'

'Not in so many words, maybe, but when we met you told me—'

'Nothing. I said she had a message for you. I didn't say I could give it to you.' His voice became quieter. 'There are many states of being.'

'Christ.' She sat down and rested her head on her arms. She had waited all those months for nothing.

His voice lowered. 'Shona, as the time gets closer I'm going to change. I need you to protect yourself. Don't come out to me in the garden, OK? Sometimes it's not me.'

'Because you're a shaman.' It had come out more sarcastic than she meant. 'Aren't you? You knew I'd been waiting.'

'And you feel I've taken advantage. I understand. But please stay away when I'm outside, OK? Just in case.'

She refused to agree. She refused to look at him.

Every time she had felt close he pushed her away. No answers, nothing. She stared at the mark on the wall and tried to remember which child had made it. It was a heavy plastic beaker, she remembered, and no-one had expected it to fragment and take part of the wall with it.

She'd been awake until two, wondering whether he would have anything to tell her, any hint about what she should do next, even though he really didn't talk about that. He lived in some mixture of the past and distant future. She lived in the present and near future. It was amazing that they could even see each other in their different worlds.

She heard him scrape the chair back and the sound of his bare feet on the tiles. He stroked her hair and murmured under his breath. She wanted to scream, 'Just tell me what the message is!' He left. She heard the gate close.

She rubbed her face and forced herself to blink away tears. Mariana would talk her out of believing it anyway.

She fetched the laptop from the back room and made some tea while it warmed up. It was like her, in need of some work and a new battery. She first looked up the address Jimmy had sent her so she could visit him, and then Greenland. There wasn't much that she couldn't find out about by looking at an atlas. She opened another page and ordered a couple of books about Greenland and shamanism on Amazon, but when she got to the payment page it didn't go through. Maynard had stopped the credit card. She didn't even remember it being a joint card. He'd been tracking everything she bought on it. He'd bought this laptop for himself and given it to her when he replaced it. Maybe he was tracking everything she did and thought. Maybe— she closed the laptop down and pushed the lid shut.

She had pretended all these years that she was independent but he'd been in charge of everything. She would work out how to wipe the laptop, get an overdraft, maybe a new credit card if they'd let her, start everything fresh and clean and new. That was her plan for the day. After seeing Jimmy.

She cycled to the address Jimmy had given her on Lexden Road and, when she got there, pulled out the letter to check she'd read it right. She had.

She got off the bike and pushed it up the wide, gravelled drive. It was four floors of large sash windows, the walls plastered white and the doorstep bordered with cast-iron boot scrapers. The front door was actually two scarlet doors, glazed with stained glass. She thought it must have been divided into flats but there was no panel of buttons, a scribbled name next to each. He'd clearly been looking out for her, or someone, as he opened the door before she knocked.

'What the hell have you been up to?' she said. 'Are you squatting?'

Jimmy smiled. 'When one knows how to hold one's tongue, one is rewarded.' He bowed and swept his arm towards the hall. 'Madam.'

She curtsied and then hesitated. 'Can I bring my bike in? It might get nicked.'

'Oh, ye of little faith.' He shook his head. 'Bloody right, I've seen two blokes casing the place just this morning. It's been empty for a while.'

'You don't have the run of the whole house, do you?'

'Of course, it's mine. Or near enough.'

'I'm not sure I like that answer. Really, are you squatting?'

'Ask me no questions, I'll tell you no lies. Get inside.' This time he jerked behind him with his thumb.

Shona lifted the bike over the black painted threshold and angled it so it leant against the coat on the bannister. The hallway was tiled like a chessboard, the architraves and coving were still intact and ornate. She looked into the two rooms they passed, walls covered in paintings and hangings, a marble woman standing five-foot high in one corner, her hands held out to the room.

'Cup of tea?'

'Please,' she said, nearly tripping down the two sudden steps into the kitchen.

A shiny Apple laptop was open on the breakfast counter next to an iPhone and an iPad.

'I heard they were the best, but I'm buggered if I can follow the instructions,' he said. 'You any good with them?'

'I'll have a go.' She looked at the glittering shine of chrome, the kettle and the coffee machine.

'Blimey,' he laughed. 'It's a good job there are no flies in here.'

Shona closed her mouth. Jimmy stopped smiling and took her by both hands.

'Seriously, any news on Cerys?'

Shona sighed and felt her lip begin to wobble. She'd almost forgotten. Jimmy sat her on a chrome bar stool and motioned for her to wait. He made two cups of tea, poured an entire packet of fig rolls onto a plate and motioned for her to begin.

'What happened just before she left?'

'Normal stuff,' Shona fudged.

'No such thing.'

Shona focused on the biscuits. 'She found out I was sleeping with one of her teachers and thought that I was sleeping with this boy she fancied rotten. He was called Dominic, now he's Kallu.' She watched his face for any sign that he was interested or hiding something, but he kept eye contact.

'Her teacher?' Jimmy tried to bite down a smile. 'Where

did she catch you? If it was in your bedroom, it doesn't count. You have to expect that kind of thing.'

Shona mumbled, 'She realised at Parents' Evening.'

Jimmy guffawed. 'Busted!'

Shona nodded.

'OK, you haven't seen the funny side of that yet, sorry.'

Shona picked up a fig roll and began to nibble on it.

'And what's Maynard's official take on this?'

'To take my house, sell it, hide his flat off the books so he can keep it and everything else he's collected. He's a company, apparently.'

'Have you got a mortgage?'

'The house is paid off, so I could get it as a settlement if he was honest. It's an asset to him, not a home.'

'So, if he's going to play dirty, have you got anything on him?'

'Yes. He was responsible for someone's death. Someone other than Meghan, I mean. But really, I've known for so long I don't know if anyone would believe me if I said it now. You were close to him for a while, can you think of anything?'

'Plenty.' Jimmy tapped his nose. 'I'll get onto that.' He turned the laptop towards him, pressed a few buttons and sighed. He went to a drawer near the sink and came back with a pen and pad. 'What's his address in London?'

'No idea.'

Jimmy raised his eyebrows and scribbled himself a note. 'Job?'

'He's been sacked.'

Jimmy smiled. 'What for?'

'I phoned up pretending to be his solicitor, arguing it was wrongful dismissal. The secretary laughed at me and said he'd admitted validating a forgery.'

Jimmy laughed. 'Excellent. When did he last contact you about Cerys being missing?'

'He hasn't. He must have explained it all to the police, or she did. I don't know. As far as anyone knows he's been out of the country since.'

'Interesting.'

Shona put the biscuit back on the plate. 'You think she's with Maynard too.'

'That's where my money would always have been, little shit. Has he left anything at your house?'

'The front room is full of his stuff. He locks the door.'

'Have you changed the locks on the external doors?'

'No. I want to, but I keep thinking Cerys might try to get back in.'

'She can phone you. We need to sort that out and get into the room.'

'I've got someone coming round. It was supposed to be last week but I forgot and went out. He was pretty pissed off but he agreed to come back.'

Shona felt an ache in her shoulders subside, although she hadn't been aware of it until now. She put her arms out to the side and rolled the twinges away.

'What do you know about Maynard?' she asked.

'That can wait,' he said. 'You need to think about something else. Drink your tea and finish that biscuit. Let me tell you about this Egyptian guy who I met inside. He was being chased by a bunch of Mossad agents in the eighties, I don't know what he did to piss them off. You don't survive that very often. He's in his sixties or seventies now, and on his sixth or seventh name. I asked him, "So, did you ever go to Israel?" and he said, "Only in a tank."'

Jimmy laughed. All Shona could think about was not asking what he'd done to end up in prison.

181

She said, 'We had a holiday in Egypt, a trip down the Nile, did I tell you?'

Jimmy nodded.

'There was a man whose job was to sit next to the tethering rope and stop rats running up it. He just sat there all day reading the Koran, waiting for rats. He looked so peaceful.' Shona drank some tea. 'I should get a job like that.'

'Good God, a job? Let's not be hasty.'

'Jimmy, do you know anything about Greenland?'

'It's not really my thing, that naïve folk art.'

'Not the art, the place.'

'The place is the art!' He laughed. 'Greenland. No, I don't think I know anything. Denmark, Sweden, all of those places, yes. I always quite fancied Svalbard. Or I would do if I ever felt like painting my own stuff. The light sounds extraordinary, but I suppose there's a reason that there are no great artists from there or Greenland. It's just too bloody cold to hold a brush. You're not going there, are you?'

'No, someone I know might be.'

'Why? There are fifty places I'd rather go before there. Does he want to go dog sledding or is he one of those climate change people?'

'I might have been talking about a woman. No, I think it's a spiritual thing.'

Jimmy spat out half a biscuit. 'Sorry. Jesus, spiritual thing. What a load of bollocks.'

'I always thought that art was your spiritual thing.'

'Don't be ridiculous. I don't believe in genius, just a marriage of man and paint, a glorious serendipity.'

'Man and paint? Not person and paint?'

'Oh, don't start. We're never going to agree on that. Did you sort the phone out?'

'Yes. I put my numbers in too and texted myself so I have your number.'

'I might not answer straight away. I keep pressing cancel instead of answer. Why did they put those buttons right next to each other? Let me know when you've booked a locksmith, OK? I want to be there when the tomb is opened.'

Shona nodded.

'Just for now, to keep the estate agents at bay, is there anything you could do to lower the price of the house? Temporarily – don't go knocking down any walls.'

'I'll think about it.'

She thought about hugging him, but didn't want to crease his shirt. She thought back to his other flats, nice but not opulent. Art materials on every surface and canvases in every corner. Not like here. It wasn't like him at all. He ate a fig roll, biting around the edges and then eating the middle in one go. The showman had faded back and she could see the man she'd known for years in the way he ate it. She must have been mistaken about seeing him in the museum. He was the same as ever.

'It's, um, a bit different seeing you here.'

'I know. It's going to take a while to get back to normal.' He rubbed his head. 'But I can stay here for as long as I like, so I'll just bed down for a while and see what happens next.' He rubbed his face, one hand on each cheek. 'I'm old, Shona. I got old, and I never expected to.'

He held her gaze for a moment and she thought that he was going to cry but he held it, blinked repeatedly and ate another biscuit.

'Come on, there's one room in this house that contains work by women. Let's see if you can spot it.'

Shona was early to collect Jude, one of the pack rather

than one of the last. She looked around, realising that she had made no effort to get to know any of the parents of Jude's classmates. With Cerys she had known all the children's names, and most of the mothers'. Only Thea recognised her.

'Are you still OK to take Callum for tea?' said Thea.

'Yes, it's fine.' Shona couldn't remember when they had arranged this. 'Tonight's fine.'

'No, tomorrow,' said Thea. 'Why would I be here if you were collecting him?' She tilted her head. 'It is OK, isn't it? You can say if you're not up to it.'

'Tomorrow is perfect. I'm not with it today, sorry. My uncle's just out of prison and I was visiting him.'

'Is he OK?'

'More than OK. He's going to be totally fine.'

She felt better than she had for ages as well, just a bit distracted. Jimmy had given her a lifeline so she could let Cerys go for a while, do the shopping and make the most of Jude. She was back in the real world and it felt odd.

Jude came out with his teacher and ran to her, beaming. She swept him up in her arms. Tomorrow she would make sure he was wearing a tie, and maybe had matching socks.

'Want to help me set up our new laptop? You and Callum can download some games tomorrow.'

'What happened to the old one?'

'It broke.' Into two satisfying lumps.

GRETA

I met Maynard a few times before Shona married him. He wasn't who I expected for her, or who I wanted for her. She'd had a couple of relationships before and they weren't any better, so at the time I was relieved that he wasn't a twenty-seven-year-old postman covered in tattoos that named all of his ex-girlfriends. Shona made a big deal of putting her arm around him if I walked into the room. She even argued with him over the absence of her own name on his arm. She didn't love him but she wanted to leave her mark – 'Shona was here'. That one petered out into longer, quieter waits by the phone which stopped ringing altogether after three months.

The second one never sat on my sofa with a beer can. If he phoned and I answered, the line went dead. Shona would sit by it until, half an hour or two hours later, the trilling started up again. She would draw out the telephone wire and sit on the floor in the hall to whisper. The wire stopped the door quite closing. I suspected he was married. I didn't suspect he was her old Geography teacher until I saw them arguing by the corner, his car door open. His school books flapped on the road whenever a car passed. She'd taken a gap year to work and save money and she spent most of it running whenever he called.

After the argument, there was no waiting by the phone. She watched the Iraq War on the BBC from 6am to 10am, then she'd switch between Channel 4 and ITV for their breakfast war reports. Back to BBC1 and the ITV news started at 5.30, an hour of *Newsnight*. There were evening bulletins and all night she watched live coverage of bombs falling on Baghdad on ITV. Somehow she pulled herself out of it and then she was off. She showed no sign of ever coming back.

Maynard at least was her age, and for a time I was grateful for that. I learned a little about him from his mother at the wedding itself when it was all too late. There were stories of a selfish little boy preparing to run away by piling up cheese in the trailer of his tricycle, but all children are self-centred and egotistical in their way. There were stories of his profligacy at university, spending all of his money for the term and having to eat porridge for the last four weeks. He told the story of his diagnosis of scurvy with pride.

He was an ordinary, arrogant boy, good looking in a carefully cocky way. He was quite unsuited to Shona, but at the time she was striving to be ordinary. He had quite a different reason to be with her.

The story came out slowly, much later. In June, he had woken Shona just before midnight at the house she shared with three other students in Brighton. They had gone out a couple of times, but then he'd gone out a couple of times with most girls at the university, so she was surprised. She was also pleased. He was attractive in that long-haired, posh boy kind of way, and Shona was determined to be like everyone else. And all her housemates chased him like mad, so she was flattered that he'd come to her. He'd taken his final exam that day and didn't think twice that Shona still had two left. He called and she responded.

He'd been drinking, but then they had all been drinking apart from Shona. He fell at her feet, declared undying love and jumped into her bed. Or something like that. He didn't leave her side but made her meals and cups of tea as she revised for her exams. He seemed to have dedicated himself to her alone. She was his choice.

It wasn't until the police arrived four days later, seeking to verify his alibi, that any doubts surfaced. As he sat beside her, Shona, the most torturously honest of people, swore he'd arrived at ten o'clock. He couldn't have hit the cyclist hidden in the sea fog that rolled in suddenly on the promenade. He wasn't there to see the intermittent flash of reflection from the pedals and wonder what it was. He hadn't veered away from the heap in the gutter, and gone to her house because it was closer than his. He hadn't stayed to make her fall in love with him.

She didn't come home for the summer holidays.

She wasn't answering the phone or replying to my letters. I opened the letters confirming her graduation but the date came and went. I took the train down to see her in August, walking from the station without any idea whether she was still at the same address. I knocked on the door for ten minutes before she let me in and went back to the sofa. She was tiny, shoulders jutting beneath her T-shirt, her hair lank. I waited for her to react to me being there. I waited days.

I found her key and went shopping. Bit by bit, I took her washing to the laundrette, apart from the T-shirt and pants she never took off. I went into Brighton some days to avoid the ringing phone on the hall table. I answered a couple of times but she didn't want to talk to Maynard. There were also letters that I didn't open. Sometimes, after the pubs closed, someone would knock on the door for as long as I had, or until the neighbours shouted obscenities from the windows. The housemates had emptied their two bedrooms and I lay in Shona's bed, wondering whether she should be sectioned.

Some days I walked through the Lanes through the tightly packed groups of tourists, grilled red on the beach and unaware of their width. Overheated children cried for ice creams and teenagers milled around the arcades. There was a fortune-telling machine that I fed large old one penny pieces before laying my hand on the soft spikes, hoping against hope that the next fortune would be different.

I brought favourite food into her house, placed it in front of her. Accidentally, she started to eat. Then she started to skim through some of the bulletins. No-one else contacted her. The lease ran out at the beginning of September and I didn't know how I was going to extract her from this dark room and get her back to my own house. On the 1st of September Maynard arrived at the door. He had been bought a flat in London for work, a reward from his mother for his 2:2.

They spoke and I left them alone, never thinking I would see him again. I think she must have told him she was pregnant before this, or he would never have been seen again. Two months later they had arranged the wedding so that the baby would be a legitimate heir. The October wedding revealed my Shona, pale cheeked in her creamy dress, stomach pressing outwards, and his family's disapproving looks.

The miscarriage confirmed to them that he'd married a gold-digging harlot. I gathered that much although I never saw them after the wedding. After Shona's trouble in the papers, Cerys was born, and they moved to Essex, and I was relieved that she would be close to me again. It turns out that this was wishful thinking. She hadn't moved back to be close to me. It was almost as if she'd forgotten I lived in Essex too.

When I did see Shona, everything seemed to be fine. She was fond enough of Maynard, helped, I think, by the amount of time he spent working away. She was committed to dedicating herself to Cerys, and that meant making the most of Maynard. But if his mother suspected the social gap between them was too large when they met, she was convinced when Maynard's career blossomed and his suits became more expensive. She tried to make Cerys her own, staying for weeks at a time to help Shona out and pass on her hard-won advice, but then Maynard's sister gave her a grandson. The visits were halted. The pressure was off Shona, but Maynard missed being centre of attention and pushed for a second child, a son. Drunk with disappointment, the day after they found out the sex of the baby at the twenty-week scan, he told Shona what it was like to kill a cyclist.

When she phoned, six weeks after Meghan was born, I had to wait for the morning bus. I hadn't been invited before. They usually came to me so that they could keep the visits brief. Maynard wasn't there. He was too important to take any time off, just as when Cerys was born, and he had a nice, quiet flat in London where he could get a good night's sleep.

The curse of our family, as I saw it then, was that the

daughters always hated the mothers. I had hated mine, after all, and Shona blamed me for not protecting her and Sean. This was the first time she had needed me. I could see it in the way she held her head. I held the baby and watched Cerys while Shona talked, told me all of it from the earliest days in Brighton to the way he avoided her now. I couldn't have been happier that she'd had a second girl. It showed that the curse had really been lifted. All I'd had to do was ignore it and it evaporated with advent of computing and reason and everyone having a phone. My mother would never have believed any of it, calling it the devil's work. I knew that modernity had emasculated him. No-one believed in the devil. No-one cared. We all held the power of our own lives, and that's what I tried to convey to Shona. Of course I'd told her at the same age that my mother told me the story of the running, but she was already too old for it, too knowing to believe it. And my heart wasn't in it to try again.

Now, in Shona's home with her curled-up baby sleeping, we talked like never before and I began to believe we could be a mother and daughter. She was tired and vulnerable in a way she'd never shown me. I loved her more than ever, now that I could show her. I could help and I could listen. When Maynard came back unexpectedly, she seemed more solid. I'd told her to make sure she got some time and space. She wasn't the only parent and deserved a long bath and a good sleep. If she was tired, she promised, she would ask him to watch the baby.

When I left, a man walked past me on the other side of the road. It had started to snow lightly and it didn't seem strange for him to have his hood up. There was something about his walk that made me recognise him, but I couldn't pinpoint exactly why he seemed familiar. I stopped and turned to watch him cross over and walk down the alley next to Shona's house.

I shook off the discomfort. It would be someone Maynard knew, someone they were expecting. Or maybe it was someone calling at their neighbour's house. There was nothing of comment or concern. It was just a man, walking down the road. My biggest worry was getting a bus before the snow got heavier.

That's what happens when you're fooled into believing in a world that is infinitely explicable. We don't react in a real way any more. If there is a loud bang, we cautiously turn our heads, scared of making a fool of ourselves, instead of running away. When we shiver inside at the way someone looks at us, we castigate ourselves for being superstitious. I denied my instincts and allowed the devil to walk past me and into Shona's house.

13

There was a brief knock at the back door before Jimmy let himself in.

'It takes me ages to open a text message,' said Jimmy. 'Next time, can you phone me?'

'You've had the phone for over a week,' said Shona. 'It's not that hard.'

'I told you, I'm old.' He saw Jude. 'You're not Shona's little one, are you?'

Jude nodded and Jimmy bowed.

'The pleasure is all mine,' said Jimmy.

Jude shrugged as if there had never been any doubt.

Shona told Jude, 'This is your great-uncle, Jimmy.'

'Right,' Jimmy said. 'Let's go and rummage.'

Jude stayed to watch CBBC with a bowl of ice cream while Jimmy followed Shona. The locked door looked odd now it was open, as if it was part of the house again. She sat on the sofa and watched him work through the boxes and the drawers. Eventually Jimmy knelt among four piles of papers. He was shaking his head.

'He's a fucking moron, that bloke.'

Shona closed the door. 'Jude is here, remember.'

Jimmy put his hand on two neat printed piles. 'These are related to his flat in London. You can get the address from here. And these are related to his work. He was sacked, yes?'

'Yes.'

'There's nothing on that here.' He moved one hand. 'These are emails from Cerys that he's printed out, mostly complaining about you.'

Shona put her hand out and he kept his hand firmly on top until she pulled her hand back. He moved to the fourth pile, scrappier and more creased than the others with half pages and hand-written scribbles.

'These relate to me. Every payment, every meeting, every idea that never quite came off. He was going to screw me over, given half a chance.'

'Over what?'

Jimmy pointed at the paintings on the walls. 'He has paperwork relating to the sales of each of these paintings to his gallery.'

'So why are they here?'

'Because the ones he sold are the copies I painted.'

They sat silently and looked at the paintings. Jimmy grimaced.

'How did that work?' Shona asked. 'Why didn't anyone notice?'

Jimmy sighed. 'I'm not sure I want to say, Shona. I'm so used to not saying anything at all, no matter what.'

'I don't want to have start visiting you in prison again. I need to know what Maynard's been up to, not what you've been up to. I know it's all connected but I'm not going to repeat anything to do with you.'

Jimmy shook his head. 'Help me up, would you?'

He sat on the sofa and she sat on the footstool.

'You can't separate what he did and I did. The brilliant idea, one of his many brilliant ideas, was to sell paintings with a renovation package. He'd have them verified and certificated and then, when they were sold, he'd arrange for them to be cleaned.'

He cleared his voice but didn't speak again.

'By you? Did you clean them?'

'He used a different name, something a bit fancier.' His eyes brightened. 'It can take months to clean a painting. It was plenty of time to do a damn good copy. And the genius bit is that they expect it to look different, to look newer and fresher. Not so fresh you can smell the paint, but, you know.' He became animated. 'And the best thing was he chose really well, only investment pieces or to a little gallery that just wants to hang it and leave it there for decades.'

'Wouldn't it be more ethical to fuck over the banks and businesses?'

'Shona, you've always had a very weird sense of who deserves to be fucked. Why them? Galleries are businesses too. And I don't see why, if the people looking get the same pleasure from the painting, that it matters. Artists are basically quite shitty people. I've met enough. They come up with all kinds of ridiculous philosophies about what they do, but in the end they are a brand. And a brand is going to be copied because it's overpriced. If there was truly something magical in their hands that powered their brush, then people would spot it. They don't. They like a nice picture of a pretty woman and that's it. That's art.'

'No, it's fraud. If I bought a pair of designer jeans and it turned out they were from Tesco, I'd be pissed off.'

'But it would be your fault for choosing for the brand and not for the quality. If you can't see the difference, stick to Tesco. It goes for everything: wine, furniture. If you're a snob, then you don't deserve the real thing. I would never have done it for a private buyer making a single, loving purchase.'

'Did you meet every buyer?'

'All the ones Maynard had marked, yes. I had to wear my false beard and beret. You could tell if it impressed them.' He stroked his missing beard and smiled.

'So what happened?'

'Nothing officially. A little gallery had second thoughts. Some great master didn't go with their colour scheme and gave the director a migraine whenever he walked past it. Or something like that. They decided to sell, and their buyer claimed it was a fake.'

'It was a fake.'

Jimmy frowned. 'That's not the word I'd use, but kind of.'

'And?'

'Maynard refused to budge. The gallery managed to offload it somewhere else but, when they complained to the company, a few other concerns started to be remembered. Just niggles and things. Now I think he was busy with other people too, not just me. I think he was far too busy generally.' He closed his eyes. 'If I'd have known …'

'Known what?'

'That's enough to be getting on with, isn't it?'

'How does this fit in with your prison sentence?'

'It doesn't. That was a stupid, impulsive and greedy move of my own making.'

Shona shook her head. 'It's ridiculous. Maynard just isn't clever enough to come up with this.'

'You never knew any of it?'

'Of course not. He worked for an exclusive art dealership and was always getting bonuses. Why would I think he was risking it all?'

'They didn't give bonuses.'

'Oh, of course not.' Shona stood and kicked the footstool. 'Why would that have been true?'

'That's an antique!'

Shona looked at Jimmy and then kicked it across the room. It shuddered against the writing desk. Jimmy pressed his lips together and rubbed his hands on his knees. Shona dropped into the armchair and closed her eyes.

Shona finally thought of words to place together. 'Why didn't you tell me?'

'You were happy.'

'I was never happy. I felt compelled.'

'You seemed happy. I thought I was helping you to be rich and successful. And I enjoyed it too much to stop.'

'Is this why Mum doesn't talk about you?'

'Could be. She suspected when he made his first big find that I had something to do with it. That wasn't one of mine. I used to have different contacts.'

They were silent again.

Shona said, 'What do we do now?'

'We could offer Maynard up to the gods of art verification and watch him burn.'

'But you'd burn too.'

'Probably,' Jimmy nodded. 'I don't want to do that, I just thought I'd say it before you did. Or we could take the paintings and sell them. He can't ask for them as he can't prove he had them in the first place.'

'Which would probably result in the same thing, when people realised there were two copies of these original paintings.'

'That depends who you sell them to. Third, I take the paintings, copy them again, give him the copies and sell these ones. It depends what kind of revenge you want, nice and quick or slow and satisfying. He might never notice, he has no eye at all. He thinks he's won but you know you have. Or would you rather he knew?'

'Fourth, we could take the whole lot to the tip,' said Shona. 'No-one benefits and no-one wins.'

Jimmy went pale and clasped his chest. 'Christ, Shona! You don't mean that, tell me you don't.'

Shona had hated the collection for so many years. Maynard only cherished it for its value. She had forgotten that some people loved art for its own existence.

'With option number three,' she said. 'I don't suppose you could include some putrid ingredient in the paint that will get progressively rank?'

Jimmy pulled a paisley handkerchief from his breast pocket. 'Shona, I'm beginning to wonder what kind of philistine you are. I need to get these irreplaceable pieces out of your grasp. Did your young man give you a new key for the lock?'

'Yes, I can lock it all back up.'

Jimmy walked to the display cabinet. 'In that case, sell this. He may notice it's gone but it will sort out your finances for a bit. And you're still married so what's his is yours and all that.' He tossed a cluster of sparkles towards her. 'Worth five grand, don't take less than four and a half. The diamonds are good quality but the design is generic enough not to alert him if he's looking at any auction websites.'

'How did you know I'm short of money?'

'I know all sorts. Forging essays, I don't know. Must be in the genes.'

Shona blushed. 'Why has he left so much stuff here? I thought he must have taken anything of any value with him.'

'The room was locked, as far as he was concerned. It makes you think that there is someone he lives with now that he doesn't quite trust. Sticky fingers, a clumsy person, someone who values things too much or too little.'

They looked at each other.

'Cerys,' said Shona.

Jimmy stood up. 'I'll come back and give you prices on everything here. Can I take a couple of the paintings?'

'To sell?'

'Maybe. I'll ask around, see what's possible. I'll ask about Cerys too.' He looked at the paintings again. 'There's one missing. He might have taken it with him, but I doubt it. He never said what he'd done with it, but I'd have heard if it was sold. It's the one I'd want to keep.'

'What's it of?'

'Of? The whole of love and life and living, that's what "it's of".' He sneered at her and then straightened his mouth. 'Sorry.' He held his hands a hand width apart. 'If you find something about this big, will you phone me? Straight away. It folds out into three parts,' he moved his hands further apart. 'I found it in Bruges. I'd pay you for it.'

Bruges. 'Did you bring it back from Bruges?'

'No, Maynard did.'

Shona frowned. 'You met him there? When we were on honeymoon?'

Jimmy turned his eyes away. 'I might have done,' he mumbled.

'So this was when I was pregnant and just before I had a miscarriage and you involve me with stolen goods.'

He scuffed at the floor with his foot. 'I didn't say it was stolen.'

'You made me into an international art thief.' Shona hid her smirk. 'Take the paintings, but tell me which are yours so I don't stick them on eBay.'

Jimmy swept his hands around the room. 'These are all original but that doesn't mean you can stick them on eBay.' He looked at her from the corner of his eye and laughed. 'Well, they're not all originally original. You can't tell, can you?' He pointed to the one on the chimney breast. 'That one,' the central one on the wall over the sofa, 'that one,' the massive landscape on the other wall, 'and this are mine. I'll leave them with you and take the other four.' He turned. 'If that's OK.'

She didn't know if it was OK. He was a confirmed thief and liar and she knew that art meant much more to him than money, or family. On the other hand, she didn't want stolen goods in the house and she had the paperwork to stuff Maynard. And if anyone was going to be able to sell the paintings it was Jimmy.

'OK. What about the bits and bobs in the cabinet?'

'All real, as far as I know. Not my area, but I know he thought they were all authentic.'

He removed the paintings from the walls and Shona fetched him towels to wrap them in.

'Can I take the papers too?' he asked.

'No, I need to see if there's anything I can use. Nothing to do with you, just his bank accounts, things like that.'

'Don't read Cerys' emails, yeah? Promise?'

Shona nodded.

'And remember to let me know if you think of where the other one might be. Soon as you can, Shona. This

199

might be my only chance to see it again. I haven't seen it since Bruges.'

'I will.'

'OK, lock up. Just be careful. I don't want anything in here getting into the wrong hands.'

In bed that night, she could think of nothing but the honeymoon she thought she was having in Bruges and the one her husband was actually having. The city was beautiful, full of towers and churches with saints' relics and holy blood. Both new and old buildings had the corners shaved off to provide a background for Madonna and child statues. Some were classically white, and others painted in primary colours. Once she started noticing them, Shona made a point of looking for them, holding her stomach in empathy. This was a city that celebrated motherhood and she could relate to that.

They laughed at the strange assortment of museums, on lights, chips and chocolate, and Maynard listed the places he couldn't leave without seeing. First Shona persuaded him to take a boat trip along the waterways, negotiating their way past quiet backrooms and secret river gardens, along with half a dozen other boats, all with loudspeakers. She wanted to swap the tourist boat for a small dinghy she could lie in and follow the swans, but the tour guides wanted to repeat their script, as well as reminding everyone that there were more than three famous Belgians.

On the carriage trip they got off at the Minnewaterpark so the horse could be watered at the fountain. They wandered away and watched people throwing metal loops on strings into the river.

'Are they catching crabs?' Shona asked the carriage driver, waiting back in his seat.

The carriage driver said, 'No, they're magnets. It's to collect the coins people throw in for good luck.'

Shona wondered whether their wishes would still stand if the money was taken. It was on the way back to the Markt that she first felt something was wrong. Just a little cramping. Maynard took her to the hotel and left her there while he toured the museums. That was why he'd chosen Bruges: for the art, the Michelangelo, the Picassos, the collection in St Saviour's that he spent an entire afternoon looking at, he said. That was the evening he'd gone out again.

'I want to see Bruges at night,' he said. 'You'll be OK, won't you?'

Shona, bent double on the bed, felt that was best. She'd just overdone it. If she could just rest, then she'd be fine. Tomorrow they could go to the convents, walk over the tiny stone bridges they'd seen from the boat, sit and eat ice cream in the shade of the bright walls. The pain worsened once he wasn't there as witness, but she didn't cry out, because what place could be safer and better for pregnant women than Bruges with its tiny streets and wide parks and mothers and babies worshipped. But Bruges was also the city that worships blood in a special basilica, with its black doors and windows too high to see through, where even the golden paintings looked dark. She had climbed the white steps to take the glass cylinder from the nun. She had acknowledged the blood at the heart of the place and now she had to acknowledge her own.

When Maynard returned, drunk and elated, a carefully wrapped parcel under one arm, she had nothing more to say.

Now that parcel she had barely seen seemed to stand out as the most important thing to take from that memory of tears and pain. She had watched Maynard place it on the dresser before he phoned down to the lobby, she had watched him hide it in the safe before the doctor arrived. She had been pleased that everyone spoke English so she wouldn't have to mime or construct an explanation, but all the time she knew Maynard had positioned himself between everyone else and that safe. She was taken away to a hospital bed, fresh and modern, which surprised her in this medieval city, and never saw the package again.

Two weeks after they got back there was a delivery of an antique crib carved from dark wood. She had thought, had hoped, that Maynard had stayed off work because he did really care that their child had melted away, but when the crib arrived safely he couldn't stay off work any longer.

Shona had wanted to sell it, send it back, burn it, but Maynard insisted on keeping it. It was the expensive crib he wanted his child to sleep in, with four finials and an overhanging wooden canopy. She hadn't wanted any baby of hers to sleep in the crib that was intended for another child. She even began to believe that he'd brought on the miscarriage by buying it too early. He refused to sell it. It was an investment, an heirloom.

Cerys used it and Meghan died in it.

Then Shona had made it disappear.

Shona got out of bed and put her dressing gown on. Jude stirred, flinging both arms above his head. She pulled the door behind her and went downstairs. The package Maynard brought to the hotel in Bruges, wrapped and insulated, must have been the same size as the one Jimmy had measured out in air. There was no reason to believe that he wouldn't have taken it to London.

She yawned and took her coffee to the back window. No sign of anything except her own reflection. Her hair created a halo, the shadows underneath made her eyes look tight and small. She couldn't see Rob's window from the kitchen but she imagined that, at two o'clock, the light was still on. She couldn't see any signs of movement in the shed either and realised that this is why she'd got up, in the hope Kallu was there. She had thought that knowing he couldn't give her a message would change how she felt about him, but she missed him when he wasn't around. She would miss him desperately when he left.

She shook her head. She had to sleep.

14

DECEMBER

Shona phoned Jimmy twice before he phoned her back. She put him on speaker to finish making Jude's lunch.

'I can't get on with this bloody phone, Shona.'

'Why don't you get a landline fitted instead? Or put me on speaker.'

'Don't be so patronising. Anyway, Cerys.'

'Yes?'

'She's definitely with Maynard, staying at his flat.'

'Is she OK? Is she going to school?'

'Yes, she's fine. She's signed up to a private school and all that. I'll text you the details.'

Shona looked at Jude who had caught Cerys' name and was making no pretence about listening in.

'Are you OK?' asked Jimmy.

'Yes. Text me now.'

'OK, but I'll speak to you later. And, Shona?'

'Yep.'

'Do you think you could phone me a bit later next time?'

She heard him yawn and then fumble with the handset before the line went dead. Why hadn't she asked how Jimmy knew who to ask? Was he watching Maynard? Was he watching her?

She placed both hands on the worktop and closed her eyes. When she opened them, Jude was standing next to her.

'Is Cerys coming home?'

'Not yet.' Shona stroked his hair.

'Can we see her?'

'She's really busy.'

Shona looked at the clock. She had ten minutes to do a fifteen-minute quick walk to school. She could get into London and back before she had to collect Jude, but she'd be clock watching all day, worried about the trains. Ever since they'd been at Mariana's she'd been determined to always be at the school gate, always be on time. She could wait until Saturday, but the Christmas shoppers put her off that idea. She tapped her fingers and picked up her phone again.

'We're going to have a day off, Jude. Do you want to go to London?'

'Is Cerys there?'

'I think she is.'

He nodded. 'Will my teacher be cross?'

'I'm going to tell a little fib. Is that OK?'

'I'll get changed.'

On the train Shona realised how little time she had spent with Jude actually being with Jude. He had changed so much since starting school and his trousers grazed his ankles rather than the soft top of his feet. She'd allowed him to get dressed himself and he chose a thick cardigan with a hood which was perfect for the windy, bright day. He was growing up despite her, she realised. She drew close to him at the window and listened to him note the things in people's gardens that he liked. She looked at him and saw Cerys in his wide-eyed persuasiveness, his smirk when he said poo. His throaty laugh nearly made her cry when he talked about school, about being chosen first for the football matches at lunchtime. She wondered how he explained away his lack of a father and the horrible man who had lived in his house and the strange one who lived in the garden. He was happy. Cerys had never been happy in this unconsidered way, not without a gift in her hand.

Mariana thought of him as a poor fatherless child. Her mother thought of him as Shona's two fingers up to Maynard. Shona had thought of him as both of these things at one point or another, but knew he was much more than this. He had saved her life. Without him she would have watched Cerys be seduced by all the goods her father would provide and then what would her life have meant? Getting pregnant with Jude had not been the weapon she intended, or the child she'd mourned for, but a liberator.

She kissed his cheek.

'Mum!' He looked disgusted as he removed it with his jumper sleeve.

At Liverpool Street she held his hand tightly as they walked down the platform but he insisted on putting his own ticket through the barrier before seriously returning it to her purse. On the train she'd googled the school Jimmy had texted and found the address, near Maynard's flat in Holland Park. Why had she thought of Edgware? Maybe he'd sold one flat and bought another. She powered her phone off, then slid it into her pocket and turned to Jude. He was looking at the tourist leaflets.

'Dinosaurs?' she said.

'Are there any guns? Or swords?'

Shona thought about lying. That wasn't how she wanted to spend their day together, but maybe a trip to the Tower of London could be fun. Too expensive for fun. She could use it for her essay, she thought, before remembering that that was long overdue. Rob hadn't been in touch. Maybe he'd had to go back to actually teaching people how to write their own essays, or he really meant it and she wouldn't be asked again.

'Or sharks?' Jude pointed to a poster. 'Can we go in the big wheelie thing too?'

She had promised to take Cerys on the London Eye about two years ago, long enough for Cerys to have stopped asking. She'd probably have been taken by Maynard now. He was good at instant gratification as long as he could be seen to spend money on it.

They travelled on the bus towards Westminster, surrounded by sullen Londoners and talkative tourists. Jude gasped when he saw the wheel, then when he saw Big Ben, then when he saw the wheel again from Westminster Bridge.

'I don't think I want to go up there now,' he said. 'It's very, very high.'

'You can see all of London. It won't feel so high when you're up there.'

Jude looked confused and then frowned. 'What?'

Shona smiled. She didn't know what she meant by that either, it just sounded like something she should say. 'Never mind, let's just walk past it and you can see how you feel.'

Jude grabbed her hand. 'Maybe we'll see Cerys from up there.'

'Maybe.'

From the riverbank, having decided against riding up to the clouds, they walked towards Tate Modern. When they reached the Millennium Bridge, Shona realised where she was heading. She couldn't think of how to sell it to Jude so she kept quiet and led him towards St Paul's Cathedral, towards the Occupy tents. They looked just as they had in the paper, chaotic and hopeful and fifty-two days old.

They sat on the cathedral steps, Jude on her lap to keep his legs warm. She wanted so much to be part of it. This is exactly how she'd imagined her life when she'd been young and, let's face it, irritating as hell. She imagined the fading stars and waking birds at dawn in the skies above the cathedral. She would breakfast on stale, bitty bread and invite the pigeons to join her, and hope they didn't shit on her tent. Later, when it was brighter and the buses came, she would lie on her side and, getting the buildings and adverts and traffic just right, they'd look like Battenberg squares with the sugar she loved to kiss off.

Here the house and everything associated with it felt like somewhere to run from, rather than hold on to. This was somewhere she wanted to belong; give up the house and memories, and place herself in proper proportion to everyone else in the world.

She couldn't ask Jude to sleep in his clothes in a small tent and use portable toilets and go without hot water because she felt it would be fun. She didn't know if she could do it herself. She had grown lazy and selfish. She had to sort herself out first. Maybe she'd start small, by learning to knit. Maybe she should go back and volunteer with Mariana. Maybe.

'Can we go now?' asked Jude.

'Yes, let's go somewhere warm.'

She led Jude to a café across the street and drank coffee as, tight by her side, he ate a muffin and drank some orange juice. Neither of them spoke. Whatever she'd felt among the tents had started something she couldn't quite grasp.

Jude looked tired and she worried that he was too cold, that she should keep dipping him into the warm Underground. Still, it really wasn't as cold as she always felt December should be. Shona thought about how she could manage a diversion to Maynard's flat or Cerys' school without alerting Jude and was shocked by the realisation that she didn't want to. If she saw Cerys, there was nothing she wanted to say. She wouldn't beg her to come home and she wouldn't create strings of promises to do anything differently. It would be the same, except for her father's visits. It wasn't even for Jude's sake that she avoided forcing some kind of resolution. She wasn't going to phone any more, she wasn't going to ask the school for information. She could wait for Cerys to make her choices. And while she waited she would make the most of Jude.

She realised he was looking at her.

'Are we going to see Cerys?' he asked.

'No, it's just us, Jude. Cerys will come back when she's ready. I'm so glad you're here.'

She resisted kissing him again, but he snuggled into her and that was enough.

On the train back Shona checked her phone. There was a long and threatening email from Maynard demanding to know why the house sale wasn't underway. At least he wasn't asking about the locks, so he hadn't been to the house. There was an invitation from Mariana to take her to church. It actually said 'Christmas markets in Cologne', but she had shown Shona photos from a trip there before and all Shona could remember were pictures of churches. She replied to Mariana 'Maybe next year' and then cursed herself. How could she have forgotten she was still angry with her? Maybe she just felt she should be angry. Mariana had the right to her opinion about Kallu, if only she didn't keep saying it.

Shona had only fifty-two pounds left in her purse and not much more in the bank. It might be enough for a couple of weeks' shopping if they ate a lot of pasta. The bills would want paying soon. Jude's school wanted a voluntary donation, that wasn't exactly voluntary, for a trip, and there were school photos to buy and Christmas cards to order that had Jude's name on, but were basically stencilled.

She didn't regret the money she'd spent in London but felt guilty for not regretting it. She knew she'd become greedy, taking money from Maynard and not ever admitting she lived off him. She was still living off him. She had submitted the sparkly brooch to the local auction house and hadn't thought what would happen if it didn't sell. She would have to sell something else from Maynard's room, no, her front room, but Jimmy still had the four best paintings and she didn't know what anything else was worth. Maybe Jimmy would end up buying the paintings, but with whose money she had no idea. She had to find a way of making money that didn't depend on Maynard, and that meant postponing any voluntary work with Mariana. She groaned. She knew what it was like trying to find a job where schools hours and holidays were taken into account. Maybe Thea needed a supporting party fairy. Maybe nothing could compensate Shona for that.

Jude was looking at her, worried.

'It's fine, I was just thinking.'

She didn't respond to Maynard. She wouldn't leave the house until it was hers to leave. She would forward his email to Mariana when they had a chance to talk about it. To Jude she said nothing either, but rested his head on her shoulder and her chin on his head as he slept.

At home he hadn't woken fully, as she'd expected, but just changed and fallen into bed. Shona looked out from the office window. Rob's light was on and his curtains closed. She could try to phone him, but suspected he'd ignore the call. And that's if he wasn't occupied with someone else anyway. She considered leaving Jude, just for a few minutes, just to run round and gauge where he was emotionally towards her, but knew that she wouldn't be able to. She'd reach the end of the street, if that, and panic. There was no-one to ask. That's what she hated most about being alone, the sense that it was seven in the evening and she was trapped there until she took Jude to school. If she had no milk, no bread, that was tough. She couldn't ask Thea, she couldn't ask Jimmy and she couldn't ever have asked Amy.

There was a long, plaintive howling. She automatically looked towards Amy's garden, lit up by the lights in her kitchen downstairs, but there was no Amy in the garden. She had been quiet lately. Shona caught a movement in her own garden. Her throat tightened and she drew back. She switched off the light in the room, closed the door to the bedroom, and looked from the window again.

There was someone, but now she wasn't sure if they were moving or if some moving thing was catching the light from next door. She could see the outline of trousers and bright feet at the bottom, almost luminous against the black grass. Kallu.

She let herself out, crept through the bedroom and ran down the stairs. She turned on the lights in the back room and the kitchen before unlocking the back door and then she stopped. She could hear him talking, muttering, both loudly and quietly and then he growled. Her shoulders tensed and she shivered. She never got used to it. She retreated to the back door and sat gingerly on the step in case he needed her. He growled and howled again, even louder. She cringed. If the neighbours had missed the first one, they would definitely have caught that. She saw one of them, Lee, looking out from his window upstairs. Shona heard him through the glass.

'It is him again. Shall I phone the police?' He turned to talk to someone behind him.

The curtain fell back in place. She imagined curtains down the street, and Rob's street too, poised to twitch at the next noise, fingers ready to point at the culprit. She had to get him inside before someone called the police. She wasn't sure that she should keep getting in the way of how things should be done. Maybe Kallu did need therapy and drugs and a diagnosis, and all Shona was doing was postponing his recovery. She held her head in her hands. She couldn't bear to lose him, but that didn't mean she had his best interests at heart. She provided a safe place for him to be mad. She was an idiot so convinced that she could find a different way of doing things, a better and fairer way, that she allowed everyone to suffer.

Lee was back at the window. She had to calm Kallu

down before they did call someone. He had warned her to stay away but she couldn't let him get arrested.

She switched off the kitchen light, let her eyes adjust and then climbed the three steps to the garden. Hearing her, Kallu drew his knees up to his chest. She could see ribbons tied to the rosemary bush he was half-hidden behind. He grabbed the ends and threw them towards her. They fluttered back down, and he looked at her. It wasn't Kallu as she knew him. Never during one of the previous episodes had he looked quite so murderous.

Shona crouched in front of him, just out of reach. 'You need to come inside.'

He snarled, his lips back high over his teeth.

'Stop it. Snap back, or whatever you do. The neighbours are going to call the police. You'll get taken away.'

Kallu said something. Shona had no idea what.

'I know you're there. They will drug you. Come on, Kallu.' She tried to smile. 'Let's go in.'

She inched her right hand towards him but he just followed it with his eyes. His snarl turned to a smile, which was worse. She turned her head to see if the neighbour was still watching, and in that second his head moved and his teeth settled hard on her fingers. It wasn't quite painful but the fear that it would become a serious and bone-breaking bite made her shake.

'Kallu, stop,' she hissed.

He bit down harder. She panicked and slapped his face with her free hand, but when his head moved he didn't let go. He turned his head back to face her. This not-Kallu was enjoying it and she realised that none of their history together meant anything at all. He was an animal and she was inviting him into her house with Jude fast asleep upstairs.

'Get off me!' She registered the panic in her voice and summoned up all the authority she could. 'I command you in the name of the spirits to release me.'

He opened his jaws and yawned. She held the wet, bruised fingers lightly in her left hand and settled back on her haunches. He was mad. She couldn't cope with him and didn't know how she'd ever thought this was under control. He caught hold of the ribbons again and threw them like before. She edged back from him and knelt on one knee. With this distance she looked at her hand, now in the light from the back room window. He'd drawn blood on three fingers. She wanted to cry with the pain, felt shaky with fear. Kallu stretched his arms in front of him, turned on his side with his back to the rosemary and closed his eyes.

Shona kept still. She didn't know if this was a trick to get her to act in some way that would provoke him. She felt the dew start to soak through the knee of her jeans and the crease of her shoes hurt her toes, but she focused on stillness and waited. Kallu breathed quietly at first and then heavily, like a child with a cold.

The lights from the houses on either side began to go out and still she knelt there until she felt that she should be running. He must be asleep. She needed to wash and wrap her fingers and lock the door like any sensible person. She made sure that she made no noise by resting her left hand on the grass as she unfolded her legs but her bent foot had gone to sleep. She managed to stand and waited for the pins and needles to build and pass. Her first attempt at a step made her ankle fold beneath her. She bit down the cry but Kallu opened his eyes. He stood up. She could see he was partly back, the proper Kallu, but she still wanted to run from him.

He held his hand out to her but she backed away. She was at the top of the steps and wasn't sure of her blood supply had returned enough to make them safe. He took a step back.

'Shona,' he said.

'You bloody bit me!'

'I didn't. My body did.' He didn't look upset, just the same as ever. 'You know I haven't got mastery yet. I'm getting there. I warned you.'

'I know.' The tears started to fall. 'I don't know if I'm right about anything any more. Maybe you do need help and you need to be Dominic again and then you can get your parents back and a normal life and I won't have to get bitten at night in my own garden.' She wiped at her face. 'I don't know anything about this, about anything. I don't think I ever did, but I thought I did and that was good enough. I loved my children and hated Maynard and that was that. But now Cerys has chosen him, even though he's a shit, and Meghan is dead and Jude, poor Jude has only got me and I'm an idiot and I have no money. We'll lose the house and I'm fucked, we're all fucked. And then I get bitten.' She shivered and Kallu approached her slowly before taking her arm. 'And now you're fine! Just back to normal like nothing just happened.'

He said, 'Come on, inside.' He helped her down the steps and to the back door. 'Can I come in?'

'No.' She'd never said no to him before. She sighed. 'I don't know.'

'I know you're playing it down. I know that I scare you. It's OK. When you want me to leave, I will.'

He switched the lights on and closed the door. He was back to a young man, a barely adult boy, with deep rings under his eyes and punched hollows in his cheeks. He shook his head wildly and yawned. The sight of his teeth made her shudder and he raised his palms to her.

'Sorry.'

Shona backed away until she could feel the fridge behind her and rested her head against it. She kept her eyes open. She knew this was possible. There had been other times when he'd scared her, and it was always temporary, but this had changed something. She thought of Mariana's face if she told her, and groaned. All this and she'd learned nothing.

He stayed perfectly still, unnaturally still. He was waiting and she wasn't sure whether she wanted to make him feel all right about this, but he was just Kallu again. Same as ever.

'When did you last sleep?' she asked.

'I'm not sure. I kind of remember Saturday. I think I locked up at work, but I've no idea. I suppose I'll find out when I go back.'

Shona pulled away from the fridge and sat down at the table, more heavily than she'd intended.

Kallu spoke more gently than normal. 'I'll put the kettle on and then sort your hand out. Have you got anything to drink?'

'I've got a couple of beers in the fridge.'

'Can I have a beer?'

'Yes.'

'Water first.'

Shona twisted herself so that she could see him as he passed behind her and then started shaking. Watching him was making her feel nauseous and slowly her eyes closed. Her ears felt thick as if there was a woollen hat pulled over them. She felt a glass of water pushed into her left hand and Kallu helped to guide it to her mouth.

216

When she'd swallowed it all and had a beer, she felt able
to talk again.

'Are you back to normal for tonight?'

'No more biting. I can say that.' He smiled.

'Do you know where Cerys is?'

'Yes,' he said. 'So do you.'

'Did you know all along?'

'Yes. So did you.'

'What else do you know?'

Kallu laughed. 'I know what the moon says to the
comets that pass by and what the snow whispers to the
earth as it lands. But I don't think that's what you mean.'

'No.' The thought of Mariana hearing that made Shona
want to laugh.

'The goddess is watching. Meghan is with you, but she
does not belong to this house, or you. She says to look for
stars and let her twinkle. She's happy and she adores you.
But she wants me to tell you I have to take someone with
me, so choose who and what you want and hold on tight.'

Shona gasped. 'You're going to kill someone?'

Kallu tutted. 'You're mental.' He held his hand to her
head and Shona cowered away. He smiled a little and
shook his head. 'You're not mental. And you think I'm
mad, I know. It's OK, it has to be like this. Don't feel bad
about it. You just can't see me properly any more.'

'I can,' she said, but she knew everything had changed.
She couldn't trust him and didn't want him in the same
house as Jude, but still she wanted to hear about Meghan,
to be forgiven by Meghan. She felt the pain of her hand
and began to cry. If he was threatening to take people
from her and she still couldn't tell anyone he needed help,
what was it going to take?

217

15

Shona kept waking in the dark. Sometimes there was nothing obvious to cause it, just a feeling of dread and the ticking of floorboards. Sometimes she thought she heard Kallu creeping through the house. Sometimes it was the phone's blue light flashing that she had a message. Jimmy had mastered texts and was asking most days whether she'd remembered anything about that package. After seeing Cerys' room turned over she felt sure that Maynard was looking it for it too. Neither of them knew, and that meant that Shona must have moved it without even realising. She must know something without understanding she knew it.

Sometimes what woke her was the thought of Maynard getting in and taking the rest of his silver and noticing the things which had already gone. He would have her arrested again, without a doubt. One night she packed everything she could get from his shelves into two boxes, wadded with old newspaper, and lay awake wondering where she could hide them. And then she realised where they had to go.

Thea caught Shona on the way back from dropping Jude off at school.

'Can I come with you to the auction? I've never been and it'd be nice to go with someone else.'

Shona had forgotten about the sale. 'I wasn't going to actually go. They'll email me.'

'Go on.' Thea tilted her head. 'I could drive.'

How would Shona explain the expensive diamond brooch she was selling? She was too tired to open it all up again, even to Thea. Since London and the creeping darkness Shona had felt she was carrying an emptiness in her chest. Except she knew it wasn't London or the dark. It was Kallu. He'd torn himself from her and she could sense he'd gone.

She tried to focus on what Thea was saying.

'I was going to go to Coggeshall. I have to drop some stuff off.' Shona didn't want to say why. Thea didn't ask.

'I can drive us to Coggeshall and then we can go to the auction. In the afternoon, isn't it? I'll pick you up in an hour.' Thea waved and left her at the corner.

Shona was sure she hadn't said it was in the afternoon. And there was something else, she thought, as she slouched at her kitchen table. It felt strange, this overlap between Kallu and Thea. In her sleepless bed, Shona mapped everything, realising this was something her mother would do. Maynard and Mariana were a pair. They crossed over too, filling a dominant personality type. Both suggested revenge and treachery. Both held the idea of fatal secrets. Maynard disagreed with every request on principle and Mariana liked to be coaxed and persuaded so that she knew she was valued.

But Thea? Thea just said yes, no strings, no questions. So did Kallu. And with Kallu leaving, it seemed to Shona as if Thea was replacing him.

Patterns soothed her mother, but seeing them made Shona nervous. It suggested a plan, a map she would follow whether she wanted to or not. And she knew where a belief in patterns and tracks and echoes had got her family.

Shona locked the back door. She would text Thea and cancel, pretend to be out when she knocked. But she hadn't even taken her coat off when Thea knocked and she answered and followed her outside. Seeing her made all the fears recede. Just like Kallu.

Shona took the boxes containing Maynard's knick-knacks to the van and stopped to take in the shocking-pink hatchback. Stencilled on the side was a fairy holding a glittering wand with seven stars around it and *Seven Stars* in silver along the side.

'Oh my God,' said Shona. 'It's hideous.'

'I've had better reactions,' said Thea. 'And much, much worse. Still want a lift?'

'I suppose. Where do you hide it?'

'I have a garage to preserve the beautiful paintwork.' She swept her hand along the van and laughed.

Thea opened the back doors and Shona pushed the box in between others vomiting tinsel and disembodied wings.

Thea was one of the most careful drivers that Shona had known, maybe because she valued her stock and maybe because any complaints would easily identify her van. She eased around corners and anticipated children running across zebra crossings even when the pavements were empty. They left the town but her speed barely rose and they were soon overtaken by a string of cars.

They pulled up and Thea undid her seatbelt.

'Do you mind waiting here?' Shona asked. 'We'll never get away if my mother gets us inside.'

'That's fine.'

Shona took the boxes, one on top of the other, from the back, closed the door with her hip, and walked to the front door. Greta answered before she knocked so she was still holding the boxes.

'Can I store these in the garage?' Shona asked.

'Leave it here, I'll do it.'

'No, can I just have the keys?'

'Shona, leave it for me to do.'

Shona held the boxes to one side. 'Just say no if you mean no.'

'I don't, I'd just rather do it myself.'

'Fine.' Shona walked back to the van.

'Wait.' Greta disappeared for a few seconds and came back with her keys. She led Shona to the row of garages behind the terrace and unlocked the one with a yellow metal shutter. Twisting the handle, she threw the door up above her head. Shona shuddered. Meghan's crib, Meghan's clothes, Meghan's first and last teddy bear, Meghan's life.

'Are you all right?' asked Greta.

'No. I'd forgotten how much there was.'

Shona put the boxes down next to the crib. The clothes bags had gaped open and any scent that they had ever held would be gone. Maybe right at the bottom … She picked up the teddy but there was nothing there but the slightly musty, oil and paint smell of everything else. She put it back in the crib.

'I'll be back for the boxes at some point.'

'What about everything else?'

'When Maynard leaves, I'll collect it all. I don't ever want him to touch it.'

Greta held a hand out to Shona, but she edged away. 'Thanks.'

Greta pulled the door closed and said nothing.

Shona got back into the van and Thea drove away without speaking. There was time to swallow back the lump in her throat and press the tears back from falling. She felt Thea pat her leg and she realised that the van had stopped again.

'Right,' Shona said. 'Let's go.'

The auction was far from over when Shona's lot came up, number 65. A specialised antique sale, Shona saw Thea's hand twitching whenever anything twee and awful was held up for inspection.

'Don't you dare,' said Shona.

Thea laughed. 'You won't have to look at it. If you ever come round, I'll cover it up.'

Shona cringed. Of course she had no right to tell Thea what she should buy. All she knew about her was that she had a son, a tattoo and a pink van. She was one of those slightly hippyish people who might have been dressed in expensive designer ranges or well-chosen charity shop buys and you wouldn't be able to tell. Shona determined to get to know more about Thea. And then lot 65 sold for £6,500.

'You had no idea it was worth that much?'

Shona shook her head. 'I was told it was expensive but I thought he was exaggerating. He underestimated.' She still felt sick.

'Who did it belong to? Was it from a family member? I can see you're regretting it.'

'I'm really not regretting it.' Shona pushed her rum and coke backwards and forwards, leaving a snail trail on the shiny varnish. 'It was mine, kind of. My husband bought it.'

'Wow! What a lovely present.'

'It would have been. He bought it as an investment.'

Legally, she wasn't at all sure if she was on safe ground. Maynard had started divorce proceedings. Yet again she'd done something he could have her charged with. And it was so much money he would be furious. What was wrong with her?

Thea lowered her voice. 'It's not exactly yours?'

Shona looked her in the eyes and shrugged.

'Still, six and a half grand and mere days until Christmas, that can't be bad.' Thea looked at Shona. 'Is it?'

Shona said, 'I think I might have fucked up. It might be theft.'

Thea raised her eyebrows.

'I shouldn't have come. I shouldn't have let you come. You might be called an accessory, or God knows what. I'm so sorry. I can't seem to make any sensible decisions. Everything gets worse the minute it looks a bit better.'

'It's OK, Shona. It will all come right.'

Shona shook her head. 'I don't know if it can. I wish I did.'

The phone rang but there was no-one speaking at the other end. Shona dialled to retrieve the number but it was blocked. That ruled out Jimmy, but somehow she knew it was Cerys. Two and a half months missing, and no reason to think it may be her, but she felt it.

Shona held on to the table to stand up and turned the key in the back door. She sat back down and tried to think through how she could justify stealing from Maynard. He'd kept his end of the deal while Cerys was at home. He had paid what he said he would. Now he could have Shona arrested and she would lose everything, and deserve to.

The door to the kitchen slowly opened.

'No!' she shouted. 'Jude, can you wait? I'll be through in a minute.' She rubbed at her eyes and cheeks. The door closed a little and then opened again. 'Jude, not now!'

The door fully opened and Shona's mother was there, not Jude.

'What are you doing here?'

'Jude let me in. You didn't hear me knocking. Is it OK?'

'Yes. I'm just not in a very sociable mood, Mum. It's been a shit day.'

Greta stood awkwardly in the doorway, one glove off and her scarf in both hands. Shona knew she should offer a cup of tea, make conversation but she needed silence. How many years was it since her mother had been here? And if she believed that she was responsible for Meghan, why was she here at all? Shona knew it was unreasonable to become angry over something so stupid.

'The devil not following you about any more?'

Greta flinched and Shona wished she could take it back.

'You shouldn't be so dismissive, you know. I'm here. I haven't been here for a long time, but I'm here now.'

Shona tried to think of something nice to say. 'I just wondered why now.'

'I hadn't seen you for a while and I wished I'd said more to you when you came today. I thought I'd bring your Christmas presents over. I didn't think about it earlier.' Greta looked around. 'And I've been told that it's safe to come.'

'Safe?'

'Your friend. Kallu. He's been to see me. He says I'm protected. And you believe him, even if you don't believe me.'

'You've seen him?' Shona tried to work out why her mother would make it up. Shona hadn't seen Kallu recently, and his words coming out of her mum's mouth? It was all wrong. She should tell her Kallu was dangerous but it felt like a betrayal.

Greta twisted her scarf. 'I could take Jude out for a bit, go and see Father Christmas in town. Not for long. I know you probably haven't eaten. If you wanted me to.'

Shona was still thinking. Kallu in her mum's house, talking to her the way he talked to Shona. There was something different about Greta, a lightness.

Greta was putting her scarf back on, avoiding eye contact with Shona. 'It's fine, I should have phoned.'

'No, that would be really good. Jude would enjoy it.'

'I wasn't going to say anything, if that's what's worrying you.'

'Well, I'd certainly rather you didn't. But thank you for thinking of him. I'll get him ready.'

Jude was reluctant to go out with his granny until Shona mentioned the grotto.

'How does Granny know where he is?'

'Grannies are much more magical than mummies. They all know Father Christmas, just like children do.'

Jude looked amazed and then tried to run out the front door without a coat.

Greta called him back and helped him into his anorak and tied his trainer laces. 'Do you have a hat, Jude? It's a bit parky.'

Shona fetched the spare key from the kitchen. 'In case I've popped out.'

Jude pulled his hat and gloves from both pockets and stood, fidgeting, while Greta dressed him.

'You didn't call a little while ago, did you, Mum?'

Greta shook her head.

Jude was ready. 'Can we go?'

Shona kissed his hat and watched them walk down the road. Jude was holding Greta's hand while keeping a step or two ahead of her. Shona waved, even though they weren't looking.

She took the new boxes she'd begged from the corner shop on the way back from school and went back to the front room to pack everything left that would fit in a box, paintings, paperwork and breakables all in together. She'd pay for Greta's taxi home and it would all be gone except the furniture. Then she might sleep.

Greta didn't stay for dinner. She'd bought some chips on the way back, she said, and shared them with Jude. She came in to wait for the taxi but they had nothing to say.

Jude had decided he was still hungry and was cutting up peppers in his samurai fashion. Shona thought that she should put a stop to it, but he kept his fingers well out of the way and she couldn't begrudge him finding a way to make cooking fun. She'd never found a way and, even though he had eaten with his grandmother and it was bedtime, he wanted to help Shona.

From the kitchen window Shona saw Jimmy come in the back gate. He had a Russian fur hat with long ear flaps even though the weather was still mild. Shona wondered if someone was dressing him. He carried a large laundry bag folded in one hand. Shona stared at him, wondering whether he really thought he was going to walk off with whatever he asked for.

'Come in!' she shouted.

'So?' he asked, shutting the door behind him.

'Six and a half,' she said. 'I did text you.'

'Six and a half what?' said Jude, still frowning.

'Potatoes,' said Shona. 'Mind your own business.'

Jude rolled his eyes and aimed another dramatic chop.

'That's pretty good. I've come to collect the rest of the stuff.' He unfolded the bag.

'Can I get in that?' Jude put the knife down and wiped his hands on his trousers.

Jimmy said, 'No, it has to keep clean. No little boys. Can I go through?'

Shona shook her head. 'I've moved most of the stuff. Everything small, anyway.'

'Why?'

'In case Maynard comes and demands it all back.'

'But you've changed the keys.'

'And he has a bit of a temper.' Shona pointed at her ears and nodded towards Jude, 'I'd rather let him in to see for himself than try to hold him at the door.'

'But I was going to price it all up for you.'

'I know. You still can. Just not now.'

Jude hadn't picked up the knife again. 'What are you talking about?'

'Let's go in the front room,' said Shona. 'No more knives now, Jude. Just break up the broccoli for me.' She moved the knife into the sink.

'I'm Camel Number Three,' he told Jimmy. 'Do you want to watch me?'

It was the third time he'd mentioned the nativity performance, as if he'd thought she might forget.

'Not sure,' Jimmy said. 'I'll find out when it is.'

Jimmy stomped to the front room and groaned. He slammed the door behind them.

'Everything's gone. Why didn't you ask me to keep the stuff? I know what it's all worth and I know what's what about the rest of it too.'

'I know. I just felt better having it out of the house. And you're the next person they'll assume has it.'

'So where is it?' He looked around at the bare walls and empty cabinets. He was pricing up the furniture as he scanned it. 'Where?'

Shona snapped. 'It's safe, that's all. And it's not yours. Why are you being such an arse?'

He narrowed his eyes. 'You're not handing it all in, are you? It's not just Maynard's head, you'll be giving them mine too.' He took a step forward. 'I need to know where the stuff is. The paperwork too. I need to protect myself.'

The heat from the house and hat combined had made his nose and forehead greasy with sweat. Shona refused to back away.

'It is safe,' she repeated. 'I'll let you know what I decide.'

'You've no idea what it's like,' he said, pulling his hat off. His hair, heavy with sweat, looked thin, his eyes tired. 'I won't risk it, Shona. It turns you mad. You end up believing all sorts just for something to think about. The next time I end up inside I won't come out again.' He pulled his hat back on and lifted his chin. 'I would do just about anything to avoid it, Shona. If I felt threatened, I couldn't say.'

'I'm not going to expose you. I've always known that you're dodgy as hell, I just didn't realise that you were endangering me and my children by fucking around with that idiot I married.'

'You were never—'

228

'Stolen and faked goods in my house, and you think they'd believe I had no idea?'

Jimmy fiddled with his collar, pulling it down with both hands. His eyes seemed unable to focus, darting from one hand to the other.

'I'm in charge now, of this house and whatever is in it. I don't want Maynard to have any of it on his terms, if at all, but I need it away from me. Got it?'

Jimmy finally met her eyes and went to leave the room before changing his mind and turning back.

'Why did you send him?' he said.

'Who?'

'That boy. Kallu.'

'Send him where?'

'He turned up on my doorstep pretending he was a bit woozy, asking me to call you. He just wanted to get inside. I knew his game.'

First Greta, now Jimmy.

'Jimmy, I didn't send him. Why didn't you call me? He has episodes.'

'He was not having an episode. He found my house, didn't he?'

'He just knows things.'

Jimmy looked at Shona. 'Lots of people know things, Shona, and they're not always truthful about how they know. You believe him?'

Shona nodded.

'You want to watch yourself, and everything else here. You have something he wants.'

'He's never asked me for anything.'

Jimmy laughed. 'The clever ones never have to. If you know anything about me, Shona, you know that I can spot a fake.'

He left the room, slamming the front door behind him. She followed him and bolted the door, top and bottom. At the back door she hesitated. She hadn't seen Kallu for days. She should check on him. She should ask why he was visiting her family. The thought of coming across him in the garden was too much. She dipped outside to the bin, grasped about for the spare key, and locked the back door.

GRETA

When I got home, I was still happy. Maynard was awful, yes, but my daughter was back. She had two beautiful daughters, not a boy and a girl, and we, together, would be fine. I bathed, went to bed and smiled as I thought about how things were going to improve.

I don't know what woke me. I just knew he was back. He was waiting to tell me something. I had to go downstairs. The streetlights were still on, so I didn't touch the light switch. It wasn't anything nice and prosaic like a burglar, so I wouldn't need lights.

Larry was sitting in the front room, in his arm chair, as he'd looked in Paris, young, arrogant and satisfied with himself. My heart sank even further than it already was. This wasn't about me. There was nothing he could do to me. It had something to do with Shona. My Shona. He smiled when I thought that.

'What have you done?' I said.

He just smiled. I thought about the religion and the folklore and the ley lines, those layers of belief we'd all heaped on ourselves, and I knew they were just distractions. They were stories. I could only ever know where he'd been, not where he was going. The only evidence was held in snow. I needed snow.

'We don't miss you.' I sat on the sofa, suddenly cold, and folded my arms. 'You're dusty bones and nothing else. No photos, not remembered by anyone.'

He nodded.

'Why come back now?'

He looked at the phone and I heard, as if from behind him, a thin baby cry. Now I became cold, right to the core. My stomach was suddenly agonising and I leant over and vomited on my feet. My head filled with the thread of sound and I was filled with loss. The cry had turned into Shona's wail. I couldn't look at him again. My eyes were squeezed tight as I tried to persuade myself, it is a punishment for me. It's an illusion. It's not him, it's not Meghan.

I finally heard him speak. 'You took me to her.' I clamped my hands to my ears, but the words were in my head. 'You showed me where she was.'

And then the phone rang.

I didn't want to go back. What if something happened to Cerys? But I did. In the two inches of snow which had fallen overnight, I saw the hoof prints on the pavement outside Shona's house, walking away. He'd been there and I'd led him.

I stayed through the tears and I stayed through the anger. I listened to her accusations, blaming Maynard, when I knew it was her father, the devil. I ordered the van she cried for and packed Meghan's clothes, Meghan's soft toys and Meghan's crib into the back of it, drove it to my house and put everything in the garage behind the house.

It was the only place where I felt I'd had power over him, the only place these things might be safe from his influence. I returned the van and asked what else I could do.

'Is everything safe from him?'

'Yes.' She was talking about Maynard and I was talking about Larry.

'I don't want him ever to touch anything that belonged to her. He's poison. He killed her.'

'He did. I know he did.'

She stared at me, red-eyed. 'Will anyone else believe us?'

I shook my head. 'You know they won't.'

She looked at me strangely then and almost pulled away. She started to sob again and I held her awkwardly.

'Mum, you've got that look than Gran had. You are talking about Maynard, aren't you? It's not anything else?'

I said nothing and she wrenched herself away.

'Oh my God, it is, isn't it? You're thinking that I've been attacked by evil. It was Maynard! Neglect and selfishness and stupid human ignorance killed my daughter.'

We heard the front door slam and both quietened. She crept to her bedroom door and stood on the landing, next to Cerys' door. I heard Maynard stop halfway on the stairs and then continue to the top. Shona said nothing. He came in the room, tired-eyed and dishevelled. He wasn't surprised to see me sitting on his bed.

'I'm just getting a few things,' he mumbled. 'Shona doesn't want me here at the minute.'

He pulled a bag from on top of the wardrobe and slung a couple of shirts in. I didn't know whether to stay or leave, so stood by the window and looked outside.

'Where's the crib?' His voice was stronger than before.

I turned round. 'Shona doesn't want—'

'Where's the fucking crib?' His fists were clenched, his eyes alert. 'Tell me where it is.'

'No.' I'd faced the devil. I wasn't going to give in to a bully.

'Shona!'

She stood in the doorway. 'It's gone. All her stuff is gone and it won't be coming back.'

'What the fuck did you do that for?' He stared at her, then at me. 'Who took it and where did they take it?'

Shona crossed her arms. 'When you tell me what happened to Meghan, I'll tell you where I dumped the crib.'

Maynard sank to the bed, his head in his hands. 'Fucking bitches. You have no idea.'

Shona stared at him as his body began to shake. I walked to the door, pushed her gently onto the landing and closed the door behind me.

Shona was still staring. 'He didn't cry about Meghan,' she whispered. She looked at me. 'Why wouldn't he cry about her?'

I was stuck then. I didn't want to take the devil back to Shona. I know she feels I failed her, but I was always here. I would have done anything for her here. Instead we both suffered separately.

I was surprised to get a letter from Jimmy a few weeks later, asking me to visit him. He'd sent a visiting card and told me which day and time to come. I put it all on the mantelpiece and left it there. I didn't write back, I'd told him I didn't want to see him, and I didn't go. I wasn't entirely surprised to see a couple of men turn up when I should have been at the prison. I knew the links between him and Maynard, but thought they'd lapsed over time and the trouble Jimmy was in. Apparently not. Maynard wanted his crib back, thought I had it, and was prepared to break into my house to get it. I thought of inviting him round, so he could have a good look for himself, but then couldn't work out how I would explain that to Shona. Jimmy had known Larry had hired one of the line of garages, but he would have had no reason to suppose I kept it, having no car. It was out of sight. It would never have occurred to Maynard.

The men finally broke in while I was sleeping and left me a broken pane in the back door, even though I'd left it open for them. I woke when they smashed it and lay quietly as they padded around my bedroom. When the devil wants you for his own, you're in no danger from anyone else.

I never knew what arrangement Shona and Maynard came to. There was some tension between them and I thought about the cyclist and how easily he'd walked away from that. I expected him to walk away from Shona too, with Cerys if he could manage it. Maybe he thought, if he stayed, the crib would eventually return when Shona got pregnant again. When she got pregnant with Jude, she bought a nice clean crib from Ikea. That was when Maynard stopped pretending everything might turn out all right and moved down to the front room, where he'd spent so many nights.

They were stuck together. Shona wanted the house, Maynard wanted the crib and they both wanted Cerys. Neither of them was any good at losing.

16

Five days before Christmas and Jude was writing his sixth wish list.

'It's probably too late for Father Christmas to change his mind, you know.'

Jude shook his head. 'He's magic, stupid.'

'Hey! He'll take out presents if you're rude.'

'You definitely won't get anything.'

School had built up a complete conviction in this mystical, generous provider of material goods. Shona had half thought that Jude would persuade the entire class that he was a fabrication and she would be the focus of dozens of accusing, tearful eyes. Instead he'd been quickly brought into the fold, as it was a more attractive idea than anything else possible. Short of showing him everything she bought before he unwrapped it, Shona was stuck. She left him to his imagination, although she was pretty sure that the magic wand he wanted would turn out a disappointment. With Father Christmas, reality wasn't a problem.

She found a film and settled him down as Mariana let

herself in the back door. Jude glanced at her and jumped up when he saw the present in her hands.

'Is it for me?'

'Of course.'

He snatched it.

'Say thank you!' Shona shouted after him before shutting the door. 'I'll just go and get your card.'

'No problem.' Mariana sighed. 'And try to find some decorations, for goodness sake. How dull it is in here. Lights, Shona, lights are the spirit of Christmas.'

Shona went to the hall, pulled the packet of cards from her bag and sat on the stairs to write it out.

Mariana was looking at the package on the table which Shona hadn't opened yet.

'No address,' said Mariana.

'Yes,' said Shona. 'I've had a few of these.'

With a long red fingernail Mariana slowly pushed it towards Shona. Shona handed her the card.

'Someone is sending me photos of Cerys.' Shona pointed to the others. 'It's not nice opening them. They've been fine so far, but still.'

'Who do think they're from?'

'Maynard, probably.'

'*Merda.* The sooner you can move on the better.'

Shona placed her hand on top of Mariana's small, rested hand. She knew that when Mariana didn't really approve of divorce but was trying to be supportive. Her large brown eyes were framed by furrowed brows.

Shona spoke quietly. 'I'll open it. Tell me what you think it's supposed to mean.'

Shona fetched a vegetable knife from the drawer and sliced underneath the Sellotape. She unfolded the stiff, brown paper. The frame was thick and black, making

Cerys' blonde hair seem even lighter than before. She had what looked like a designer bag over one shoulder and was made up with some mascara and lipstick. A couple of girls stood next to her, smiling for the camera.

Mariana said, 'Her smile isn't like theirs.'

Shona looked. She was right. It was a photo smile with a watchfulness to her eyes.

'What do you think they are for?'

'I think in a strange way they are a sorry, but also to make you feel you can keep in touch. Also, there's an implicit threat. You are getting these while Maynard gets his way, or thinks he is. When that changes you will lose her, as far as he's concerned. But—' Mariana held her hand up '—not necessarily as far as Cerys is concerned. She's old enough to make contact on her own and to get on a train. She doesn't look short of money. It will be up to her, not him.'

Shona looked at the photo and wished she had some kind of clue about Cerys' feelings towards her now. Mariana took the photo and placed it on the table.

'So, you want me to look at the latest letter from the solicitor?'

Shona drew it from the envelope and stood up to put the kettle on. Her mobile rang, vibrating against the draining board. Shona looked and turned the phone over to cut the sound. Jimmy. Shona held the phone in both hands until it stilled and then switched it off. Something was disturbing her about his reaction to Maynard's collection. He had treated it like his own property, as if no-one could deal with it but him. She thought that he had plans that he wasn't telling her. She had no idea about his situation, his income. She was starting to suspect that he intended to sell the paintings to keep the money for himself. He'd taken the ones with any real price and if she confronted him she might never see the money. If she accused him, he could make things very complicated for her. She'd taken the paperwork which linked him to the paintings and to Maynard, but she didn't want to get him sent back to prison.

She wanted to talk to Mariana about it, but there was something which stopped her. It had been two weeks since Shona had seen Kallu that night in the garden. She almost asked Mariana if she had been visited, but she would have said.

When she looked back to her, Mariana was watching her as if waiting for something. Shona smiled and Mariana went back to the papers.

Shona offered Jude the last piece of pizza but he shook his head. He chewed on his thumb, the way he did when he felt tired or close to tears. She thought he might be thinking about Christmas without Cerys, just them two. She wasn't enough for him and had always known that, but having Cerys around had hidden it.

'Are you feeling all right, Jude?'

'Yeah.'

'So, Camel Number Three, do you want me to read you a story or have a bath and then a story?'

'Just a story.'

'OK, brush your teeth.'

In bed she pretended she couldn't find the book straight away.

'How would you feel about having your own bedroom?'

Jude frowned at her. 'What do you mean?'

'I mean, we have three bedrooms and it's silly for us to share one of them.'

'It's two bedrooms, one just has a cave.'

Shona looked at his face. 'Are you scared of the office?'

'No.' He shrugged. 'I like caves.'

Shona wondered whether she should tell him he was moving rooms or keep asking him what he thought. She didn't remember ever being asked as a child what she thought about anything. Equally she didn't want Jude to grow up thinking that whatever he wanted would inevitably happen with no effort on his part.

'Now that Cerys isn't here, I think you should have her room. You can take all your toys from here and put them where you like. Or would you rather stay in here?' He still wasn't looking at her. 'I think you're too old to share a bed now, Jude. What do you think?'

He looked at his hands. 'I like sharing with you. I would get lonely.'

'Do your friends have their own rooms?'

He stuck his bottom lip out. 'Dunno.'

'I think you should ask Callum what he thinks. And then he can come to play and you can have secret games in your own room, and he can stay for the night.'

Jude's chin rested on his chest and he kept his eyes fixed firmly in front of him. The air was squeezed between his palms. Shona stroked his hair and his flicked his head away from her hand.

She hadn't looked in his schoolbag for three weeks before this afternoon and had found a party invitation for the previous weekend and two requests for late dinner money. His reading book hadn't been changed as apparently they were waiting for her comments in his home/ school book and one plimsoll had been lost and needed replacing. She tried not to cry. She had failed him over and over and he hadn't said a word. She needed to forget about Cerys who would turn up when she turned up, and sever all ties with Maynard twelve years after she should have done. Jude needed a little bit of attention other than food and warmth and she couldn't spend it all on people who weren't here. Meghan was gone, Cerys was gone, Maynard was gone and yet they were more present in her head than her beautiful little boy who adored her.

'Mum? Are there going to be people in the garden again tonight? I don't like them.'

'Did you hear someone? It wasn't Kallu?'

'No, it wasn't Kallu. It was strange people.'

'Why didn't you tell me, wake me up?'

'You were crying in your dreams and I didn't want you to wake up all sad. Did you wake up sad?'

'No, I didn't.'

Jude smiled and hugged her arm. She hadn't noticed the rings under his eyes this morning, although he had been quieter than usual. And he'd made a fuss about what he wanted in his sandwiches, which wasn't like him.

'I've found your story,' she said, pulling the reading book from his bag.

He looked at the book. 'Stay after this, Mummy.' He leaned his head against her shoulder and she couldn't argue with him. She knew this was the problem. She needed him, and she liked him more than she wanted to be his parent.

She kissed his head and read and ignored the message alerts from her mobile phone. Everything could wait.

17

Jude spent an hour choosing his library books. He still liked the low-slung wooden boxes of books which stood upright. Shona was worried that he should be looking for older storybooks now, fewer illustrations and more words, but decided to let him be. Shona took one of the soft but uncomfortable oblong seats and watched him flip each book forward so it banged against the one in front. He did it quickly but never had to reverse back to one. He spotted what he wanted and she began to wonder what selection process he was using. She couldn't remember making easy decisions on the basis of a cover, but so much more effort went into them now. Her early teenage years had been full of dull beige books with all the colour contained in the words. A small line drawing at the opening of a chapter was as decorative as it got. Even the teenage section in the library was careful to display lurid, sometimes gruesome, covers to attract the eye.

'Done.' Jude had his three books clamped to his chest.

'My turn. You can have a look at them while I'm choosing mine.'

'Can we go up in the lift?'

Shona shuddered. 'It's just for buggies.'

'You're scared.'

Shona stuck her tongue out and guided him to the escalator.

Kallu had phoned to meet them for lunch in town. Shona was pleased they were meeting somewhere neutral, and public. They were late, but he was later. She had found a corner table to place the bags of library books behind and worried that, out of sight, she would forget them. Jude promised to remind her. She unrolled her scarf and tucked it into the arm of her coat, her gloves into her pockets and heard the crinkle of paper. This latest letter informed her that Maynard was getting the divorce underway on the basis that they'd been separated for over five years, using his flat in London as the proof. Now he was openly admitting that Cerys was with him so that he wouldn't have to pay Shona any maintenance and was claiming that he deserved his half of their house. Only it wasn't *his* house to Shona.

She looked at her watch, wondering whether Kallu had been and gone, when he arrived. Kallu wasn't wearing a coat, just a beige jumper as thick as a sheep. He smelled of leaves and soil.

'I ordered for you,' Shona said.

He always ate the same thing in this café and she never did, choosing the special on principle. Today she wished she'd had the same as him, her onion soup being too runny and, if it was possible, too oniony. Jude had eaten his sandwich and taken his place at the drawing table hidden under the staircase.

'How are you?' she asked.

He shrugged. She was never sure what he thought of when she asked that, how he was physically, spiritually or metaphysically. He ate his toasted cheese sandwich in the same way as always, savouring each bite. She'd read this book where the girl could taste the history of production in her food and she wondered if he could taste the grass that the cows ate. Sometimes he couldn't eat it. He would put it down and drink his water instead. He was losing weight, she thought, but not in a worrying way. His face was thinning and hardening into that of a man, the veins on the back of his hands becoming prominent. His hair curled around his shoulders, newly trimmed. She wondered who did that for him now and how well they managed to save every wisp for him. What did he do with the clippings? She remembered the smell of burnt hair at her mother's house.

'You've got a question?' he said.

'Yes,' she said, but which one?

Kallu said, 'I've seen people around the house. Two men or one man, it varies. One man was in the garden last night but he couldn't find the key under the bin.'

Shona signalled towards Jude and put a finger to her lips. She whispered, 'What did he look like?'

Kallu shrugged. Shona knew now that she wasn't scared of him. As long as she stayed inside she was in no danger.

'I moved the key. Do you want a new spare?'

'I won't be needing it. Keep it inside. He tried the windows but you'd remembered to lock them. I watched you.'

'Did he see you?'

'No, he didn't come towards the shed. I don't think he would have seen me anyway.'

244

'No?'

'I was in Amy's garden.'

'Why?'

'Amy needs me.'

Shona fought down the queasy jealousy and broke the last of her bread into pieces.

'Why won't you need the key?'

Kallu smiled at her. 'I'm leaving very soon.'

'Where are you going?'

'Wherever you send me.'

'I want you to stay.'

'No, you want me to make everything right. You want to know that Meghan is with you, that Cerys will be with you and that you will never lose Jude. You don't own the house but the house owns you. You can do this. Jimmy hasn't chosen a side yet, he's trying to beat both of you.'

'What about Maynard?'

'What about him?' Kallu laughed, held his hand out and blew across the top of it. 'Jude's not the only one who needs to know the truth. You can't search for it if you can't release it back to the world.'

Shona looked towards Jude. He looked away when he saw her.

Shona hissed, 'You can talk about truth. Did you even see your mum at Christmas? I'm not the only one who is letting people down.'

Kallu swallowed his last mouthful. 'I never said you were. And on Christmas Day I turned up for work, realised, and then saw my mum. You both have to let me go.'

'I'm not your mother.'

He looked at her. 'I'm not what you want me to be. I just am.' He kissed her cheek and left the table, pulling the café door gently closed behind him.

Shona felt her throat tighten and closed her eyes to stop them overfilling. She raised one hand to her forehead to squeeze her temples. Again he'd gone and she never felt she'd said what she meant to. Was that the last time, or would she have another chance? She heard her table being cleared, the shuffle of people leaving the café. When she lifted her eyes, Jude was standing in front of her with his drawing of a Christmas tree and red stick figure smiling next to it. The waitress came over.

'Would you like anything else?'

'Is it all right to stay a bit longer, Jude? I'll get you a cake.'

He nodded and she turned to the waitress.

'Yes, chocolate cake and a coffee, please. And can I borrow a pen and a bit of paper?'

After a bath and twenty minutes of Shona reading, Jude had half settled in bed.

'You are sleeping in here with me, aren't you?' It was the fifth time he'd asked. For the fifth time she said yes. His eyes were closed now but Shona knew from his breathing that sleep was some way off. They'd talked about the men, people who'd come to the wrong house Shona had said, and Jude had nodded seriously in an unconvinced way. Shona stroked his hair and wondered when she started to lie so easily to him. He was still, but his hands were grasping the edges of the duvet when there was a knock on the door. His eyes opened wide and he sat up.

'Not again,' said Shona.

'Who is it?'

'I'll check. It's OK,' said Shona. 'Lie back down.'

But he clung to her arm and there was something in

his eyes which prompted a sudden hope in her. Could it be Cerys?

She picked him from the bed and carried him downstairs. She put Jude on the bottom step and opened the door. It wasn't Cerys. She tried not to let her face fall.

'It's Thea,' she said lightly to Jude.

Thea held out a drill, its flex wound around it. 'Sorry it's late, but I only just remembered.'

Shona put Jude down and took the drill. 'Brilliant, thanks. Do you want to come in?'

Thea smiled shyly. 'I have a date.' She pointed towards the car, engine still running. 'She's called Asha.'

'Have fun.' Shona tried to smile.

Thea frowned. 'Are you all right, Shona?'

'Yes. I'll speak to you tomorrow. Really, have a great time.'

Thea waved to Jude and walked back to the car. Shona closed the door.

'I need to just do a bit of drilling. It can wait until tomorrow or do you want to watch?'

'I'll watch.' Jude chewed on his thumb. 'What's it for?'

Shona lifted the plastic bag from the coat rack and pulled a bolt out. 'I was going to put this big, fat bolt on the door, just so we know we're completely safe.'

'What if they come back when we're not in?'

'I don't care what happens when we're not here. It's just a house and it's just stuff.'

Jude put the lock back and looked at the drill. 'I wish Cerys was here.'

'Me too.' Shona sat down next to him. 'Cerys is busy somewhere else.' She took a breath. 'She's decided that she wants to live with her dad. She's in London and she'll be back, but for now she's really cross with me.'

'Is she cross with me too?'

'No, not at all.'

'But I hate her daddy. I told her.'

'That's OK, she knows he's not very nice to you.'

'If I had a daddy, I'd share him with her.'

Shona bit her lip. He hadn't mentioned his daddy for over a year but it was bound to come up now that he was at school. He wasn't the only fatherless child, but he was clearly constructing a heroic image in his head that beat all of the fathers he saw. She waited for him to ask again but he didn't. He was waiting.

'Do you want to help?' she asked.

He jumped up. 'Can I do the drill?'

'Not this time. You can choose the bolts. We'll just do one door tonight, which one?'

'The back door.'

He ran through to the kitchen while Shona grabbed the small plastic wallet of screws. He walked back slowly.

'What about Kallu? We can't lock him out.'

'Kallu will have to start knocking on the door like other people.' Shona put her arms round him. 'He knows why we're doing this and he doesn't mind. We'll only lock it when we go to bed and unlock it first thing. Cerys has got a phone, so don't worry about her either.'

Jude nodded and eyed the drill again. 'Are you sure I can't do just one hole?'

'Very sure.'

Once Jude was asleep she went to Cerys' room. She wasn't ready to call it her room. She'd boxed up the school books and revision notes. Cerys' clothes from the floor were now in a suitcase and, having gone through them, Shona still couldn't identify any that she'd taken with her. Maynard must have bought her an entirely new wardrobe for her new life. The make-up, scattered across the desk and floor by the window, was all in a plastic bag.

She was still shaken from those few seconds when she'd truly believed that Cerys was back, that it was all over. She could feel it tug at her as she looked around the room. There were still at least four more boxfuls to pack up. Shona hadn't managed to put more than a couple of empty plastic bottles in the bin bag. She couldn't bear to throw anything away.

The suitcase wasn't quite full so she decided to see if there was anything left hanging in the wardrobe. Made from antique oak, it had to be dismantled to get it out of the room. To get it in, Maynard had got men round to remove the windows from their settings. Shona had never understood how a wardrobe deserved such attention and dedication, but Maynard wanted the best of everything for their house. In the beginning, anyway.

She turned the trefoil key and the right-hand door swung open. There were some boxes of barely worn shoes at the bottom. She felt with her fingers for the upper and lower latches, and the left door swung too.

Shona stepped away and looked around the room. She was unsure whether she wanted to know what else was in the room. What had Maynard been looking for? Were the people outside looking for the same thing? It must be the lost piece that Jimmy mentioned, but Shona couldn't understand why Maynard didn't know where he'd put it. It was difficult to believe that he'd give it to slapdash Cerys to look after. Someone believed it was here though, either Jimmy or Maynard. She could imagine what Maynard would do to get it back, what Jimmy would do to look at it. They weren't safe. She should take Jude and leave everyone to ransack the place and they could make do with whatever they left.

She imagined Jude, asleep with a hand flung across his head. She needed to allow him space to grow but she couldn't leave him to face whatever was going to happen. She knew it was coming. But she also knew she wasn't going to leave. This was her house, her daughters' and her son's. She would make them think it was gone and she would take her house back.

The least hard thing to do now was to strip the bed. Shona undressed the duvet and pillow and pulled the sheet from the bed, trying not to smell Cerys as it pinged away from the corners. She balled up the material and left it outside the door. The clean linen was on the chair which yesterday had been covered in clothes. Shona tried not to imagine that she was making the bed for Cerys, as she had when Cerys had spent a week away on a school trip or a night at a friend's house. She was making the bed for herself. Or for Jude. For someone other than Cerys.

The bed made, she lay down on top of the duvet and kicked her shoes onto the floor. The main light lit up the inside of the windows but she could just see the movement of the tree outside. The radiators were clicking, cooling down for the night, and Shona closed her eyes, promising herself that she wouldn't fall asleep. Jude wouldn't wake up alone.

Her mind drifted.

She was pulled back from sleep by the sound of Kallu's voice, at a slight distance. He must have got inside somehow, despite the locks. She froze. He was talking, so wouldn't be in a trance, but how could he get in? She jumped up and ran to the landing, expecting to see him on the stairs. The stairs were lit by the streetlights, but there was no sign of him. She could still hear him, more faintly now.

She covered her mouth. He was talking to someone. Had he teamed up with Jimmy or one of the other men? Her hands grabbed the bannister. He couldn't betray her. She backed up quietly and stood in front of Jude's door. He was louder again, and she went back into Cerys' room.

He wasn't in her house. He was in the next room. He was in Amy's bedroom. Shona looked at the wall, imagining the scene that would match the lilt of their words. The lack of the fire wall meant that she could almost hear them breathing. When the words stopped and the sounds started, she switched the light off and slammed Cerys' door shut.

In the kitchen she took a deep breath and wiped her face with her sleeves. It would calm her to make another list. She put *Aladdin Sane* on, just loud enough to hide any noises from next door, took her notebook and turned to a fresh page. She kept getting distracted by the lyrics which all seemed to point to the sighs she couldn't stop hearing.

She shook herself. A three-piece artwork. She tried to remember how far away Jimmy had spread his hands when he described it and noted that down. Maynard must have hidden it somewhere, somewhere that he didn't have control over, inside something that had been lost or moved or given away. The crib.

She pushed her chair back from the table and grabbed her phone. Jimmy answered with a curse.

'Where did Maynard get this painting from, the one you said was missing?'

'Bruges.'

She could hear him breathing heavily.

'Why?'

She cleared her throat. She knew, but just wanted him to say it. 'Definitely on our honeymoon?'

He held his breath. 'You know, don't you? You know where it is. Can I come round? Can I see it?'

'I don't have it here. I think I know what happened to it.'

'Can you find it? I'll pay, Shona, I'll pay as much as you want. Can I come round now? Shona! Tell me where it is. I've been waiting years for this. Maynard told me it had gone, the fucker. I knew he was lying. I can be round in five minutes.'

His urgency was unnerving her. He was most likely one of, or responsible for, the people creeping around her garden and maybe her house. The connected lofts meant that there was easy access to her house from Amy's, and Amy was in no state to suss out when she was being used. All that time spent on doors and locks and she should have been looking next door.

'Shona?'

'It's not here. Let me think about it, Jimmy, OK? I don't know if I want to find it.'

'For fu—'

Shona pressed the red button. She returned to the table and opened up another book. Now she was in charge. She knew what no-one else did and everything would come to her. She could focus now.

18

JANUARY 2012

'Did you show Fernando the papers?'

Mariana sighed. 'I did, and I've read them too. I think you're going to have to sell up. It's a very, very good company. And he hasn't even mentioned the adultery.'

'I can't lose my house. He's got his own flat, his own home. This is mine.'

'It's his house too. He's on the deeds, he paid the mortgage. He has the legal right to half of every square metre.' She sighed. 'His flat belongs to his business, legally. It's tied up very tightly and in his mother's name primarily. He's had very good advice, or bad advice. It's not ethical but it is legal.' Mariana stroked Shona's shoulder. 'It will be OK.'

'No, it won't. I can't afford to buy a house with half the money.'

Mariana tutted. 'Yes, you can. You can get exactly what you need for you and Jude to be happy. You just need to look in different areas.'

Shona spread her arms. 'I won't be able to buy this house.'

'Children move houses all the time. They cope, as long as the parents allow them to cope. They just need, *Jude* just needs you to smile and tell him that it's different but still good. Still somewhere he can feel safe.'

Shona scraped the chair back so it hit the wall, moved away and flicked the kettle on. She stood by the window and bit on her thumb. She heard Mariana behind her, taking her coat off and placing it on the back of the chair before pulling it out to sit down. She decided.

'I know where something is that Maynard really wants.'

Mariana squinted. 'What kind of something?'

'It's dodgy, though. Really dodgy. Do you want to know?'

'How am I supposed to know if I want to know?' Mariana looked suspicious and busied herself with her handbag before pulling out a packet of chocolate biscuits. 'How many biscuits would I need afterwards?'

'The whole packet.'

She sighed. 'It's really illegal, isn't it? Do you need to tell me?'

'No. But I think that using it would mean that I get my house.' Shona sat down next to her. 'There's a painting. I think, from the description, that it's a religious icon. A stolen icon, most likely.'

'You haven't seen it?'

'No. But I know at least two men who rate it very highly.'

'Why wouldn't Maynard return it and be happy with the fame of finding it?'

'He never loved art. He loved the money and there's enough people with money who do love art to make it worth his while. I think he got it for someone specific. Someone who has never forgiven him for losing it. Or he just doesn't like losing.'

Mariana opened the biscuits and bit into one. 'You realise that you're in possession of stolen goods?'

'No-one gave it to me.'

'You know perfectly well how the law works. Ignorance is not a defence, and you can't even claim ignorance. And now, neither can I.'

'It isn't in my house and I haven't touched it, yet. I'm not interested in it, but maybe I can use it as leverage.'

'Where do you think it was taken from?'

'At that time probably a church,' Shona said. 'Originally, anyway.'

'And you want to use it to gain from in the divorce?' Mariana finished the biscuit and picked out another. 'I don't think I want to be involved in this hypothetical conversation any further. Stealing from churches is stealing from history at the very least, the lowest of the low, and I think you, Shona, should do the right thing and return it. Have Maynard arrested, return the painting, get divorced and just start your life properly again.'

'What about the house?'

Mariana thumped the table, the biscuit crumbling. 'What about the house? It doesn't belong to you, it's shared property and has to be divided. You won't get any of his flat as it belongs to his company. You won't get any of his income as he's been sacked. You don't deserve anything other than half this house as you cheated on your husband and had a bastard child outside your marriage and you can't expect sympathy or payment for that.'

Shona sat, stunned and shifted on her chair. Mariana's fury wasn't over.

'You used to be decent and honest. You were a friend and I would have done anything to help you. Now I don't even like you any more. You're deceitful and unfaithful not just to your husband, but also to your friends.'

In the silence Shona blushed. 'You know.'

'Yes, I know.' Mariana's frown crumpled and she held her hands to her face. 'I don't know how you have looked me in the face all these years without the slightest trace of guilt or even self-consciousness.' She took a deep breath and pulled her hands away. 'You have two children who are alive and one who is dead. Accept it and move on.' She pushed her chair back from the table and started to put her coat back on.

'Does he know you know?'

'Does my husband know that I know you fucked him or that he's the father of your son?'

Shona cringed. Mariana bent down towards her.

'He worked it out. Anyone who looks at them together can work it out. I truly believed you'd tell me eventually, but you didn't.' She gestured towards her breast. 'My marriage belongs to me, no matter who tries to get in the middle of it. I'm a good person and I believe in forgiveness but I do not believe in supporting people who don't want to be forgiven and just make things worse. Cheating, lying and now theft. Where do you see this ending?' She put the biscuits back in her bag and slammed the back door behind her.

What would the church or cathedral or wherever benefit from the return of this panel? Shona didn't even know where it had come from. One cathedral in Ghent had a panel stolen and so they had commissioned a replacement, which had proved satisfactory since 1945, by a copyist. An acknowledged fake which did exactly the same as the original had, to those who could see something in it.

Which Shona couldn't. Jimmy was right. It was just paint on board. And money.

She had no right to keep it and she didn't want it. She didn't want to return it. Now two other people, Jimmy and Mariana, wanted it too but last week no-one knew it existed. She shouldn't have told Mariana, or Jimmy. Maynard must know by now as well.

Shona didn't know where she saw anything ending. She did know that it was a relief, a cowardly one, not to have to tell Mariana about Jude. She also knew that avoiding the problem hadn't made it go away. Fernando knew and she would have to face him and, oh God, tell Jude. Mariana, Cerys and her mother – she owed something to all of them.

She found her mobile in the front room and listened to another message from Jimmy. Once she'd finished she noticed that she had a second voice message that must have come through as she was listening to the first. She didn't recognise the number but called up to listen to it. There was a lot of background noise and the sense that someone was walking along, the sound of material being brushed against the speaker. Then a man's name saying 'Cerys', and the line went dead. She'd had another photo of Cerys in the past week, looking away from the camera, pensive, so different to the early photos where she was hair-swingingly happy. She hoped that the photos were a sign that Cerys was missing her, maybe regretting having left home. Was she thinking about her mother, her brother, even her room? Shona knew it was probably a brief fit of pique over a pair of shoes, a badly expressed question that had annoyed her, but why send it? She looked again at the ones on the fridge and saw, she thought, a change, a quietness in the later photos. She felt she was getting her back, but it would never be the same.

Greta knocked on the back door before opening it and shook her umbrella off.

'Is Jude ready?'

'I think so. I'd better warn you, he's overexcited about this.'

'Don't worry. He'll sleep well and be ready for school in the morning.'

Shona called Jude. He came in, sweating under his hat and scarf.

'How long have you been wearing all of that?' asked Greta.

'Hours,' groaned Jude.

'We'd better get you to the bus stop so you can cool down.'

Jude stepped outside. Shona gestured to Greta.

'Do you need any money? He'll demand all sorts of things but you don't need to say yes.'

'Every time I took you to the zoo you got to choose a toy. I know how it works.' Greta waved and left.

Shona tried but couldn't remember ever going to the zoo with her mother. She couldn't remember choosing a toy to cherish or ignore. Every time she spoke to her mother recently she wondered how much of the childhood she remembered was real, and how much she'd forgotten or never really seen in the first place.

She went upstairs to turn Jude's bedroom into one for him alone. All her books and clothes were moving into the front bedroom. Her office would be packed up and filled with his toys. She was ready to let go.

When Shona came back from the shop, the smells from her kitchen were homely in a way they hadn't been for years. This was a meal someone was taking time over.

At the table Jude had a blocky figure he was posing, her mum had a bowlful of potato parings and Jimmy had his furry hat squashed between his hands. The lights in the kitchen blanched all the deep darkness of the evening. Shona noticed new fairy lights around the neglected rubber plant by the table.

All three looked up at her and immediately the scene was altered as they jumped up to pull the table from the wall to free up the fourth chair.

'What's going on?' Shona said, pulling off her hat and scarf and draping her coat on the corner of the kitchen door.

'We had a lovely day,' said Greta. 'Now Jude's going to help me with the carrots.'

'I got a lion!'

Jude started rubbing at the carrots under the running water as her mother fetched the onions from one of the drawers in the fridge. There hadn't been any in there when Shona had left. The chicken in the oven fizzed. Greta turned the radio on, just high enough to allow them to talk freely.

Jimmy was watching them too. Shona looked at his sad smile. He looked well, but tired.

'We need to talk,' she said.

He looked at his hat. 'So, are you going to give it to the police?'

She waited until he looked at her before answering. 'I need to know what you think about this. I don't know where it's from, I don't know anything about it and I don't have my hands on it yet. But, if I can get it back, I need it to be around for a couple of weeks so I can get my house off Maynard. I won't give you away but I need him to truly believe that I would in a heartbeat. I don't know whose side you're on, or if you're just on your own side, but can I trust you?'

'I've just spoken to my sister for the first time in twenty-two years.' His eyes filled and he blinked rapidly. He whispered, 'She's still mad,' and smiled. 'I was never on Maynard's side. I always thought that everything he did, we did, would work out for the best for you as well. Even after everything with Meghan, I thought – well, never mind that. I'll support you however I can.'

'Even if you ended up in prison again?'

He lowered his head. 'Don't ask me that, Shona.'

Shona nodded. 'Fair enough.'

He looked up. 'Can I see it again?'

Shona looked over, but Jude and Greta were busy. 'We'll talk about that. I need all the information I can get on how you or he found it, who it was for and how he paid for it. If I'm going to persuade him to sign the house over, I need to terrify him with what I know. Will you help?'

There was a slight hesitation. 'Yes. Not who it was for though. I can't give you that.'

'Shona, can you set the table?' said Greta. 'Are you eating with us, James?'

'That would be lovely.'

Greta started to dish up and Jude carried the plates to the table.

'No more questions though,' said Shona to Jimmy. 'I need to write everything down after dinner so I can get things moving. Time's running out. OK?'

He nodded.

GRETA

Wherever he went, James sent a postcard. Everywhere he went came back on a small illustration, a piece of card, to Coggeshall, centre of demons and ley lines and hoof prints. The first time he came back he lifted the postcard, a pen drawing of Canterbury cathedral, from the mantelpiece and put it in a rosewood box. It was exactly the right size for a postcard standing upright.

'All the postcards I send you need to go in here. You will keep them, won't you?'

'All right.'

I wondered whether the box was mine or just a holder for his postcards. I never felt they were mine but that I was keeping them safe for him, box and all. So every time a postcard arrived I put it in front of the previous one. As the years went on, long after I married and moved, the postcards got larger and I had to trim off more and more to fit them in without bending them. There were never many words to worry about. That wasn't why he wanted me to keep them. I wondered whether it was some memory prompt he felt he might need in later years, but it was odd for such a young man to think about being old. No teenager ever believes that it will happen to them, maybe no-one in their twenties either. There was another reason.

One by one James' postcards arrived: Berlin, Toronto, Holland, Montreal, Besancon, Geneva and New York. No-one in our family had ever been beyond England's borders before, apart from my trip to Paris. Then in 1971 I happened to read an article on the soaring prices of fine art, and the flurry of robberies in the 1960s. The cities all sounded familiar. I didn't see Jimmy from one year to the next, had no way of contacting him. I waited for the next postcard, Zagreb in September 1971. It took three days until I found it reported in the newspapers at the library. I began to research all of the thefts in the cities on the dates of the postcards. The more I found out the less I believed that James could be involved. James would never cut a picture from its frame; he would never throw a painting in the boot of a car. James loved paint on canvas more than a normal person could love their own child. The next postcard took five years to arrive, Chicago in November 1976. In it James mentioned being in prison. He didn't say where or what he had been sentenced for. He didn't need to. I was his accessory. Then again, I had every power over him.

I got them out and began to read them. Then I got my maps out again and found the lines that drew everything together, but they didn't help. I decided to just leave him to it. I had enough to cope with, trying to stop Larry murdering my son, trying to stop my daughter from idolising him. We all had our own problems, and our own secrets, and I could keep James'. For a time.

It was a bit easier to get in touch with James in the 1990s. He had friends in Brighton near Shona and they saw each other quite often in the last year of her degree. She started to call him Jimmy then. I wouldn't hear from her for months at a time, but if I did phone James had always been round the weekend before or the one before that. I tried not to feel jealous, but to be pleased that at least one element of our family still worked. James got on with Shona and always had. He was caught up in his art, and never in a quite legal way, but what she didn't know was never going to hurt her. I got the occasional postcard from James, from Amsterdam and Boston, and Shona worked hard. Then Shona moved to Maynard's flat in London, near to James, and they carried on meeting.

I don't know what made me phone her when I got the postcard from Frankfurt. James had been to Germany a number of times and there was nothing different in the anodyne message. Blue biro, four words, *Wish you were here*. But I didn't think of being in Frankfurt, I thought of Shona.

I looked up her new London phone number in the small notebook I used to keep track on Shona and Sean's lives. No-one else was in there. I dialled, my fingers nervously feeling the unfamiliar holes of the disc sweeping the numbers, weighing the heavy receiver and lifting it to my ear. Shona answered quickly. She was surprised, maybe worried. I could hear the radio in the background as she rushed through a series of questions.

'Did you want something?'

'No, nothing. Just a chat.'

'I'm busy.'

I could hear her run the tap, filling the kettle. 'Nothing's happening then?'

'No, just enjoying being on my own. Maynard's on a work trip to Frankfurt and back in two days. That's all.'

I made myself reply something so she could ring off. I went back to the box of postcards. I had to get James away from her. I wrote to him and told him that I knew what the postcards meant. I said that I'd send them to the police if he didn't stay away from Shona and her stupid husband. I thought that was enough to break their association and leave Maynard to make a business of his own. But I was far too late. Maynard already had a taste for stealing and fraud and money. Everything that James could teach him was used.

I never asked Maynard about it and I never told Shona. I never told her that her family had everything it needed because her husband was a criminal, that it could all be taken away in a breath. She'd had the worst father, the weakest mother, a criminal uncle and I couldn't tell her. I heard about his successes while Cerys was small, I heard about how his mother tried to mould her and borrow Cerys and make her into her father's child rather than her mother's. And I said nothing.

The postcards still sit on the mantelpiece but I don't have to add to them any more. Sometimes I think of Larry smiling at them and wonder what he had to do with it all. How did he help James to find that world and draw everyone around Shona into it? It could have been James on his own but, in my experience, if Larry was nearby he was involved.

I wanted Larry dead and was pleased when I buried

him. It was over. I didn't have to be scared of his shape in the chair or stand in front of my children so he had to fight to reach them. We were free. But after he died I found myself watching for his shadow, listening for the clip of his feet, smelling the cigarette smoke that still drifted behind him. I knew that when I died he'd haunt my children, then my grandchildren. The cycle hadn't been broken but was still binding us.

Who do you ask for help to defeat the devil? The churches don't believe any more and you can hardly defeat him with tarot cards. A paper cut, maybe, if you threw them just right. Death by a thousand cuts sounded like a good, convincing way to kill something but my aim wasn't great, I didn't have enough cards and I wasn't quite sure how physical he was.

I occasionally saw him standing where his chair used to be but there was no shadow, no matter how many lights I put on. He had no reflection in the window or glass covered pictures. There were no mirrors. Sometimes I saw through him with just a hint of his outline.

My mother had religion. I had maps and books on the occult and dreams of snow, the importance of snow, that revealed steps and tracks and people, and other visitors. I had focused on trying to understand where he had been, but as I looked at James' postcards I realised that this had been the wrong approach. My great-grandparents had run when they discovered they were hunted. I knew I was being hunted, so why wasn't I running? Because he was already here. 'You took me to her,' he said. He could only follow me. Somehow we were linked.

After all these years of being taunted, I now knew that he couldn't move on to anyone else until I was dead. That's when I began to plan. Maybe I could draw him away from Shona, trap him in some distant place, bind him while he was still tied to my shadow. My mother's stories were full of wise people who had tricked the devil. I wasn't wise, but I was willing to sacrifice everything, even my soul, and that is its own kind of power.

I'd killed him once. It felt so unfair to make me do it again, but only I could.

19

Maynard had finally lowered the asking price and there was a sudden flurry of requests from the estate agent to see the house. Shona had heard them turn up to find the door bolted a couple of times. In any case, they had given up trying to get in. Shona had his attention. She'd ignored all of his attempts to phone her, insisting on a meeting. She'd stretched it out, allowed him to think of what he would give up, who he would give up. They were set for a verbal confrontation on the 6th of January and then Shona postponed. The 13th sounded better. They arranged a meeting at The George, eleven o'clock, for tea and maybe an early lunch. She wasn't sure what she'd be in the mood for and The George covered all options – coffee, food or sudden strong spirits. Even a bed.

Everyone seemed to be in the right place. Jude was at school, Thea was buzzing with facts about her new partner, Asha, Jimmy was on alert and Mariana was nowhere to be seen. Or more exactly, when it came to her, heard. Shona hadn't tried to contact her. She knew Mariana and it wasn't a good idea to chase her. When she was ready to talk about Jude, Shona would know about it. Shona had got used to her absence in those years after Jude was born, and then got used to her being there again. She missed her. She would find a way to make things OK short of agreeing to have Jude baptised, which was a possible condition of Mariana's continued favour. But it had to wait. Maynard came first.

She left home far too early, in an unnecessary rush, and had to go back for her scarf which she wrapped over her nose. It was quite warm but the wind, swinging from the west, was stronger than she expected. She set out again, trying to walk slowly along the road, having to keep checking herself. There was plenty of time. She walked up past the police station, down the underpass and still she was an hour early. The shops had 'last' and 'final' displayed over the windows but she wasn't interested. As she walked past the library she felt pleased there would be no more essays. It was the last of many threads of her life. She was tying them together in the bright, cold sun and moving on.

She went into a café across the road from The George to wait until it was time. She took a seat next to the window to watch for Maynard. She thought of Kallu, but she heard little from him now either. He'd left his job, but that was all she'd found out. She was cross that he would leave without saying goodbye, but, simultaneously, entirely expected him to do that. Still, it would hurt. He may have left already, but she knew he was taking someone and no-one else had gone yet.

Ten to eleven. She drank the last of her tea and put her bag over her head and shoulder so the strap crossed her body. She wanted to be ready to run. That's when she saw Maynard kissing Cerys goodbye, fiddling in his wallet for cash and then waving. Cerys turned from him, didn't wait for the traffic lights, and darted across the road and out of Shona's sight. Her eyes filled and she sat still to concentrate on blinking them back.

She was four minutes late in the end, after all that waiting. The joy of having the power for once had faded away.

He stood when he saw her.

'Oh, sit down, Maynard. I'm not your mother.'

'I ordered you a pot of tea.'

'Of course you did.'

Maynard clicked his fingers together. 'Offending your feminist sensibilities again. I do apologise.'

Shona took off her bag, scarf and coat and took her time settling down. When she was ready, she looked at him. He glowed with excitement. She'd seen that look before, on honeymoon when she thought it was related to her in some way. When he came back from a multitude of trips with shadowy, secret men in dark rooms and smoky pubs and who knows what else. It was the excitement of greed, of the quest and the acquisition of something marvellous. There was something else in his eyes. Seduction. He intended to charm and wheedle something out of her that she'd said he could have, just so he could feel as if he won it from her, the weak woman who stupidly loved him enough to marry him, instead of accepting it from her in a fair exchange. A boring business deal that he'd made sure he could avoid as a way of making sordid money. He made exciting, dirty money. He probably made exciting, dirty love now to rows of exciting, dirty women who liked the way he glowed when he took something from them.

For the first time the idea of a man being inhabited by

a devil made sense. There was no way he was going to get that painting.

'Here's the deal,' said Shona. 'I get the house and contents, including the paintings and bits from the front room. You get the furniture from the front room as well as your other property and contents.'

'No.'

'Oh.' Shona looked down at the table. 'It seems fair.' She tapped her finger on her cup. 'Is there any other furniture you'd like? Cerys' wardrobe, or the crib you bought on our honeymoon?'

His eyelids fluttered. 'You said you got rid of the crib.'

'I did get rid of it, in the sense that I got it out of my house.'

Maynard swallowed hard and poured milk and then tea into his cup. Shona noticed the tremor.

'Would you like some?' he asked.

She nodded. He poured and then settled back into the armchair, his cup in both hands. She let him think it over.

'Where is the crib?'

'Why, is it important?'

'You knew how much I wanted that. It was important to me. I thought it had gone.'

He wasn't making eye contact, but talking to his cup.

'I saw it as Meghan's, not yours. But you can have it.'

He sipped the tea and then drank it down.

'I'm just going to get a whiskey. Do you want anything else to drink?'

Shona shook her head. The tone he was using, considerate and generous, reminded her of those early months together. Before the miscarriage, before the crib, before Meghan. She watched him at the bar, shifting from one foot to the other, running his hand through his hair. His smile when he returned was fixed and wide.

'We've been over for a long while,' he said. 'I like to think it's time to become friends and go our separate ways. I do have somewhere else to live and it's only right that you should too. I will see my solicitor when I get back to London and get him to write all this up, but I'd like to draw it all to a close. I get the furniture from my room and the crib. That's all. You can have the house and everything else.' His smile got slightly wider. 'What do you say?'

Shona said, 'You do also get to keep the most expensive things you acquired while we were married, the bank accounts and the flat, and I get the house.'

'Isn't that what you wanted?' He held his breath.

'I just want to be clear. It's a deal,' she agreed.

He pulled his keys from his pocket. 'Do you want the key for my room?'

'Yes, that would be helpful.'

He unlinked and handed it to her. She put the tiny, useless victory in her pocket. He exhaled, went to clink his glass on her teacup, then thought better of it and had celebratory drink by himself.

'What about Cerys?' asked Shona.

'I'll talk to her about coming back home.'

'I didn't say I wanted her back.'

Maynard's jaw slackened. 'Oh, I thought…'

'Let's just leave that up to her.'

Maynard put his glass down and fumbled for his phone in his pocket. 'No, wait. She's here. Let me call her to meet us.'

'No need.' Shona stood up. 'I have to go now, in any case.'

'Are you sure?' Maynard stood as well. 'I'll get the paperwork sorted immediately. You should get it through in a day or so.'

'Fine. Just remember that Cerys isn't part of this deal. I don't want any reference to her in the papers. She's old enough to choose.'

Maynard nodded and held his hand out.

'It's not business, Maynard. It's just the end of a marriage.'

Outside The George she phoned Jimmy. It went to answerphone. 'I need to book you up for a few days. A restoration project. Phone me back.'

Next she phoned Mariana. Another answerphone. 'I need your help for a couple of days, Mariana. I'm going to come and find you now.'

She saw Cerys standing across the High Street. She thought about running over to her and begging her to come home. She thought about promising her the world. Cerys kept her hands in her pockets, and Shona saw Maynard reach her, put his arm round her shoulders and guide her away. Cerys turned round to look back. Shona raised her hand, blew her a kiss and walked away.

20

Maynard was due at 2 o'clock. Shona was watching the garage door from Greta's kitchen window. Jimmy emerged from Greta's garage at half past one, red-eyed and sniffing, and slumped past Shona into the front room. Mariana emerged a couple of minutes later, a package in her arms. In the kitchen she didn't put it down, but stood, holding it to her.

'I owed you this,' said Shona.

'You didn't quite give it to me. I won it.'

'I knew you would. How did he take it?'

'He cried. I let him hold it for a while, but he cried when he handed it over.'

'It's not the money. He really does love it.'

'I know. But it's not his to keep.'

Shona nodded towards the front room. 'Shall we go in?'

Mariana nodded. Shona picked up the tray of tea and biscuits and followed her through. Greta had her arm around Jimmy and was sitting on the arm of the sofa.

Shona put the tray down and handed everyone a mug. Mariana shook her head, and even refused a biscuit.

Shona said, 'You can keep all the paintings you've got, Jimmy.'

He coughed. 'I thought you had to give them back.'

'No, he didn't mention paintings. Nothing but furniture.'

Jimmy raised his head. 'Thanks, Shona.'

'I know you're upset, but it does need to go back. I owe Mariana that.'

Jimmy glanced towards Mariana with her beatific smile and grunted. Shona started to relax. He wasn't happy but he seemed to be tempted to give in on this. Maybe it would be OK. It could only ever have gone to Mariana. Shona settled back into the armchair and again noted the boxes, the empty shelves. Even in the kitchen things had looked strange, pared down. She looked towards her mother, but Greta looked past Mariana and stood up.

'He's early.'

Shona stood to look as well. Cerys was in the car, looking towards the house. Behind Maynard's sleek black car was a white Transit.

'The papers are in the kitchen,' said Mariana.

'Aren't you coming?'

'No, you don't need me any more.'

She wasn't letting go of the package.

'I'll come with you,' said Greta.

Greta opened to the front door before Maynard could ring while Shona fetched the papers.

'All sorted?' he said.

'Yes,' said Shona. 'Come round to the garage.'

The sofa, the cabinets and desk. She had banked on him focusing only on the crib. That's exactly what he did. He stroked it and examined it for signs of change or damage, but she trusted Jimmy's steady hand.

He stood up and smiled. 'I'll just get the movers.' He walked back to his car and returned with two young men in white overalls and Cerys. Her hair was still blonde, but there were dark roots. She glanced at Shona but didn't say anything.

'Hi Cerys,' said Shona. 'How've you been?'

'Fine. Is Jude here?'

'No, he's at school. I didn't know what you were doing so I didn't want to make a big deal of things and upset him. You're very welcome to come with me and see him though.'

Cerys shrugged. Maynard stopped watching the exchange and headed towards the garage.

'You have to sign for everything first,' said Shona, holding out a pen with the papers. She'd made sure the crib was at the front so he could see it easily. As he legally agreed that she had returned everything itemised, she had to clasp her hands together to stop them shaking. Then she turned to Cerys as they took the crib, the tea chest, the cardboard box, the display cabinets, the chaise longue, the coffee table with two mug rings and the bureau, emptied of papers, back to the van.

'How are you really, Cerys?'

She shrugged. 'All right.'

'Good.'

Cerys looked at Shona as if she expected to be asked something else, but Shona turned back to the removal. Maynard was quietly berating the overalled men, straightening the blankets that covered the furniture, and being generally dismissive.

Shona turned back to Cerys. 'Enjoying London?'

'Not really.'

'That's a shame.'

They stood in silence until the last item had been taken, guided by Maynard.

'Well, see you later then,' said Shona.

'Mum?'

Maynard came back up the drive with a large bag and dropped it at Cerys' feet.

'Well, thanks for asking me, Dad!' shouted Cerys.

'You belong with your mother, until you're older anyway. I'll ring you.'

He walked away and they listened to the sound of two engines starting up.

Cerys didn't look upset. 'I'd decided to come back anyway.' She fidgeted. 'If I can. I know you didn't want to talk to me in town.'

'I did want to. I just made the decision not to chase you. You knew where I was.'

Shona realised the engines had then been turned off again. Maynard got out of the car and gestured to the van to stop.

'He's forgotten something,' said Shona.

Maynard ran back up the driveway. 'I just saw Jimmy inside, through the window. Was it? Is he in there?'

'Yes.'

Maynard screwed up his fists and made a grab for the papers she still held in her hands. Shona put them behind her back and he stood in front of her, forcing her to back up to the wall.

'The deal's off, give me those papers.'

'You signed for everything. It's over.'

He pointed a finger towards her chest. 'You knew. You got him to take out the painting and, what, let him keep it? I'll make sure he goes back inside for this. I'll make sure you go down for it too.' He spat at her feet.

'No, you won't, Maynard. You're behind this theft and many, many others. You lost your job because they had suspicions. They would be more than open to learning anything about you that would confirm what they already believe.' She stepped forward, pressing against his finger. 'You're fucked.'

He opened his mouth and then closed it again. He turned to Cerys. 'Come on.'

Cerys looked at Shona. Shona shrugged.

Cerys turned to Maynard and said, 'I don't want to go with you.'

Shona felt the tears build in her throat.

'What have you said to her?' Maynard grabbed Shona by the throat, banging her head against the wall. 'What did you just say?'

Cerys picked up her bag and hit him with it. 'Get off her!'

Maynard blinked and released Shona, then stepped back. 'I'll make your life hell. I'll get your bastard taken away and I'll fucking burn your house down with you in it.'

Shona said nothing. Maynard said nothing. There was a light tapping on the kitchen window. They all turned to see Mariana with her phone held towards them.

'What's she doing?' asked Maynard.

'She's videoing you,' said Cerys.

Maynard turned and ran to his car. Shona brought the papers back in front of her and smoothed them out. Her breath was shuddering and her throat burned, but she still refused to cry.

Cerys whispered, 'Can I come home?'

'You don't need to ask.' Shona picked up the bag and showed Cerys through the back door. In the front room Mariana was back in her place and still glowing, Jimmy was still heartbroken and Greta was the only one to notice Cerys come in.

'Good to have you back, Cerys.'

'Thanks.'

'Mariana, could you drive us back now?' asked Shona.

'Sure.' Mariana stood up and awkwardly pulled the keys from her handbag. 'Could you drive?'

Shona nodded. 'Come on, Jimmy.' She handed the keys to Cerys. 'Can you open the car?' When the room was empty, she hugged Greta for slightly longer than she'd intended.

'You'll be fine now,' said Greta. 'Go and enjoy it.'

'Thank you. Come over soon.'

Mariana sat in the front passenger seat, her package tightly held beneath the seat belt. Cerys looked happy and Jimmy looked utterly miserable. Shona smiled as she looked at them before she sat in the driver's seat.

'Be kind to the clutch, Shona,' said Mariana. 'And no hard braking.'

They dropped Jimmy off first, Mariana and Cerys gasping as Shona pulled into his drive. Once he was inside Mariana gave her seat to the package, safe behind its seat belt, and took over at the wheel. They pulled up close to Shona's house and Mariana turned to say goodbye through the open car window.

'Are we OK, Mariana?' asked Shona.

'We're getting there. I will contact you in a couple of weeks, when everything has calmed down. Fernando and I think you should come to dinner. With Jude.' She looked at Cerys. 'You would be very welcome, Cerys, but I will not be offended if you have better things to do.'

Shona leaned through the window and kissed Mariana on the cheek. Mariana nodded, pressed the button to close the window and pulled away.

Shona put her arm around Cerys and led her into the house. Cerys cried properly when she saw how her room had been packed up into boxes.

'I've been using your room so Jude could have his own. You can have it back.'

'No, it's fine. I'll have the downstairs room. Dad's room. I knew things would be different.' Her voice sounded thick.

'We'll get you a new bed. I'll go back in with Jude until—'

Cerys sat down on the bed. 'No, it's OK. I left and I can't blame you if you changed things.'

'Maybe I can get hold of a fold-out bed today. The sofa might be better though. I'll ask around.' Shona's alarm went off on her phone. 'I need to get Jude. Do you want to come with me?'

'Does he hate me?'

'No, he misses you terribly.'

'I'd like to come.'

'Good.' Shona put her hand on Cerys' shoulder. 'I'm not going to ask, and it's not because I don't care. Just tell me what you want when you want.'

'I missed you,' said Cerys.

Shona hugged her and kissed her head. 'Blonde suits you,' she said.

Cerys and Jude sat at the table as Shona placed the fish and chips in front of them. She'd asked Cerys to choose whatever she liked, was prepared to try to cook anything, but this was her choice. She could barely swallow anything

279

for the tears and the bruise that was forming on her throat, but she tried. They all tried. Jude was too pleased and Cerys was too tired. But they were fine in their way and sat at the table long after the chips were too cold to pick at. Jude jumped up to fetch a present he'd been talking about and then sat back down again, blushing.

'What's the matter?' asked Shona. 'It's in your room.'

'Does Cerys have any presents?'

Shona winced. 'No. I'm sorry, Cerys. I didn't want wrapped presents just sitting there. You'll have to tell me what you want.'

'It's OK. I should have told you where I was.'

'We knew,' said Jude. 'We didn't see you though. London was too big.'

Cerys looked at Shona, who looked away.

'Where are you sleeping?' asked Jude. 'Are you staying?'

'I'm not sure where I'm sleeping yet.'

'Have your room. I'll sleep on the sofa until we sort things out.' Shona watched Cerys' face, waiting for a sign of her displeasure, her regret at coming home, but there was nothing. She just seemed smaller, somehow.

The back door opened, making them all turn. Kallu walked in, wrapped in a blanket like a poncho, his hair frosted stiff at the front.

'I have a date for leaving,' he said. 'I'm so pleased to catch you all before I go.'

Cerys looked away from him, listening to Jude's questions but forming none of her own. Shona had watched his face and she knew that he had known Cerys was here, back at home. Ten days and he'd be gone. Cerys was back and the balance of her life, this endless round of arrivals and departures meant, of course, that someone else had to leave. But he'd said that he'd be taking someone else with him, someone that she would give him. It couldn't be Cerys, never Jude. Who would be leaving with him?

She breathed in deeply and tried to stay happy, stay calm.

'We'll have to have a proper goodbye, Kallu. Next week. Would that be OK? So we have a chance to do this properly?'

'That would be nice, Shona, but there's really no need. I'm not leaving many people behind.'

'You have to. No loose ends, please, Kallu. I need to know. Are you going alone?'

'I'm not going alone and the person I'm going with doesn't know it yet. I don't even have any tickets.' He laughed. 'I do have a passport, so that's a start.'

Shona was stunned. He couldn't have organised that, could he? She shook her questions away.

'Are you hungry?' she asked.

'Thank you, no. I have to leave now.'

He turned to Cerys, lifted her hand to his lips and kissed it as he stood up so he was bowing. She blushed scarlet and he said nothing else before leaving.

'He's weird,' said Jude. 'Will he come back?'

'Who knows?' said Shona. 'Let's get these beds sorted.'

She carried the fresh sheets upstairs and stripped both beds. Something was niggling at her, something she had forgotten. She stood by the window in Cerys' room and tried to work out what it was. Her head turned to the wall. Amy. She'd forgotten all about Amy. There had been no noise from the house since Kallu was last there.

She left the sheets and ran down the stairs.

'Be back in a second!' she shouted, letting the door slam behind her.

She hesitated at Amy's door before knocking. She could be dead. She knocked loudly.

'Amy, it's just Shona!'

The door opened almost immediately. Amy was dressed in tight jeans and an overly large grey T-shirt. Her hair had been cut short around her jaw line and her skin had cleared.

'Amy, you look great!'

'I've been away for a few days. I'm feeling good. Well, getting there.'

Shona wanted to ask, were you with Kallu, where did you go, what happened? Instead she said, 'I'm so pleased.'

Amy smiled. 'I'm not sure how it happened. Sorry for all the stuff.'

'It's fine. I'm just glad you're so well. Do you want to come round? Cerys is back.'

'No, I'll leave it thanks. Just having a good clear out before I put the house up for sale.'

Shona gasped. 'Are you going to Greenland?'

Amy laughed. 'No! Sussex. I'm going to stay with my sister for a bit.'

'Brilliant. That's brilliant.'

Amy shrugged. 'Better get on then.'

Shona nodded and returned home. No-one was going with Kallu, then. Everyone was back or heading where they should be.

21

The farewell meal was only supposed to be small, Shona, Cerys, Jude and Kallu. Then her mother invited herself. Shona invited Mariana and Fernando, while dreading the inevitable questions from Jude and Cerys. In the end, Mariana said they couldn't come. She emailed a photo from a Belgian local paper of a priest and the long-lost icon, reunited at last.

Jimmy was still ignoring all phone calls and messages. He'd come around.

Thea brought Callum and Asha, who never left her side now.

Shona had sold more of Maynard's pieces of silver and spent a good portion on food for this goodbye. She'd filled up the freezer as well, and the cupboards had a great deal of pasta. She had to make the most of it and spend time preparing for her new job as a junior in Mariana's office. She knew that the subject of fatherhood would come up again, but she was ready to deal with it now. She'd see how it went, anyway.

Cerys and Jude came in first. Cerys, not quite installed back at school, had collected Jude from his. Greta arrived next, followed by Thea, Callum and Asha.

'Is Kallu still out there?' asked Shona.

'Yes.' Greta put her suitcase inside the doorway to the back room.

'Mum, what's the suitcase for?'

Greta looked around evasively. 'Ah, I do need to have a chat with you, Shona.'

Shona's heart sank. She didn't want to think about where to squeeze in her mother, not just after they'd all nearly got used to their new rooms. There was always the shed, now Kallu was officially leaving. She opened her mouth to say something, but then Kallu came in and she busied herself at the table again.

He stood next to Jude and put a hand on Cerys' shoulder.

'Amy said she might come, but I don't think she will. She's much better though.'

Kallu gently took his hand from Cerys and sat next to her. Jude and Callum were in the back room. Greta sat down opposite Kallu, next to Thea, who had her hand in Asha's. Shona handed everyone a plate.

'Help yourselves.'

She left them to it and went to finish off icing Kallu's cake. She watched the way Cerys didn't look at Kallu and froze whenever he brushed against her. She was still very much in love with him and Shona's heart ached for her. Kallu was going and Shona knew he wouldn't ever be back. At that age love was all about destiny and waiting, because only sacrifice made you worthy.

And her mother, what was wrong with her? She was trying to catch Kallu's eye to mouth things at him. Jude and Kallu were the only ones eating.

Shona dipped her knife back into the boiling water to smooth down the icing and pushed the cake to one side. She filled the kettle and switched it on.

'I'll help,' said Greta, and got the mugs from the cupboard.

Shona folded her arms and waited for her to finally spill whatever it was that needed to be said. Greta filled mugs with tea bags, and then tapped her fingers as she watched the steam build as it escaped from the kettle. Then she nodded her head, fetched an envelope from her bag and handed it to Shona.

'What's this?'

'It's the money from all the stuff from the house, except the little we need to get on our way.'

'We?' Shona looked at the envelope and back at her mother. 'Oh my God. You're going with Kallu? How did you arrange that?'

'I was leaving anyway. I was packing up before you knew that he was going. We've spent a lot of time talking. He didn't need convincing, like some people.' She smiled. 'He's going to Greenland. I couldn't have thought of anywhere so perfect. I was only going to go to Scotland,' she laughed.

'This can't work, Mum. You and Kallu? In Greenland?'

'I haven't gone mad. He knows what to do. He understands more of it than I do.'

'Are you sure?' Shona turned her mother towards her so she could whisper and the children couldn't hear as well. 'Are you sure this isn't to do with all that devil stuff?'

'It is absolutely to do with it.' Greta pressed her lips together and exhaled through her nose. 'Kallu explained it. While I'm alive he's stuck to me, and while I'm near you it strengthens those bonds to let him make the leap.

I've long thought that I can lead him away from you and, if I could go a really, really long way, I should. Kallu and I, we can do this.'

'You don't even know him.'

'I do now.'

'But, seriously?'

'I can believe what I like and, Shona, if I believe that going to the snow saves you and your children from having to go mad in your turn then I'm going to do that.' Greta took out the tea bags and added the milk.

'Does Kallu know what to do?'

'Of course. I've paid for the tickets and got some warm clothes, obviously. He says he'll cover everything else.'

'You're just taking that suitcase? There can't be much in there.'

'It's enough to get there. Most things I'll buy when we arrive. It's always best to buy things for a particular climate in the place where people understand it. The snow, Shona. Imagine it.'

Greta's eyes were shining. Shona turned to the window.

'Has everything else gone?'

'There's still the garage. I didn't sell that. It didn't seem to be mine to sell. Here's the key.' She passed it across.

Shona looked down at it, a silver Yale key, holder of her mother's best-kept secret and scene of her only triumph.

'Sell it, keep it, I don't mind.'

'You're not coming back, are you?'

'No.'

Greta went back to the table and started to eat. Shona could see the reflection of all of them in the window. Occasionally one would look at her, but there would be no more private talks. Everything else would take place in public, between all of them. Kallu went into the back room and brought in a fifth chair and placed it between Cerys and Greta. She sat in it and put some food on her plate.

Thea and Asha were sharing a chair and a plate and as close to each other as they could get. Shona saw Kallu watching them too.

'The goddess of the seven stars,' he said. 'Look after her. And Mariana is important too. She needs you.'

'Not that she'd ever admit it.'

'That's exactly why it's down to you.'

Shona dipped a carrot stick into an onion dip and bit off the end.

Kallu leaned over and spoke quietly to Shona. 'Can I ask you a favour?'

'Of course.'

'Upstairs.'

She followed him up to the bathroom. He knelt on the floor and handed her a pair of scissors. She didn't ask but silently began to cut his hair, which hung just below his shoulders, short to the neck, the scalp, letting it curl into the bath. It was such a ritual that she didn't dare speak. She was releasing him, voluntarily and willingly. It was the end and the beginning. The final lock fell and she knelt beside him, looking at the pile of hair.

A husk, thought Shona as she shivered. 'What should I do with it?'

'Whatever you like. It's not important.' He leaned back on his heels. 'Shona, Meghan says, "Look at me. I'm right here. Watch me shine."'

Shona closed her eyes. Another message she didn't understand.

'Meghan came back for you. He is sitting in your kitchen right now. He adores you. There are many states of being, Shona. Ever since he arrived, you've been ready to be whole again. Don't fight it any more.'

Shona opened her eyes. Jude.

Kallu ran both hands over the roughness of his choppy hair. 'Bit mad, cutting my insulation off before I head into the dark north.'

'Will you take care of Mum? She's not going to last long. She's barely been out of the house in decades.'

'She's been saving herself for this. Her life force is poised. She's ready and she'll love it. And of course I'll take care of her. I promise.'

Shona thought, If it was ever going to happen I would have to kiss him now – but had no urge to. He was a hack-haired boy, a weird child whisking her mother into the wilderness, and she envied them both without desiring either their journey or him.

It was so dark in the kitchen. Only the fairy lights around the rubber tree were on and a couple of candles which hadn't burned down. Winter needs special lighting, she thought, pricks in the darkness to follow.

Kallu was looking at Jude but talking to them all. 'We will chase the wolves into the dark forest, like the child wearing a cat mask. Guided by a fairy, the child pulled the sword from the end of the rainbow, where the skull was buried. They flew into the dark to challenge the witch who turned into a wolf.'

There was something happening that Shona couldn't describe. A feeling of completion. The tents of St Paul's were still there, another light in the darkness. People would still fight their way through.

Kallu was hypnotising. She didn't care about where the truth lay. Her mother had hope for the first time ever.

Cerys shuddered and turned away, turning her phone in her hand. Thea and Asha whispered to each other. Jude and Callum listened, as if to any fairy tale, eyes sparkling in the lights. Shona gazed at Kallu and then at Greta. She put her arm around Cerys, who sank back against her, and they all listened to completely different stories made from the same words.

The house she had fought for was only a house now. She knew that she could move too, away from Maynard and Rob and away from death. Meghan was a memory come back to find her, and Jude and Cerys were with her for as long as she deserved them. Mariana and Thea and Amy would be there, in one way or another. Fernando too. Her mother and Kallu wouldn't be because they had their own futures and deaths to chase. Shona would forge their tales in the way Greta had adapted the tales of her childhood and keep them alive for her children.

GRETA

FEBRUARY 2012

The snow is astonishing. Nothing else is as I expected.

Five hours' flight from Copenhagen and we are nowhere near. It takes more flights, more boats, to get where we are heading. We aren't there yet. I am tired. I think of my great-grandparents and try to be glad that I'm not pulling all my worldly goods behind me. I have a small backpack, which replaced the suitcase I had packed. Kallu showed up with this bag and selected the few things I would need. He was brutal, but I trust him. He made me put on all my clothes, so I could hardly squeeze into my plane seat. The first plane I've taken since I went to Paris with the devil, and my last flight.

Who accompanies me this time? I don't know. I neither know nor understand this half-boy, half-man with his short choppy hair and eyes which reflect what he sees. When I first looked in his eyes, I could see Larry standing behind me. When I told him, Kallu bought a pair of sunglasses and, for some reason, in them I only see myself. There's snow here but he says that it is nothing compared to the snow that awaits us, with no gaps to see cars and houses, roads and streetlights. I felt bubbles in my stomach when he said that and realised I haven't felt excited in over a decade. Not since Shona had Meghan.

I've missed it, anticipation and life. I look out of the window on the plane and feel fear falling beneath me. All the lines and connections I've drawn are clear from this height. Kallu sleeps next to me, a blanket pulled up to his chin. He looks like an old man. I stroke his hair. He gently growls.

Shona was sad to see me leave but she trusts me. Doesn't quite believe me, but hopefully she won't ever have to. I'm leading the devil away from her, and between Kallu and the snow and the ice and burning moon we'll win. There won't be visible sun for months where we're heading. It's February, near the end of the long night of the year.

Here there is a little light. It seems as if the icy snow is glowing. The harbours are full of dogs, alive and dead, their fur and shit coating the heaps of plastic bags. There are torn nets and broken bottles licked by drunks, seal innards and screaming women. There are no trees to break up the landscape, just the houses tiny against the mountains which lead nowhere and everywhere.

Among all there is the unspoken. We haven't seen him following us. Kallu has his seal fur jacket drawn back from his already sunburned face. He watches the boats arriving with their disappointed noise and departing in hopeful silence. He knows when our sled is ready. The dogs bark for meat.

I am scared.

I'm leaving Shona, the daughter who never loved me until the end, and Sean, the son who loved me and who

I let down. Both of them have children who don't know me, and that's what I deserve. But I can make it right and they'll live on and maybe think of me.

I've spent my life in the darkest of corners in the light of the sun and but only now can I see it. I can be the moon and goddess of the seven stars that spin out from the sun. I am everything, the bad become good and the weak become strong. Kallu beckons me.

I am ready.

I take Kallu's hand and feel my death in the tips of his fingers. I become a little brighter.

The silence of the sky and the cracking of icebergs, the severity of sea and darkness against light makes my eyes water. I will fade and burn in the heat of the snow along with the devil which follows me. We can't see his hoof prints yet, but Kallu says he's coming. He will come. I have to believe that he will. But I know that, underneath, Kallu has found out something else and there is doubt. I don't know whether it's doubt of himself or me, of this world or another. His face is shadowed, even when he sits right in front of the fire.

I just watch for the prints and try to be ready for something I know has to happen but will never understand.

My dreams are so hot I have to wipe their remnants from my face. Kallu remains curled up, sickly bright. He has been there for days.

I dreamed of Cerys smiling at a man who doesn't drink and can move his fingers one at a time on a tabletop. In my dream I could make him move and took each foot, one at a time, and walked him off a cliff.

The gentle drumming fills my ears unless I can focus on

the dogs which howl outside. We have no more seal for them to eat. We have nothing.

Finally, Kallu unbends himself and goes outside with a knife. I hear the dogs snap at him and cry. I hope he's cut them free, but I can't hear them run. The drumming is too loud.

There's something about the way he walks when he comes back in, just a little loose, a little swaggering. I realise why he won't let me look in his eyes now. We are locked together in a tent in the snow and maybe one of us will leave. And maybe neither of us.

All I face now is the brightness where life meets death and I just need the space to take him through with me. He may end up taking me. Kallu has bound us and I will burn whichever way it goes.

I am ready.

I am gone.

All families have secrets...

On holiday in Northern Ireland, Nancy and Bernadette discover their family is involved with disappearances and murder. The sisters have not spoken to each other since that last disturbing summer. Thirty years later, Nancy is making a return...

Paperback ISBN: 9781910124321 RRP: £8.99
Also available in eBook

www.sandstonepress.com

 facebook.com/SandstonePress/

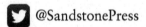 @SandstonePress